Camel Red

To Paul

Greg Page '04

Camel Red

Gregory David Page

Lowell Books
Jacksonville

Camel Red

Published by Lowell Books

ISBN 0-9760428-0-0 (ISBN 0-595-66341-9)

Printed in the United States of America

Contents

Many people have contributed important details in the preparation of Camel Red, particularly Azelia Heron, who passed away while the book was being written. Others who supplied factual information were Larry Heron, and doctors Joseph Murray and Bradford Cannon. Angelo Bastoni, Roger Burt, and John Sears supplied important detail regarding the history of the 87th.

Special thanks to Sue, who made it all possible with encouragement and support throughout. And to the brave men and women who continually risk their lives to serve the cause of freedom throughout the world.

FOREWORD

Few of us are born with the speed, strength, and stamina it takes to become a professional sports figure. Lawrence J. Heron was such a man, a very special man who took great personal risk to protect the lives of endangered comrades. In doing so, he gave up his most precious personal assets and a brilliant future in sports. His story does not end there. With the help of his lovely and selfless wife, he persevered through many obstacles and turned his story into one of triumph over tragedy.

Camel Red is a tender love story involving two people who, through a flood of painful trials and tribulations, never lost their faith in God. The book introduces us to some of the greatest wartime surgeons to have served their country and the contributions they have made, which continue to benefit us to this day. It involves a legendary chaplain who volunteered to serve God on the battlefield, and the strange twists that fate took in reuniting old friends during battle.

After becoming wounded by enemy machinegun fire in northern Italy during World War II, I spent three months convalescing in a hospital. During the thirty-five years I represented the people of my state in Washington, I have on many occasions visited veterans hospitals where I have seen first hand what price America has paid for the peace we enjoy today.

I donated my services as the Campaign Chairman of the National World War II Memorial because I strongly believe we must continue to honor the sacrifices our veterans have made. Of all the honors that have come my way, none has surpassed the pride I felt wearing my country's uniform. I will never forget that the peace we enjoy today was secured at a precious price, and that we must constantly recommit ourselves to honor the sacrifices of our veterans. No one epitomizes such brave men and women more than Larry

Heron, arguably the most severely wounded man to have returned from World War II, and the only man ever to have a Disabled American Veterans' chapter dedicated in his name while he was still alive.

We owe our freedom to individuals like Larry and we cannot thank them enough. This book can teach us many things about the spirit of Americans in the face of adversity. Though the story takes place in a different era, the lessons apply to what is happening in our world today. Most people have little sense of what it takes to fight in a war, the suffering it causes, or the courage it demands. Everyone could benefit by reading *Camel Red*.

- Senator Bob Dole

1

A Death Wish

The flowers from her son arrived on June 26, 2000, marking the day fifty-six years ago when her husband had become World War II's most severely wounded soldier. Five days later they have wilted, yet she cannot bring herself to throw them out. She feels that she has much in common with them as she looks at herself in the bathroom mirror. It seems she's aged several years in just these past few weeks. Her breathing is labored. Her lungs pump like organ bellows. She holds her sides and grimaces in pain.

"Just the gall bladder acting up again," she tells her son, Larry Heron, Jr., as he loads her oxygen tank into his car and helps her climb aboard for the one-mile ride from their Hopedale residence to the local hospital in the neighboring town of Milford, Massachusetts. "Don't look so worried. The doctor says I'll be just fine. He wants to keep me a few days to run a thorough checkup, just like last year."

Her oldest daughter, Patty, drops by the Milford Hospital early on Saturday morning. Carol, the second oldest, arrives on her sister's heels. "Nothing unusual," Azelia tells them. "Just haven't had much energy lately." Each breath is a gasp, as though she's breathing through an aqualung, and her skin is as white as a Geisha's, her cheeks blotched red. This is nothing new. Their mother has been hooked up to oxygen tanks the past five years, and every year at this time she's been brought here for checkups.

Two weeks after he died, she was rushed to the hospital hemorrhaging through her nose and mouth. She lost three pints of precious blood that day.

It took the doctors two years to diagnose her condition as pulmonary fibrosis.

"What a shame," her friends said. "She deserves far better after all she's been through."

When her youngest daughter, Debbie, drops by Room 201 the next morning, Azelia asks, "Have you been praying for me?"

"Every day."

"That's not what I mean. Tonight I want you to pray that when I go to sleep, I won't wake up in the morning."

"Mom!" Debbie protests. Despite how weak and emaciated her mom had appeared in the past, today she seems even more shrunken. Skin hangs loosely from her arms. The veins on the backs of her hands look ready to burst through skin that's an unnatural pallor.

"It's all right, dear. Every new day I wake up trapped in this body and tied to that oxygen tank with nowhere to go and nothing to do except watch television. And every night I pray that I won't have to face another day, that God will allow me to sleep beside him once more."

Debbie understands. Her mother's life is filled with misery. She believes that when she dies, she might have a better shot at finding happiness. Before she cries herself to sleep that night, Debbie prays, "God, please help her to find the peace and happiness she seeks."

On July 3rd, Larry's concern for his mother escalates. Her color matches the white of her bed sheets. She struggles for each breath as though an elephant were sitting on her chest.

"Don't worry," she tells him. "I'm fine." Moments later she asks, "They've forgotten him, haven't they?"

"No, Mom. People still remember."

She sighs. "No. The Honor Roll's been torn down. Nobody wants to pay to maintain it. Last year they voted down a proposal to put up a new memorial in its place." She draws a breath. "Since Father Connors passed away, they stopped holding the annual memorial for the 9th Division."

Larry's brows furrow. He leans forward and takes her hand.

"The Lawrence J. Heron Chapter is gone," she continues. "The DAV has moved to Medway. There are so few of them left alive. Most are in hospitals or homes waiting to die. No one seems to care any more, what they did, how they suffered. It's all been forgotten."

Her son tightens his grip on her hand and holds back words that he knows will sound meaningless.

She shifts her body and adjusts the plastic tubing under her nose and ushers in another breath. "We only had a short time before, before..." She can't bring herself to say it. It is not necessary. Larry understands. So much promise, just to have it stolen from him in the prime of his life.

"Was it worth it?" she asks.

"I never heard him complain."

"But people should at least remember what he did, all he gave up, all he suffered. Is that too much to ask?"

"He always said he was the luckiest man in the world to have married you. You meant more to him than any of the things he lost. You were the one person he cherished most. Because of you, he never felt bitter or lost his faith."

"He loved all his children and grandchildren as much as he did me, but he never got to see what one of them looked like," she sighs. "Not one. That he would die without seeing..." Her voice trails off and she closes her eyes while a single tear takes a familiar path down her cheek.

Larry gives her hand a light squeeze. "It's OK mom. I truly believe he is looking down from heaven and can see us now. I often feel his presence."

"June 26, 1944, was the day that everything changed. That was the first time he died."

That night she can't sleep. Her mind keeps drifting back to a time when life held meaning, back to days of happiness, to the place where it all began.

2
Where It All Began

It all started July 10, 1926. The sun was a caldron of fire in a stark blue sky over Hopedale. On a foot-high stone wall that ran a hundred feet along Hopedale Street, he placed one foot carefully before the other, arms flailing by his sides like a tightrope walker balancing against a slight breeze.

Towering elms bordered both sides of the newly surfaced street, a contiguous canopy casting dappled sunshine onto the sidewalk below. A cocktail of harmonious scents wafted from fresh cut lawns, flowering lilacs, and a variety of colorful flowers. His mother kept pace, a hand extended to brace him should he fall. He paused as a gaggle of high school runners jogged past, numbered shirts and shorts bouncing each time their feet hit the macadam.

Thirty yards ahead, a woman about his mother's age crossed Adin Street, named for the town's founder, Adin Ballou. It was the street of dreams, a half-mile stretch that afforded taunting glimpses of Draper family estates behind concrete walls, wrought iron gates, pampered trees, tall shrubs, and lofty evergreens.

The woman walking toward them was an attractive brunette, neatly dressed. As she drew closer, a shiny black Model-T putt-putted past as creamy and smooth as though it had just been driven off the factory floor. Suddenly, a striking little girl came into view from behind the woman. She appeared to be about his age. As the distance between them narrowed, the challenges of funambulism lost favor and he leapt off the wall to take his place beside his mother.

As the girl drew closer his pulse quickened and he twisted his body for a closer view. His world would never be the same from that moment: eyes as blue and bottomless as the deep sea; hair to her shoulders that reminded him of corn silk under a summer's sun; a blue ribbon in her hair and a short-sleeved white dress with soft blue trim that complemented the cobalt of her eyes. While his heart ricocheted around in his chest, he could only stare.

His mother checked her out and smiled. "I don't blame him," Emma said to the woman. "She is beautiful."

Larry Heron felt his face flush.

"What's her name?"

"Azelia."

"Pretty name."

"Named after the flower but they misspelled it on her birth certificate, so we just left it."

"How old?"

Azelia let go of her mother's hand and approached the wall where she leaned with her back against it and returned his stare.

"Just turned six," Livia Noferi said.

Azelia cocked her head and a smile issued from the corners of her mouth.

"So, she will be starting school in September?"

"Yes," Livia said politely, "and your boy?"

Emma patted Larry on the head, a proud smile blossoming. He made a face and twisted away as though her hand were on fire.

"Larry turned six just last month," she said.

The girl attempted to pull herself up onto the wall but lacked a foothold. A wasp buzzed her hair then moved off in search of sugar.

"Isn't that nice? They'll be in the same class." In a town the size of Hopedale, elementary school classes numbered around twenty-five children who customarily remained together through high school.

The women exchanged names and pleasantries while Larry Heron worked up his nerve to speak. He hesitated as a truck rolled past, the driver clanging a loud bell and shouting, "Fruits and vegetables. Come get your fresh foods!" Just then Larry said aloud, "I like you." The mothers weren't supposed to hear but the words gushed into the sudden quiet, loud and clear. The mothers laughed. Azelia Noferi blushed. Larry Heron's face turned crimson and he ran towards Adin Street without looking back.

He would see no more of her until school started in the fall, when his interests will have shifted to shooting marbles, tossing baseball cards, and otherwise matching his capabilities against boys his own age. But fate had taken a first major turn. Two paths collided on that day, with the promise of all the fury, love, and emotion that life can bring.

John Heron was a good Welsh name. Irish Catholic. He'd taken a bullet in the Boer War that had just missed his heart, leaving an exit hole in his back. The Queen of England pinned him with one of several medals he'd earned while fighting in various campaigns during the war. The medals plus a nickel would have bought him that famous cup of coffee.

John married an English girl named Emma Schofield and they had five children that never made it to adulthood. All were lost to scarlet fever, whooping cough, or pneumonia. Barely able to make ends meet, John seized an offer to relocate free of charge to Fall River, Massachusetts to work as a laborer in a woolen mill, where five more children would be born: John, Fred, Leonard, Ethel, and Lawrence, in that order. All turned out to be exceptional athletes.

Upwards to 20,000 people would flock to Fall River on a given day to watch Heron's older brothers make opposing soccer goalies wish they'd stayed home. When Draper scouts got wind of their athletic prowess, the world's largest manufacturer of textile looms offered John a job. Once again they were relocated, this time to a Draper house in Hopedale, Massachusetts. The boys were immediately added to the semi-pro soccer team, and thus began an era of Draper soccer dominance.

Endowed with super-genes and influenced by a sports-minded father and brothers, it came as no surprise when Larry Heron began setting new records in schoolboy football and baseball. It started when Hopedale's Sacred Heart Church opted to pay his full four-year tuition to St. Mary's High

School in the neighboring town of Milford. Hopedale was too small to field a team of its own and Heron wanted desperately to play, so after persuading his parents to buy in, he readily accepted.

That's when he first met Fr. Edward T. Connors. It was Heron's final season with St. Mary's. Loyal Milford area fans had raised funds to replace uniforms that literally hung in tatters from the player's backs. When they finally appeared in their new uniforms, the press labeled them the "Rags to Riches Team" and gave much of the credit for the team's success to Larry Heron, their rugged team captain.

The "Saints" won game after game that season until Heron fractured a rib while scoring two touchdowns against Angel Guardian. With Heron side-lined, the team lost then dropped their next game to Hyde Park.

Fr. Connors was St. Bernard's athletic director and Heron gave his school fits whenever they competed. Connors would not soon forget that the previous season Heron and his Saints had destroyed Northbridge High in their annual Thanksgiving Day match-up. Northbridge was his alma mater, the high school where a much younger Ed Connors had lettered in football.

But none of this had affected his righteous judgment. "I was looking forward to seeing Heron play," he told Father McCarron. "He's one of the most exciting backs in the league."

Come game day, St. Bernard's upset St. Mary's handily. As the teams headed for their respective locker rooms, Connors approached Heron sitting dejected on a bench and introduced himself. "I did not feel the thrill of victory today," he said. "I had been looking forward to seeing you play. Perhaps next year."

"Thanks, but this is my last year, Father."

"Well the season isn't over. You can still take it out on some of the other poor teams," he chuckled.

Heron was impressed that the priest would have preferred to see him play even if it had cost St. Bernard's the game. In parting, Fr. Connors said, "Perhaps we will meet again in some other place and time – if not on the playing field."

Heron was back on the field the following Saturday to score two touch-

downs against Hopkinton and lead the Saints to a 14-6 victory. The Saints'
next and final game was the classic Thanksgiving Day match up against
Connor's Northbridge High. On game day, Heron told Azelia, "I'm going to
score two touchdowns, just for you. That's a promise."

"Just to see you play is fine with me," she answered.

The sky was a grainy gunmetal wash over Whitinsville's Picnic Point Field
on Thursday, November 24, 1938. A nor'easter blowing through for the past
two days had left the field crusty and uneven, but the biting cold did not deter
the four thousand shivering spectators who filed into the stands and pressed
the field to watch.

On St. Mary's first possession, Heron carried the ball thirty-yards to the
fifty yard line. Two plays later, a trail of defenders lay sprawled in the turf as
he crossed the goal line on his feet. In eight minutes, St. Mary's had moved
the ball seventy-five yards to put them out front 6 to 0.

That score would hold through the fourth quarter when Northbridge attempted a pair of desperation passes back-to-back. The second was inter-
cepted by the Saints' quarterback who ran the ball to his own 31 yard line. A
pass play moved it to midfield where Heron took over and picked up three
grueling yards with half the Northbridge team on his back.

With less than two minutes remaining, his promise to Azelia was about
to vanish like a puff of hot air. To make matters worse, the Saints' quarterback was then sacked and on the very next play overthrew his receiver. As
Heron separated himself from the ensuing pileup, a moose in a Northbridge
uniform shoved past him jeering, "I'm going to smear you so far down in the
muck next play, you'll be speaking Chinese!"

With nine seconds remaining, the ball was snapped to Heron who carried it around the right end then twisted from one tackler, bounced off two
more, and shook loose from a fourth. Moose was the last man to beat. Heron
stiff-armed him, but Moose clamped his arm and a tug of war began, with
Heron stopped just short of the goal line.

Just when all seemed lost, two Northbridge players slammed into them
and all four toppled forward, the momentum carrying Heron and the ball into

the end zone. As time ran out, he had pulled the sword from the stone, just as he had promised her. *Just for you!*

Azelia would never forget that day.

Thursday afternoon was crowned with bright sunshine. Squirrels carved jagged paths across the Community House lawn seeking the safety of giant elms. A charm of goldfinches in search of thistle landed en mass in the swaying branches of a mature lilac.

The Community House was a brick building with white trim that resembled a courthouse, the type of structure that would be incomplete without the huge American flag that waved from its tall white flagpole near the front entrance. The building's original purpose was to provide temporary shelter for families of newly hired workers, who were waiting for their new homes to be completed. Over time it had evolved into a gathering place for residents with meeting rooms, a theater, lounges, bowling alleys, and a gymnasium. Every Saturday morning, full-length feature films would be run for the children, at no charge.

No cars were in sight that day as he crossed Dutcher Street and bounded the front steps of his family's modest two-story wood-framed house on the corner. The scent of his mother's cooking caught him even before he opened the front door.

The house was modestly furnished, comfortable in its simplicity. The front hall led to a family room, living room, dining room and one bedroom; there were two more bedrooms upstairs. When the door closed behind him Emma Heron wasted no time calling from the aromatic kitchen in the rear of the house, her voice underscored with a sense of urgency.

"There's a letter on the hall table for you from the University of Notre Dame," she said. He felt his pulse quicken and his blood drain as he tore open the envelope and scanned the letter.

"Well?" she asked impatiently, as he entered the kitchen. "What do they have to say?"

He finished reading and handed it to her. "Take a look."

Emma wiped her hands on her apron and spread the letter open on the kitchen table. *Congratulations. You have been selected to receive a full scholarship to the University of...* She hesitated. "Oh, my God!" The letter went on to explain the academic requirements and expressed the hope that Heron would soon join the ranks of the Fighting Irish.

"Oh Larry! I can't wait to tell your father! He'll be so proud - not that he isn't already."

He returned her hug and took a kiss on the cheek.

"What is it?" she asked, noting a look of dismay. "Why so solemn?"

When he merely shrugged, she added, "I thought this is what you wanted."

"It is, Ma. I...I'm just wondering how I'll be able to afford room and board, even with free tuition. Maybe next year. What smells so great?"

She returned to the stove and resumed stirring the simmering pasta sauce with that unnerved expression that meant she was not going to allow him to change the subject.

She added chopped garlic and a mixture of oregano, rosemary, parsley, and basil from two small bowls she had prepared in advance. A third bowl held a bit more garlic to add near the end so the flavors would peak when they sat down to eat. In a fourth bowl was some grated Parmesan for the table. "You have to take these things when offered," she commented.

He scooped up a morsel of sauce with a wooden spoon, blew on it then took a taste, the flavors exploding in his mouth. "Ummm! Mom! You've got to write down these recipes before I go off and leave you." Her way of preparing food was to add a pinch of this and a portion of that, seldom with the benefit of a measuring cup or spoon. Without her cooking, the quality of his life would be sadly diminished.

Ignoring his request, she continued, "Don't worry, we'll come up with enough money, even if I have to take in wash."

"You would, too." He laughed and his powerful arms encircled her gently. "You're right. We will work it out somehow." With his parents' support, the scholarship, and the savings from his new job at the Draper Corporation - it just might be possible.

Suddenly the phone jangled with fire alarm intensity. "Heron residence," Emma sang cheerily into the mouthpiece. The smile that always lit up her face when she answered was replaced with an instant frown. "What? What? God no! Oh no!" Her face turned ashen and she gripped the two pieces of the phone so tightly that her knuckles matched the ivory on their upright piano. "How did it happen?"

There was a distended pause, then, "We're on our way."

"What is it mom?"

Her body collapsed onto a chair next to the kitchen table and her chin fell to her chest. She seemed to have shrunken physically into a vulnerable, defenseless person no longer solid, composed, and in control of her emotions. With glazed eyes she said, "Call a cab."

"What is it?" he repeated.

Turning glistening eyes toward her son, she said in a whisper, "It's your father. It was his heart. They rushed him to the Milford Hospital. Tried to save him but..." Her voice trailed. She grew more distant as her mind drew images of John waving to her from fields of ambrosia.

Heron bent to embrace his mother and felt her body quiver. He remembered his father quoting Yeats: "In days of great joy, take comfort in the fact that disaster is just around the corner."

The Drapers had been maintaining the Hopedale Cemetery since 1886. Its manicured lawns were as neat and green as could be found on any fairway. Rhododendrons, lilacs, and hydrangeas lined pathways that meandered past neat rows of well-maintained graves. Majestic elms and aromatic lilacs provided the right amount of shade and color.

Turnout for his father's funeral exceeded Heron's expectations. Chief among those he was pleased to see was Fr. Connors, whose words of condolence lifted his spirits and pulled him from the depths of despair.

After everyone had departed, he stood before his father's casket silently asking forgiveness for breaking a promise he'd made one fall night as they walked home from the State Theater after watching the "All American." Pat O'Brien played Knute Rockne and Ronald Reagan played George Gipp. The highlight was Rockne's pep talk to his losing football team at halftime, years after Gipp had died of pneumonia.

"None of you ever knew George Gipp. It was long before your time, but you know what a tradition he is at Notre Dame. And the last thing he said to me, 'Rock,' he said, 'sometime when the team is up against it and the breaks are beating the boys, tell them to go out there with all they got and win just one for the Gipper. I don't know where I'll be then, Rock,' he said, 'but I'll know about it, and I'll be happy.'"

As they proceeded home, awash in the emotional aftermath of the movie, John said, "I want you to know how proud you make me, son. You play like a pro. Each week you just get better."

"I love the game, Dad."

"Ran into Coach Morris at the barbershop last week. Said he has to drive the other kids but not you because you already push yourself to the limit."

His father glowed with pride. "Some day you'll play for Notre Dame. I can feel it. Hey, look at that!" A falling star streaked across the heavens then disappeared in the blink of an eye. "The Drapers brought us here because your brothers were exceptional athletes and now you'll carry on the tradition by playing for the Irish."

"Maybe they won't want me - I'm only one quarter Irish."

They laughed simultaneously.

Then John turned serious again. "Not to pressure you, son." He raised a hand as if to bat down any rebuttal. "I'd be proud of you no matter what team you played for, but after watching that movie I hope it's Notre Dame." It wasn't just the movie. He had always wished his son would someday play for the Irish.

"Don't worry, Dad. I'd never pass it up."

"Promise?"

"I promise."

Heron brushed tears from his eyes. *Sorry Dad. I know you'd want me to look after Mom.* He had lain awake last night thinking about his future. The money he had been saving for college would soon be gone. He had no choice but to hold onto his job at the Draper Corporation.

Like the vast majority of residents in town, the Herons lived in a Draper-built home rented for $3.50 a week for as long as at least one member of the household remained an employee. For that reason, he would have to pass on his dreams and continue working.

That night he sat on his bed staring at a newspaper clipping with a picture of the 1926 Worcester County Sportsman soccer team. It had been taken just before the team set sail out of East Boston for England. The date was October 3, 1926. Eight of the ten men huddled in their white soccer uniforms were Draper players, one was his brother, John. Fred would have gone as well, had he not taken ill.

His father had been so proud of that picture. He'd be prouder still to have seen Heron playing for Notre Dame. Tears welled in his eyes as the full impact of the loss hit him. His dad was gone forever.

3

The Winds of War

World War II dominated the headlines as well as the minds of all Americans in 1942. It was the year that nationwide gasoline rationing had gone into effect. Earlier that month, the U.S. Navy had won the strategic battle of Midway. War movies were plentiful and increasing in popularity.

Fr. Tom O'Malley entered Fr. Connors' office in the rear of St. Bernard's Rectory and found the priest seated at his desk, lost in thought. On the wall behind him hung a framed diploma from Holy Cross dated 1927 and a certificate from St. Mary's Seminary in Baltimore where he had earned his priesthood and ordainment.

"What's wrong Father?" his good friend asked.

Connors cocked an eye and frowned. Usually, he would welcome his friend with an upbeat smile, a pat on the back and an invitation to sit down to a cup of his famous coffee.

"My God. We're losing our kids," Connors said. "Our future." *White Cliffs of Dover* drifted from a radio in a corner of the office where he served as associate pastor.

Fr. O'Malley knew Connors as well as any man. He crossed the room and sat down in an old but solid wooden armchair and placed the morning mail on his desk. "I know what you are feeling. So many are dying, missing, or returning home wounded. These are terrible times."

The pile of mail suddenly spilled over and fanned out across the desk, the second letter from the top catching Connor's eye. His hands darted for it

14

and he tore it open expectantly. As he read, a smile tugged his lips and the crow's feet reappeared at the corners of his eyes.

"What is it?" Tom O'Malley leaned forward, eager to share the news.

"Here. You read it," Connors said, grinning widely.

The letter came from the Most Reverend Thomas M. O'Leary, Bishop of Springfield. *Dear Reverend Father: Your wish to tender your services to the United States as a War Chaplain has our approval. We have made known to the Military Ordinariate that you are seeking a Chaplain's commission with our knowledge and consent.* The letter went on to release Connors from his present job and declared him free to take up his new duties as chaplain. He was to write to His Excellency, The Most Reverend Military Delegate, Bishop John F. O'Hara, and wait for instructions.

"How about a cup of coffee?" he asked Fr. O'Malley.

On July 15, 1942, Connors received his chaplain appointment from the War Department. He proceeded to 207th General Hospital at Camp Livingston, Louisiana and reported to the commanding officer on July 29. Soon thereafter, he wrote to his bishop: *Thank you for the opportunity to represent the Diocese and to work with our young men. There are many wonderful opportunities in this life. I hope that I don't miss too many.*

Then on October 27, he forwarded a change to his APOE address, adding: *It is such a joy to go on various tactical formations with the men. It gives me a chance to become acquainted, and men are brought back to the church. Each day I am grateful for the priesthood. I have asked to go where the fighting is – and hope that I may be there soon.*

They needed to get away, have some fun - forget about death, anger, and sadness. Azelia was very proud for having arranged the trip to Massachusetts' premier amusement park. The Nantasket carousel included two rare Roman Chariots; each pulled by two horses carved by the Dentzel Company, and the scalloped canopy was considered the most beautiful of any carousel ever constructed.

As they walked arm-in-arm through the park, she suddenly stopped to listen to words spewing from the mouth of a barker. "I'll guess your weight within two pounds or you can pick from this wide assortment of dolls and stuffed animals. Ten cents. How 'bout you Ma'am," he called to Azelia. "Step right up."

Azelia laughed and turned to Heron. "Should I?"

"Go ahead," Heron said. "But you know these things are rigged."

"He won't come close," she whispered. Then to the barker she said, "All right."

"Right over here, Ma'am." He surveyed her head to toe, so intensely that her cheeks flushed red. Then he took her hands and pumped them up and down a few times while keeping his eyes closed. Heron flashed her a smile. This was all part of the act.

The barker hesitated for effect then said, "One-hundred and six pounds."

Azelia leaned over and whispered to Larry, "Wrong. I weighed myself this morning and I am one-twelve."

"Step right on these scales, Ma'am."

The monster scale had a round face with a bouncing pointer that settled at one hundred-seven.

"Ah! I was within one pound. Who's next? Let me guess your weight. I will come within two pounds or..."

Azelia gave Heron an enigmatic look. "He cheated."

"What did I tell you?" he asked.

They rode the Dodgems, electric-driven bumper cars that smashed into other cars loaded with strangers screeching in glee. Then they eagerly left the bumper cars and just as eagerly rode through the Tunnel of Love. When they exited, Azelia's face was flushed and Heron was grinning sheepishly.

"Test your strength!" shouted another barker who strongly resembled W.C. Fields. "How about you, sir?" he said to a giant, the size of Paul Bunyan. "You look like you could win one of my giant pandas, great teddies, or stuffed giraffes. Just ring the gong at the top of the pole." The pole was marked *WEAKLING* at the bottom and progressed up to *SUPERHUMAN* at the gong.

The big man paid, rolled up his sleeves and raised the mallet high above his head. He smashed it down with all his strength shooting the ball upward. It reached *STRONG MAN*, one down from *SUPERHUMAN*.

"Try again? Come on. You can do it."

The giant shrugged and disappeared into the crowd.

"How about you, sir?" the barker gestured at Heron, who shook his head, no.

"Why don't you try?" Azelia asked. "You want to. I can tell."

"It's fixed. That big guy couldn't do it."

"It's going to bother you if you don't at least try. I don't care if you don't hit the gong."

Heron handed over his money and took the mallet in his hands with one eye surveying the barker to see if he was signaling someone. Then he wound up and brought the mallet down as hard as he could, shooting the red ball straight up the pole like a rocket, dinging the bell so hard that it left a dent.

Azelia squealed with delight.

The barker's face took on a sullen look. He said, "Hey, you don't have to break the damned thing." Reluctantly, he handed Azelia the large stuffed panda bear she pointed out.

The smile instantly returned to the barker's face as he faced a new crowd. "See that folks? You too can win. Step right up and take your chances. How about you sir?"

The beach was just across the street from the amusement park. They bought cotton candy and crossed over to where seagulls soared above the breaking waves in search of food. Sailboats were moving up and down the coast and a large freighter could be seen on the far horizon. Heron had been here several times with his father to dig for clams, so early in the morning that they'd have come and gone long before the amusement park had opened. It seemed different now with throngs of people talking and laughing. The sun had never been this high or this bright on those occasions.

A breeze caught her hair and whipped a strand across her forehead. She absentmindedly brushed it back and tilted her head against the wind. He could have looked at her face for all eternity and never have tired of it. She was thoroughly captivating.

Her head was on his shoulder and the panda on her lap when the bus pulled away from the beach. She couldn't be prouder. She could search the world and never find another like him. To have found her man in Hopedale in the early years of her life seemed improbable. For God to have made him so very special would always astound her.

On Monday, July 6, the phone rang with the same demanding intensity as on the day John had passed away. This time Emma refused to be her cheerful self when she answered it. "It's for you," she called to her son as he sat in the living room reading the Sunday paper. She returned to the ironing board beside the hot stove, moistened her finger and tapped the flat part of the iron to test the level of heat.

Heron heard the sizzle as he took up the earpiece. "Hello," he said into the stationary mouthpiece with the receiver pressed to his ear. The man on the other end identified himself as a scout from the Boston Braves. "Mr. Heron, we've been monitoring your play for most of the season and we want to invite you to try out for the team." Heron was having a sensational season with the Draper semipro baseball team, leading the Blackstone Valley League in home runs and stolen bases.

"We'd like to bring you to Boston as soon as possible. I think it's safe to say that in your case, the tryout is a mere formality. I am convinced we'll soon have you in a Braves uniform."

Ordinarily, Heron would have jumped for joy, but at the moment he was barely listening. No matter that the Braves could pay him handsomely - more in one year than he could make in five years working for the Drapers. No matter that this was the answer to his prayers. The offer had arrived a day too late.

"I'm afraid it's impossible. Yesterday I received my draft notice." He was to report to the Boston Army Base on Wednesday, July 14th for induction.

Undaunted, the representative suggested Heron apply for a deferment. "No," he said. "It wouldn't feel right – like shirking my duty."

The representative reminded him that Ted Williams had received a deferment as sole support of his mom. Why not Heron? Heron had followed the story closely in the newspapers. In the end, Williams joined naval aviation and was called to active duty in November 1942.

His final answer was thanks but no thanks. Perhaps later, but first he had a duty to perform. The very next day the phone rang yet again. This time the caller identified himself as a scout for the New York Yankees. Heron gave him the same answer.

Sports were not all that would have to be relegated to the back burner; the wedding of Lawrence Heron and Azelia Noferi, planned for September, would have to be postponed until his first furlough.

On their last Saturday together, the Ford he had borrowed from Fred rode as though it knew its own way. North on Dutcher, left on West Street, and then over dirt roads deep into the Hopedale Parklands past Maroni's Grove, a walk-in shelter with three stone walls, a concrete roof, and a huge built-in fireplace.

They left the car parked by a clump of tall pines and strolled the causeway to the old Rustic Bridge, a setting David Henry Thoreau would have loved to write about. The narrow Mill River rushed past boulders projecting from the water, forming small eddies that swept under the bridge to join the placid pond on the opposite side.

Azelia sat on one of the two low rails of stone on either side of the bridge and Heron plopped down beside her. They listened to the wind whispering through the pines and watched as birds silently glided through the evening haze en route to their nests. The shimmering surface of the water reflected the forest of trees surrounding it. Fish leapt but they each turned too late to catch more than a telltale ripple. Overhead a graceful hawk soared on a thermal in ever-narrowing circles without ever having to flap its wings. Heron placed his arm around her. The strong scent of ozone was intoxicating. "Remember me when the stars come out to play and moonbeams skirt the bay. Remember me," he said.

"Where did that come from?" she asked.

"Not sure. Perhaps I heard it in a movie. You know, the one where the departing hero tells his girlfriend to look up at the moon at night. Gazing at the same object from distant places would somehow keep them in touch."

"But night falls at different times on the other side of the globe."

"No matter. We each will have looked at the same object on any given day."

"And each night when I look up at the moon I will tell it how much I love you." A shiver made its way down her spine though the temperature was still in the eighties.

Returning to Maroni's Grove they stood beside the car listening to the sound of a rushing brook that wound its way from a pristine spring upstream. Suddenly a gust of wind lifted a page from a discarded newspaper off a picnic table. It became airborne and hovered like a manta ray before plunging to the ground at their feet. The headline read: *ARMED FORCES ALLSTARS BEAT BRAVES 9-8. Ted Williams' last inning homerun wins it for the All-Stars.* Included on the list of All-Star players were Joe DiMaggio and Babe Ruth.

A second gust turned to a page that read *GERMAN PANZER DIVISIONS DRIVEN OFF; Allies unite bridgeheads and secure objectives.* The susurrus of war hung in the air; they could almost hear a clock ticking. An eerie whistle of the wind sent a chill passing through them, this time portending something evil.

Heron tightened his arm around Azelia and took one last look around, thinking how much he loved Hopedale, its symmetry, peace, and quiet. It was not an easy place to leave.

On the morning of August 4th, Fred drove Heron, Azelia, and Emma to Union Station in Worcester under an emotional cloud made drearier by a sudden cloudburst. The procession entered the station wordlessly and followed Heron as he made his way toward the platform. The slightest whispers and the tiniest footsteps echoed off walls that stretched heavenward to meet the station's vaulted ceilings.

John Volpicelli, David Rubenstein, and Arthur Fertitta were all waiting on the platform when they arrived.

As the engine built up steam, Larry held Azelia in a tight embrace and kissed her goodbye one last time. "Hurry or you'll miss the train," Rubenstein's mother shouted. Heron finally broke away and sprinted toward the train as it began leaving the station without him. At the last second, David Rubenstein reached out to help him safely aboard.

Azelia wept unabashedly.

Mrs. Rubenstein placed a hand on her shoulder. "Don't worry, Azelia," she said. "He'll be fine. He'll come home to you." There was something comforting in the manner of Mrs. Rubenstein's words, while at the same time foreboding.

The suicide of a key post office employee following an embezzlement created an ominous scandal and left an opening that needed to be filled immediately. "We need someone bright, well organized, and capable of expeditiously tidying up the botched books," postmaster William Larson said to high school Principal Winburn Dennett. "I was hoping you might recommend someone."

Without hesitation, Dennett answered. "I know just such a person. She's sharp, extremely ethical, and trustworthy. Besides, she plans to marry soon and could use the money." Dennett agreed to call her right away and explain that the job would last for only a few months.

Azelia accepted the offer and remained in the job for the next five months. Postmaster Larson wanted her to stay longer. "I only wish I could find more like you. You're extremely well organized and efficient. But I can't compete with what Draper is offering."

She thanked him for the opportunity but her job here was done. Anyone could step in and maintain what she'd started. The Draper Corporation was breaking tradition. It had expanded the openings for women because of manpower shortages caused by the war, and it was eager to hire the woman who had recently sorted out the post office fiasco.

Azelia was happy to begin as a secretary in the tool design department. The routine kept her busy and took her mind off Larry for very brief periods. Besides field hockey, she had played basketball in high school and was an excellent pitcher, having captained the high school softball team her senior year. So it came as no surprise that she soon became the star pitcher for the *Jigs,* a Draper softball team that competed against teams with names like *Main Office, Mechanics*, and *Shuttle*. If she had been born a generation later she might have played professional sports or had a shot at becoming an executive. But women in her day were lucky just to find a job.

4
Six Months at Rucker

On August 9, 1943, the sun slashed through stratus clouds to bleed a fiery red on the far horizon. Twin buses entered the gates of Camp Rucker carrying fifty-two draftees from New England, the Mid-Atlantic States, Indiana, and Wisconsin.

The twelve hundred grueling miles from New York left shirts stained and bodies emitting foul odors. Record-breaking heat and humidity forecasted from Washington, DC, to the Keys promised no relief.

Pvt. Heron exited the bus and glanced at the Bulova Azelia had presented to him last June on his twenty-third birthday. A quarter to six a.m. Fifty-five hours since his last bath.

"Damn the southern heat," said William E. Shanahan from, Taunton, Massachusetts. "Damn the southern humidity. And those stupid Barbasol, Nehi, and Dr. Pepper billboards. Didn't southerners ever hear of Coke or Pepsi?"

"Christ, if we could bottle this smell, we could use it to win the war," Angelo Bastoni muttered as he sucked in a breath of fresh air. He bent to separate his duffle bags from where the driver was piling them on the curb. "It's strong enough to give mosquitoes second thoughts."

"Yeah. We'll call it *Angelo's Revenge*." Shanahan commented as he lifted his bag from the pile.

Raising his arm above his head, Steve Fiske, the farm boy from Chesterfield, Massachusetts said, "I would be the first to surrender."

"Phew! Lower your arms." Roger Burt quipped. "Or somebody please fart and clear the air."

"Ha. Ha. Real funny, Burt." Fiske gave his arm a friendly poke.

Spoken words and laughter belied an undercurrent of nervous tension borne by fear of the unknown. These men had been inducted into an army about which they knew very little, with no control over their own destinies. Lives interrupted. Like Heron, many had recently taken new jobs or put aside plans to attend college. Separated from the safety and security of their friendly hometowns, they were on a path that could lead straight to death's door.

The newly formed 87th Chemical Weapons Battalion, whose principal weapon was the 4.2-inch mortar, required plenty of space for lobbing shells at targets – open space was about all that was before them for as far as the eye could see.

This was "Wiregrass Country," named for the stiff grass that prolifer-ated wide portions of Alabama, Florida, and Georgia like strands of copper wire. By the end of 1941, the Federal government had purchased 65,000 acres of Alabama farmland, and last year the Corps of Engineers had built a 4,600-acre cantonment naming it after Edmund Winchester Rucker, a con-federate soldier from Tennessee.

"I'm starving," groaned John Sears, from Plymouth, Massachusetts. Sears stood well over six feet and moved with a lumbering gait. He reminded most people of James Stewart, the actor who had enlisted as a private in 1941 and was rapidly advancing up through the ranks. Most draftees were between the ages of eighteen and twenty-four. The forty year-old Sears had told Heron, "The army scraped the bottom of the barrel when they drafted me."

"I'm ready for some grub," said Burt. Prior to being drafted, the no-nonsense twenty year-old had been an auto mechanic living in Plainfield, Massachusetts. He was a wiry five foot seven with hazel eyes and brown hair. Forthright and likable, Burt had first met Heron at Ft. Devens.

Shanahan cocked an eye at Burt. "Yeah. Me too. Only I don't know what first, food or bath?"

"You'd better eat while the mess hall's still serving."

Heads turned toward the soldier who had appeared from nowhere and whose voice was as coarse as a Sherman tank swiveling on loose gravel. "Welcome to Rucker," he said. "My name is Sgt. Volcjak. The sooner you finish role call and stash your gear, the sooner you'll eat. The army moves on its stomach you know, so fall in!"

Sgt. Carl C. Volcjak stood six feet tall, thickly built; his square cut face was seamed with lines of stress and browned by the wind and sun. An Army cap rode at a jaunty angle atop his military crew cut. Three months ago he'd been promoted to private first class, corporal a month later, and sergeant a month after that.

Hands on hips, shoulders thrust back, head erect, the sergeant read names alphabetically off a clipboard, his sanguine gray-black eyes conveying sternness and competence. As the final "here" echoed back at him, the roar of a cannon sounded from somewhere distant. "That was Big Bertha. She'll be your wake up call every morning at this time except Sundays," he said.

"Training at Camp Rucker will include mortar practice and squad tactics, simulated support of infantry house-to-house fighting, jungle combat, and assaults on fortified positions. You will undergo strenuous calisthenics four times a week. The obstacle course and the physical fitness course at the beginning and end of your training will show how much you've improved. Exhausting road marches with full field equipment will prepare you for battle."

"Grab your gear and fall in," the sergeant ordered. They lined up as instructed, still with a sense of extreme dislocation. It took but a few moments to stow their gear in Barracks #12. Its ceiling was a maze of ductwork and electrical wiring. Not exactly the Hilton but it would do as a place to rest after a hard day's work.

As they marched the short distance to the mess hall, the camp came alive with soldiers streaming from barracks like colonies of ants from disturbed nests. Roll was being called, orders barked, and cadence shouted as neat columns moved smartly past.

Mess hall food, though nourishing and substantial, was not exactly five-star. After chow the men lined up outside Barracks #12 to be interviewed by company commander, Captain John T. Stiefel. They were ragamuffin dirty, smelling like lockers stuffed with soiled laundry, and strongly resembling a bread line in the midst of the Great Depression.

The captain stood square-jawed and tight-lipped, his forthright blue eyes smiling in the manner of Fr. Connors. Despite the heat, his starched shirt showed sharp creases. Though everyone else was soaked, the captain was neat and dry. Heron wondered if he was missing sweat glands.

"Good morning men, and welcome to Camp Rucker. I know you're anxious to wash and get into clean fatigues so I will make this brief..."

The screech of brakes drew attention to the jeep jamming to a stop amid a cloud of dust behind the captain. An Army major hopped out and bolted forward. The captain about-faced and saluted Major James T. Batte, commander of the 87th Chemical Weapons Battalion (Motorized), which had been activated on May 22, 1943.

Ramrod straight and wielding a swagger stick like an extension of his hand, Batte addressed the company commander. His eyes were hard blue coals. "Why aren't these soldiers cleaned up and in starched fatigues?" The major wore full dress, his chest gleaming with medals, shoes spit-shined, swagger stick menacingly tapping the side of his leg.

"Sir, they arrived by motor coach at 0530 and have not had time..."

"What time is it now, soldier?" Batte looked past Captain Stiefel as though he did not exist and snapped the stick jauntily under his left arm.

"Oh nine hundred, sir."

"Forty-five minutes remain if you intend to get them cleaned up and in proper uniform in time for indoctrination."

"Yes sir." The captain saluted as the major turned to depart. Then he did a snappy about face and ordered, "Fall in here at..." The captain checked his watch, "Oh nine thirty." He continued. "In combat fatigues and helmets." The major had already climbed into his jeep and was being whisked away.

Sweat glistened the captain's forehead at last and his mouth was drawn into a tight thin line. The Pennsylvanian who had risen through the ranks impressed Heron by keeping his cool. Though his face was placid, there was enough heat in his eyes to fire a massive boiler. He said, "Clean up quickly and get into starched fatigues. Look sharp. Dismissed."

After beating all recorded cleanup times, the men were reassembled and marched several blocks to a set of green bleachers where they were ordered to fall out and take seats. As they settled in, a staff car pulled up as if on cue. The driver climbed out and opened the rear door smartly for Major Batte. The major exited the car carrying a leather binder in one hand and the ever-present swagger stick in the other. He marched briskly to a podium, arranged some papers, and began to address the men.

A hush fell over the stands.

"Men," he said, reading from papers he had stacked on the podium. "Welcome to the 87th Chemical Weapons Battalion." A smile curled back his thin lips revealing even rows of sparkling white teeth. But that was not what held their attention. The stern eyes and rigid body language were conveying all the personality and warmth of a bronze bust in the heart of Yukon Territory.

"Here you will find excellent teaching facilities and competent instructors, amusement and recreational facilities. Your religious preference will be respected and our chaplains are here to minister to your spiritual needs." He paused while a helmet clunked down a few steps before an embarrassed private Tom Fletcher swept down to scoop it up. When the chuckles died down, he continued. "You will find your officers just in their treatment and anxious to teach. Many started out as privates who by hard work and diligent study have achieved their present ranks."

The smile evaporated. His eyes pierced, his voice swelled. "You can do the same, but not by goldbricking, playing sick, or being a sloppy, inefficient soldier. If you are a Dumb Joe now, you will be a Dumb Joe when the war ends. By paying strict attention, you can emerge an efficient soldier, more likely to return from battle."

The major cleared his throat and continued. "The Fighting 87th has traditions to build. It is a chemical warfare battalion armed with the 4.2-inch mortar that fires projectiles containing gas, smoke, or high explosive."

He paused to scan faces for a reaction to the word "gas." There were the usual frowns and turning of heads. This group appeared to be even younger than the last crop, yet all seemed eager.

"Your mission is to render support to the infantry." His voice grew more intense. "You must strike quickly and with fury, like tough first class field soldiers. We don't give a damn how our gases and powder are made, or by whom; our job is to shoot them at our enemies, and shoot to kill."

Now his voice softened and his body lost its rigidity, as if the worst was over and he was about to coast to a finish. "May you enjoy good health, happiness and good luck while you are members of the Fighting 87th. I know you are anxious to show those damn Germans and Japs that here is one battalion that can out-fight the infantry and out-shoot the artillery, and who are just as good and tough as they come."

The major was convinced that he had instilled a sense of what the 87th was about and had ignited a curiosity as to the types of chemicals the Army planned to employ. It was common knowledge that poison gas had been outlawed by international convention. These opening comments always raised questions. Before training ends, they will find their answers.

In the weeks and months that followed, Heron would learn that in 1874, the Brussels Convention had outlawed the use of poisons and all weapons that might cause unnecessary suffering. Twenty-five years later the Hague International Peace Conference added projectiles filled with poison gases to the banned list. But when the Germans launched a major chlorine gas attack at Ypres, Belgium during World War I, all bets were off. Both sides began using chemical weapons and continued using them through the end of the war.

The rationale behind the formation of the 87th became clear at a lecture given by Captain Stiefel on a balmy Wednesday afternoon. "The Treaty of Versailles banned chemical weapons but not their development, production or possession. All countries retained the right to retaliate in kind should an enemy attack them or their allies with such weapons. Unless they do, we are restricted to the use of high explosive and white phosphorous, or 'smoke,' as WP is sometimes called."

"How long after the enemy initiates a poison gas strike would we get access to such weapons?" Private John Sears asked.

"Immediately," Stiefel answered. He paused for a moment then added, "We'll be carrying mustard and phosgene gases into battle with us just in case. Let's hope we're not forced to use them."

Pvt. Heron was one of seven men reporting to a squad leader, four gun squads to a platoon, three platoons to a company, sixty-four men operating nine mortars. Each platoon had its own fire direction center and operated separately to maximize geographic coverage. When moving forward, one platoon would fire while another repositioned.

The squad soon learned to set up and fire in minutes with unbelievable accuracy. They were dropping high explosive rounds on fake fortifications, tanks, and targets being towed to simulate an enemy on the move. They fired white phosphorous to create smoke and simulate driving an enemy from hiding by dousing them with particles that would eat their flesh. They were all able to distinguish between the shells by the gray or olive colors and the coded bands of green, yellow, and red that indicated the chemical fill.

The 4.2-inch mortar had a rifled bore so the shell did not require a fin. This allowed it to be fired with far more deadly accuracy than its predecessor, the old British Stokes mortar. The assembled mortar weighed 330 pounds. The heaviest of its three main parts was 175 pounds. The men were amazed at the ease with which Heron would single-handedly lift the heaviest part on and off a jeep whenever the platoon advanced its position.

5

He Marches to a Different Drummer

On Tuesday following a tense day of practice firing, Sgt. Volcjak approached Heron. "The Major wants to see you in his office right away," he said.

"What's up Sergeant?"

"No idea."

What did the commanding officer want with a lowly private he couldn't pick from a crowd? Had something happened to Azelia, or his mother? His mind was in a whirl rejecting such concepts, pushing them down, striving to stay calm.

His footsteps echoed off unpainted walls and linoleum floors as he walked past a tight warren of small offices in the one-story rambling building until he spotted Batte's nameplate tacked to a mahogany-colored door. He knocked and a voice invited him to enter.

Lieutenant Bonafin was seated inside thumbing through a manual. The room was neat and sparsely furnished. The lieutenant gestured him in. "Sit down," he said. Then he rose and left to go in search of Batte.

The scent of cleaning chemicals awakened Heron's senses. The office was as antiseptic as a medical facility. A silver frame on a side table held a five by seven photograph of an attractive woman Heron supposed was the Major's wife. Several plaques with Batte's name and dates inscribed on brass plates were centered on the two walls on either side of the desk, each surrounded by framed certificates of achievement and pictures of the major being pinned with medals.

His attention fell on a certificate showing Batte had graduated from VMI in 1940. It was common knowledge that the major had dropped out of West Point as a plebe in 1935. In all the photos he sported the half-inch spiky brush cut that had earned him the nickname "Old Knobby." Old Knobby was all of 31 years old, not much older than the mostly twenty-year olds under his command.

A radio playing somewhere down the hall sent *I'll Be Seeing You* wafting in through the thin walls. From outside came a cacophony of engines, shouts of cadence, and stomping of boots as soldiers marched past an open window. He could hear the *pop, pop, pop* of distant gunfire and the drone of a plane used for reconnaissance passing overhead.

Finally the door opened. Old Knobby entered, followed by Lt. Bonafin. The sudden opening stirred a mild breeze that set the fringes of beige curtains dancing.

Heron rose to attention. "At ease, soldier. Please sit down." The major spoke dispassionately and flashed a disarming smile. "How are things going with you?" he asked.

"Fine, sir."

"Good. Good." The major moved around his desk and lowered himself into a swivel chair that looked too large for his slight frame. Standing up, he appeared taller than he really was because of his slim stature. The oversized chair shrunk him even more.

Lt. Bonafin drew a chair even with Heron's as the major became preoccupied with an imaginary dust particle and absent-mindedly brushed it from the shinny surface of his desk. There were no signs he was about to deliver bad news.

He opened a manila folder and drew a sheet of paper toward him. "I see you were an outstanding ball player," he stated. "Captained the football team your senior year. You swamped Cathedral High, shutting out Angelo Bertelli, Notre Dame's star quarterback, the man they call the 'Springfield Rifle.' You not only beat them, you didn't allow one first down."

Heron refrained from adding, *I didn't do it alone*, sensing the major was on a roll.

"Just as you've set records for the most home runs and stolen bases in the Blackstone League, you maxed our aptitude tests and topped the best recorded times through the obstacle and physical fitness courses."

"What have I left out Lieutenant?" he asked Bonafin.

The lieutenant twisted in his chair to face Heron. "You were swamped with scholarship offers," he said. "Boston Braves and New York Yankee scouts made offers just when you were drafted."

Heron was amazed. These officers had certainly done their homework. He never imagined the army would run such a thorough background check. What else did they know about him?

The major remained solemn. "I'll come right to the point – *Corporal* Heron."

A look of surprise crossed Heron's face.

"Yes, you've been promoted. Keep up the good work and you'll soon make sergeant. But that's not why I've invited you here." Batte leaned against the back of his chair and rested his hands on the arms.

"I like what I see in your progress reports."

Heron shifted self-consciously.

"Captain Stiefel and I have discussed this thoroughly. He agrees, as does Lt. Bonafin. Stiefel thought it better that I be the one to talk to you about it."

The major leaned on his desk and tented his hands. "I won't pursue anything unless you agree to go along." Lowering his voice conspiratorially, he added, "I'd like to sponsor your entry into West Point." He leaned back. "Of course there will be tests. You'll have to compete. But you have the right stuff. The Army needs leaders and you could make the grade."

He paused to let his words sink in.

Heron was deeply moved. Azelia would want him to accept, if for no other reason than to keep him out of harm's way for a period of time.

But he felt he had no choice in the matter. He smiled politely and cleared his throat. "Uh. Sir. I am honored that you think so highly of me...that you would recommend me. But I am afraid I cannot accept."

The major made no effort to mask his disappointment. "Though you have all the makings of a warrior, you also have a history of turning down great opportunities," he said. A rasp crept into his voice that had not been there before, as if to hint annoyance. "You've refused scholarship offers from Notre Dame, Texas A&M, Trinity, Boston College, Holy Cross, and many other fine institutions." A pause. "And now West Point."

Heron cleared his throat. "There were reasons, sir."

The major hesitated then smiled grudgingly. "I'm listening."

He squirmed in his chair, not comfortable talking about himself. The lieutenant shifted his body in silent sympathy. "I would like nothing more than to play ball for West Point or Notre Dame." He looked down at his folded hands. "But it is not an option."

"Go on."

He told Batte everything, the promise to his father, saving up to be married, his father's sudden death, working to support his mother, and how the Draper Corporation rents houses to employees for next to nothing and maintains them free of charge – as long as someone in the family works for the company. "The benefits remain in effect as long as I am on duty, and will continue uninterrupted once I return to the job."

"I see. It seems you are responding to a higher calling. Rather noble of you, young man. I might have misjudged you had I not been made aware of the circumstances." His voice grew softer, calmer. "It would be a good thing for the Army if you chose to stay in, even after the war. There are always battlefield commissions and other ways for you to become an officer. Like the Draper Corporation, the Army takes care of its own." He smiled with a practiced cordiality that did not extend to his eyes.

"Thank you, sir. I'll do my best," he promised.

Heron went right to work on his commitment to perform. On Wednesday, he came away from the rifle range an expert marksman. The following Monday, he led Tom Fletcher through the first of a series of exhaustive nightly drills to help the flabby lobsterman from Bar Harbor firm up. No one could understand how a man who made a living hauling lobster traps and performing other heavy-duty tasks each and every day, could not muster a single sit-up.

Heron was greatly admired by his comrades. Tough, blessed with good looks, intelligent, and possessing the physical attributes most men covet, he was nevertheless unburdened of a swelled head. He treated every man as his equal, including Fletcher, the man who wore an apology tattooed on his forehead and seemed to hate himself for taking up too much space on the planet.

After a month of regular workouts, Heron had Fletcher knocking off ten sit-ups with relative ease. He lost ten pounds of flab as well and was beginning to rebuild his self-confidence.

As time ticked past, relationships between all the men grew stronger. They worked, struggled, and lived together. They went into town and got drunk together. They even got into a few scrapes together.

One foggy Saturday in early December, Heron and David Rubenstein thumbed a ride into Dothan, about twenty miles southeast of Rucker. There was next to nothing going on in town except Christmas lights, so they made for a place called the *Red Barn,* where *Pabst* and *Schlitz* signs graced the front windows.

The place had ratty floors that hadn't seen a mop in decades. At one end of the room stood a Wurlitzer. Confederate flags adorned both upper corners of a large mirror behind the bar. Heron spotted a sign on the wall that read: "No Colored Served Here." Nodding his head to draw Rubenstein's attention to the sign, he whispered, "Let's make it a quick one."

Before Rubenstein could respond, a burly man on Heron's right asked, "Where you boys from?" He had a hard, raw-boned face badly in need of a shave.

"Rucker," Heron answered. An inner voice warned him not to mention Massachusetts.

"Let me buy you a drink, soldier," the man said. It was not a question.

"Oh that's not necessary," he answered without rancor. "Thanks anyway."

"You refusin' my hospitality, boy?" Burly asked, pugnaciously. He was a towering man. Late thirties, early forties. His black sleeveless undershirt fit snuggly, displaying rippling biceps.

In the interest of civility, Heron replied, "Hey. No problem. You can buy us a drink if you'd like."

"I offered *you* a beer. Didn't say nothing' about the Jew boy." His eyes were fixed on Rubenstein's gold ring with the Star of David.

Heron tensed and looked at the bartender who averted his eyes. Suddenly it grew so quiet you could have heard a flea scratch itself. "Come on Dave. Let's go," he said.

Emboldened by the presence of his three smirking friends, Burly said, "I would feel insulted if you was to walk out of here after I offered you a drink, boy." He turned an amused smile toward his associates who nudged one another and laughed encouragingly.

"Thank you," Heron said. "But a truck load of buddies will be picking us up any minute to take us back to camp." He looked at his Bulova to support the statement.

"In fact, we'd better go meet them right now." He started for the door with Rubenstein close behind. But on the heels of Heron's assertion, Burly reached up and grabbed Rubenstein's lapel and a brief moment of silence was shattered by the sound of fabric tearing. "You don't leave 'til I say so." His manner of speech was petulant, intolerant.

"Take your hands off him," Heron ordered.

The redneck grinned, displaying yellowing teeth. This was the reaction he had been hoping for. "Suppose you make me?"

Rubenstein, who was slight and bookish, struggled to break Burly's grip but was no match. The redneck grabbed his other lapel with his free hand and pushed Rubenstein onto a barstool. "Sit!" he barked and picked up a bottle the bartender had opened and began pouring it down Rubenstein's front. Rubenstein reared up ready to fight but Heron already had a tight grip on the man's arm. "Enough," he said quietly, his eyes brandishing an inscrutable gaze that could have beat out those of Charlie Chan and Fu Manchu.

"Sure," Burly said, grinning like a shark. He raised his left hand defensively then smacked the base of the bottle against the lip of the bar with his right, breaking off the end. Rubenstein sidestepped as Burly turned to face

Heron. "Jews, niggers, and northerners are not welcome here," he sneered. With the speed and menace of a rattler, he stabbed straight at Heron's face with the jagged edge, an inside move he knew was impossible to block.

With unflinching speed, Heron's left arm shot out to deflect the arm, preternaturally so, redirecting the bottle harmlessly to one side. Then both hands closed on Burly's wrist like a vise, forcing it behind him to shoulder level with a twist that sent the bottle crashing to the floor.

Burly's distorted face turned a shade of purple incongruent with human skin. He made a strange guttural sound, which brought his two companions down off their stools. With his arm twisted behind his back, he began whimpering in pain, no longer fearful looking. All eyes were regarding Heron with a new appreciation.

The man who stood out as the largest, whose appearance was even more menacing than Burly's, inched closer. He was taller than Heron, thick through the body, with no neck. His flat head bore a wartime crew cut, and his forehead was also flat and shiny, reminding Heron of a bar brawler that used to prowl the dark alleys adjacent to the Milford Hotel.

Just then, the bartender brought the barrel of a double-barreled shotgun into view, stopping Flat Head dead in his tracks. "Not in my bar," he said, with a motion of dismissal. He nodded his head at the picture of a young soldier mounted on the wall behind the bar. "My son, Mickey," he said to the soldiers. "Somewhere in Sicily last I knew." Then he added, "Now get the hell out of here and don't come back."

Heron released Burly who raised his arms in the posture of a supplicant. To his friends he whispered, "Wait until they leave. We'll follow and get them outside."

The rednecks spotted the Jew through a fog rolling in. He was thumbing a ride. "The other one must be taking a leak," Flat Head whispered. Burly crossed the street. The others followed, Flat Head bringing up the rear. Behind him, Heron moved in swiftly. "Looking for me?" he asked, truculently, with the forbidding look of a panther. Flat Head took a swing that hit nothing but air. Before he could recover, Heron brought a knee up sharply into his groin. The big man tumbled to his knees and let out a gurgle.

A moment later, he was back on his feet, rushing forward with hands outstretched to take Heron by the throat. But again he missed his target, only this time his legs were kicked out from under him. Cursing loudly, he hit the pavement. Before he knew what was happening, his right hand was twisted behind him to the base of his neck. Heron leveraged the arm to bring him to his feet then ran him into a nearby fence. His head glanced off a corner post and his shoulder cracked against solid wood. "Jesus! My shoulder's broken!"

Heron let go.

Burly had already disappeared up the road. The others darted after him like hounds after a fox.

Moments later a two-door red Lincoln convertible with a black top stopped to offer the men a lift. The passenger window rolled down and the driver asked, "Where you boys headed?" She was a heavy-set bleached blonde with short choppy hair and abundant makeup. She spoke with a southern drawl, her words slipping over her tongue like wet molasses on a cool day.

"Camp Rucker," Heron answered. "Is it on your way?"

"Going right past it," the driver said. "Get in." Both women looked to be about twenty-something.

The passenger stepped out and pushed her seat forward. She stood about five feet tall and reeked of cheap perfume. Her hair was brown with red streaks. Once the car was in motion, Rubenstein asked, "Where y'all from?"

"Montgomery," the driver said. "My daddy's the sheriff." She said it as though he were the King of England. "Ever hear of Sheriff Thompson? He's quite famous," she beamed.

"Can't say I have?" Heron replied. He glanced over at Rubenstein who shrugged.

"Should we know him?" Rubenstein asked.

"It's been in all the papers." The driver giggled. "You never read about the lynchin's?" It was as though she were asking if they'd ever been to a carnival.

"What lynchin's?" Rubenstein gulped.

"Two niggers caught with a white girl about six months ago, wasn't it, Melinda? It made all the papers."

Melinda replied, "Right around Easter."

"Happened to another nigger a few years back. They said he raped a white girl in his shack. Her daddy called my daddy and...well."

The two men fell silent. It was not what sheriffs did back home, but they were aware such things did happen. There had been five thousand lynching incidents in the United States since 1882, many in recent years.

Melinda asked, "Where y'all from?"

"Ah, Massachusetts," Heron responded.

Rubenstein kept swiveling his head around to peer behind them for headlights.

"So what do you girls do – for work that is?" Heron asked.

"I'm a cosmetologist," Melinda announced flatly.

Silence.

"I work for a funeral home. Make up dead people," she added.

Dead silence.

She swiveled her head around with each phrase, as if to toss her words past the rumblings of the Lincoln. "It's no worse than working on live people. Actually it's easier. Never get no complaints. Ha. Ha."

"Down right spooky at times though. Like when you press the flesh, it stays pressed. Leaves marks. Weird."

"It takes skill," she went on. "I can make them look just like the photos people give me."

Rubenstein said, "That's real interesting." He actually felt sympathy toward her. What other work could there be around here for a young woman?

The soldiers were taking turns looking behind them for a motorized posse to appear but none materialized. It was with great relief that they finally climbed out of the car a half-hour later. Thanking the girls for the ride, they moved gingerly toward Rucker's gates.

"I'll bet they lynch Jew boys, too," Rubenstein said, as the Lincoln drove off.

"Welcome to Alabama."

When they passed through the gates into Camp Rucker, it was as though a safety net had closed behind them. The south would forever bring to mind images of sharecropper shacks, confederate flags, and bodies swinging from ropes in dark shadows.

All future trips were to Panama City, which Heron found delightful. Though unlike the shores of New England, the Florida seaside held a sweet charm of its own.

6

Finding Time to Wed

As weeks rolled into months, Heron never lost sight of his dreams and aspirations. In a few years he would return to sports. Meanwhile, he would stay in top physical condition by running laps at the track and lifting weights at the base gym.

On Thanksgiving Day, he reversed the charges after spending nearly an hour waiting to cram his wide shoulders into a tiny outdoor phone booth. Even with the door closed, he could barely hear her voice above the din of passing vehicles and the chatter of men queued up outside the booth.

Christmas Day was especially difficult. After completing his call to Azelia, he ran five miles at the track then went to the gym to lift weights and throw some punches at the bag before returning to the barracks for a steaming shower. It was seven o'clock when he left the mess hall following a hearty Christmas dinner, returning to the barracks to reread her letters by moonlight.

Thousands of recollections were loosed in his mind like startled pigeons, as he recalled many happy years of courtship. Dating in the thirties and early forties meant playing tennis on clay courts in the town park, ice-skating on Hopedale Pond, enjoying hotdogs and fresh popcorn at the Wednesday evening band concerts, or strolling through the park on a clear night and looking up at the stars.

That night they held a Christmas party. A tree that looked like a reject from a paper factory was set up in one corner of the barracks. It was garnished with colored paper, garlands of popcorn, and silver balls from rolled cigarette foil. John Sears dressed up like Santa. There was laughter and cajoling as the men wished aloud for such items as a red fire engine, a night with Betty Grable, an end to the war, a month's furlough, money, and liquor.

Santa handed out gifts bought with donations, some useful, others not, like cigarettes, candy, prophylactics, beer, Vaseline, trusses, Kotex, and foot-long toothbrushes. Meanwhile, Burt, Healy, and Bastoni handed out beer that Cookie had kept stashed in the cooler in cases marked *Evaporated Milk.*

The fun and games were few and short-lived. By the end of January, the 87th had become a crack outfit proficient in the employment of the deadly mortar.

At 0600 on February 1, the battalion departed Rucker on buses and arrived at Camp Forrest, Tennessee nineteen hours later for phase two training. Early the next morning, the men were dragging carbines under barbed wire with live machinegun fire passing inches overhead and explosive charges going off nearby to simulate actual combat conditions. On the 12th, an Air-Ground Liaison Test was administered by the 11th Detachment, Special Forces, during which the men practiced coordinated attacks with artillery and infantry units. At the completion of this exercise, the 87th was cited for its outstanding performance.

On February 13, Heron was one of 450 officers and enlisted men to depart on a furlough originally scheduled to last two weeks, but at the eleventh-hour it had suddenly been cut to eight days. Something big was up. But he had more immediate and far more important matters to consider.

When he saw her in her wedding dress, his stomach did somersaults. No amount of rehearsals could have prepared him. He was bowled over by how much more beautiful she was than he had remembered. With her hair pulled back under a simple yet elegant white wedding crown that accented her bright blue eyes, she looked like a movie star. Her stride down the aisle was sure-footed. And her great shape was evident to where her gown flowed regally.

As they stood side-by-side taking vows, she found herself trembling.

Does he like me in this gown? Will I disappoint him on our honeymoon?

The Milford Hotel, regarded by many as a less than desirable place for a wedding reception, was decorated that day with white ribbons. A bouquet of flowers adorned each table. The bride and groom were caught in a swirl of music and danced as though they were the only two people on earth. Sparks passed like electric currents between them. Heron stood tall and held her tightly to his chest as they moved to the strains of Stardust, his hands caressing her strong sensuous back.

Part way through the night, she shook out her hair and it fell to her shoulders, smooth and clean smelling. It bounced as she spun, and sent a whiff of fragrance past him. "The Milford Hotel worked out just fine," she said. "No one is likely to ever forget our wedding."

Azelia had been aghast when her mom first suggested this place of darkness for the reception. Even now it emitted the strong scent of stale beer, its floors were crusted with a film of grime, and circular stains marked the long mahogany bar. But the food was good and the price was right. Owner Joe Sardini had offered it for free, out of friendship with her father.

"Your hair smells of jasmine," Heron whispered in her ear. He had no idea what jasmine smelled like. It was often mentioned in books and movies. All he knew was that her hair smelled heavenly and it set his heart pumping faster.

"You smell good too," she remarked, leaning her head against his cheek.

He kissed her hair and thrilled to its softness.

And so they were man and wife at long last. Two people clinging to one another like swimmers lost at sea. Not knowing what the future had in store.

The best wedding gift came from Heron's brother Fred who must have suffered weighty pangs of conscience for allowing his kid brother to discard a bright future to single-handedly support their mother. He gave them his old car and bought a new one for himself. Heron never asked for, nor expected help from brothers Fred, John, and Leonard. They had long since married and moved on. For his part, Larry was just as thrilled with the old Ford as Fred must have been with his new one.

Azelia sat at the wheel and turned the ignition. She adjusted the choke and the throttle while Larry bent at the front to crank the engine. It started on the third crank and they took off for their honeymoon in their car with its arthritic engine.

Heron found it difficult to take his eyes off the remarkably beautiful woman riding next to him. He was the proudest and happiest man alive. On the outside, she was cheerful and bright, but beneath the surface was an undeniable strength underscored by a hint of vulnerability.

The couple spent their abbreviated honeymoon at a friend's cottage in Chatham on Cape Cod. The days were sunny, balmy, and breezy, the nights romantic. The afternoon of their arrival began strained and awkward. Azelia remained anomalously silent as she unpacked.

He was not sure how long it was before she emerged from the bathroom in a white silk robe that clung to her exquisite body like a second skin. He swallowed hard. Without makeup her features were even more exquisite – nose perfect, lips full, intense blue eyes warm and exciting.

He stared into her eyes longer than he had intended then blurted, "Want to go through this list of restaurants Johnny gave us?" He seemed as nervous and fidgety as a kitten in a dog kennel.

"Later," she said taunting him with half-closed eyes and a wicked smile that surprised even her. Deliberately, wantonly, she stripped the covers and stretched out on the bed. Her hair cascaded around her shoulders and her robe fell open revealing long lithe legs, the muscles flexing in a way that set his heart pulsating. Sports had served her well. Her body was taunt and fluid, and as strong as tempered steel.

It was like seeing her for the first time, her smooth chin, her full and exotic lips slightly parted, teeth even and white, her eyes perfectly set and proportioned. He reached out to caress her mouth ever so gently, then kissed the hollow of her neck. It was like lighting a match in a propane-filled room.

Afterward, she whispered, "I love you, Larry Heron. Always have. Always will."

"I love you, too, Mrs. Heron," he said tenderly.

That night they went for Italian. The moon was bright and the air fragrant following a brisk afternoon shower. They started at the bar with a glass of Champagne then moved into the dining area where he ordered a bottle of Chianti. When the waiter returned for their food order, she selected the insalata caprese and fettuccine Alfredo, and he chose a small antipasto and chicken cacciatore.

Light from a candle set off her high cheekbones and delicate chin, accenting her glowing hair. When she caught his admiring glance, she leaned forward and gave his hand a loving squeeze.

Come Back to Sorrento drifted from speakers in each corner of the room. People gave them knowing glances, as though they were illicit lovers instead of husband and wife. At the end of their meal, the owner stopped to ask if they had enjoyed it.

"We loved the chicken cacciatore," Heron said, pouring the last of the wine. The garlic-laced smells emanating from the kitchen were so strong that he felt he could eat another helping.

"And I helped him finish it," Azelia added.

"It was my mother's recipe – my favorite. I'm so happy you are enjoying yourselves." He bowed and disappeared into the kitchen. Moments later he emerged carrying a new serving of cacciatore and a pitcher of red wine. He placed both on the table and said, "This one's on me." It added just the right touch and when they finally left the restaurant, it was in an exceptionally cheerful frame of mind.

She awoke the next morning and felt the mattress but he was gone. The cottage was quiet, too quiet. She called his name and checked each room but he was not to be found. After throwing on some clothes, she carried her search outside where her eyes were drawn to the ocean lapping the shore. Out of the corners of her eyes she caught him jogging along a far stretch of beach. If this had been summer and fifty degrees warmer, he'd have been fifty yards out in the ocean, cutting through the water like Johnny Weissmuller.

A hundred yards out, a large red buoy rocked by choppy waves sounded a bell while seagulls circled above a small fleet of fishing boats headed out to sea. She inhaled the freshness of the salty air and wondered why every day couldn't be as simple and serene as this one.

After he had showered and shaved, he bundled up and went out on the front porch while she took her time getting dressed. He sat in a porch swing and swayed gently, watching a group of gulls in the vast blue sky, lofty birds powered by white oars fanning the air. Far to the west, he could see puffs of charcoal-colored cotton and thought of war and death and man-made thunder fast approaching. And suddenly, an ominous dread fell heavily upon his shoulders and his heart began beating disquietly.

The next morning opened once again with bright sunshine and unseasonably warm weather. She slipped on a pair of slacks and threw a sweater over a plaid blouse. He wore corduroys and a sweatshirt over a flannel shirt - just enough to keep out the chill as they strolled the beach listening to the surf. Sea gulls shrieked overhead as waves tumbled lazily against the shore. The calming sounds and the warming rays of the sun seemed at odds with the chaos of a world gone mad.

Heron snapped a picture of her sitting on the bow of an overturned row-boat, her loosened hair outlining her face, with its glowing highlights exacerbated by the sunlight.

They sat in companionable silence, taking in lobster boats, sails, gulls, and breaking waves. Then he cupped her face in his hands and felt currents of electricity pass through his fingers to the tiny nerve centers in his body. The sweetness of her was like a narcotic to which he was completely addicted.

They decided to eat in that night. Azelia cooked a small pot roast to help extend the week's meat rations. The dinner table was covered with a linen tablecloth and napkins, fancy silverware, and lit candles.

They drank David Noferi's homemade wine and listened to Frank Sinatra records. After diner they danced; Heron held her close. They moved as one. And the war was forgotten, as basic emotions carried them to their own private places in their minds.

The record changed and the next tune captured the mood of the evening,

Dream when you're feeling blue.

Heron filled their wine glasses and they moved to a sofa fronting a large picture window. He leaned back, inhaling the sweet musk of her, as though sniffing a newly opened bottle of wine. "The scent fits you perfectly. Innocent," he said. "Perhaps fecund, with just a hint of carnal desire."

She laughed mellifluously and kissed him on the lips.

He raised an eyebrow and pursed his lips in a perfect imitation of Clark Gable. "Scarlet," he said. "I do give a damn! Yes I do!" With that, he lifted her in his arms and carried her to the foot of the stairs leading up to a tiny bedroom.

"Put me down this instant Rhett Butler," she said with mock primness.

"In my own good time," he said, twitching his lips and shifting his jaw, à la Gable.

He carried her up the stairs to the bedroom, dropped her gently on the bed, and fell beside her. They both laughed and he kissed her tenderly.

"Oh Larry. I love you so much. I wish you didn't have to..."

"Shhh," he whispered and kissed her cheeks. He tasted salt from fresh tears. "I love you more than words can say," he said. Then they hurriedly undressed.

They were back in Hopedale early the next morning, the day ending with tearful goodbyes at Worcester's Union Station. Again, Heron had to run to catch a departing train. Once aboard, he sat gazing absently out a window as the train gathered speed, and was suddenly stricken with extreme loneliness. An icy finger snaked its way down his spine as he shrunk down into the heavy collar of his overcoat like a turtle into its shell.

He arrived back at Camp Forest for the start of more specialized training on February 22. The next day, Lt. Colonel Batte resumed command of the battalion. By the 25th, the strength of the outfit had reached 624 enlisted men and 41 officers, and the days were filled with intensive training and repeated inspections. A month later, the battalion departed Tennessee via rail for a permanent change of station to Camp Shanks, New York. The day before, he had managed a hasty call to Azelia, updating her of his whereabouts. "I've been granted a weekend pass. How do you feel about meeting me in New York City on Friday?" he asked. "I checked ahead and there are plenty of rooms available at the Claridge."

"I can't wait!" she said.

In 1944, Worcester's tallest structure was a tower that cast its incongruous shadow over Union Station in Washington Square. Resembling Florence's Palazzo Vecchio, the tower was all that remained of the old station, demolished in 1909. When the new station was finally completed in 1911, at a cost of $750,000, it was considered the grandest in the nation. Twin terra cotta domes rising on either side of the main entrance were filled with rows of stained glass that illuminated ornate sculptures below, and a giant canopy of arched ceilings sparkled like enormous jewels between the two domes.

It was Thursday, March 29, a day Azelia had been anxiously awaiting. The main floor of the station was lined with rows of dark wooden benches. People jammed the platform. Many were in uniform, hugging, kissing and shedding tears - reminders of the day Larry left to return to Tennessee. She'd been too absorbed at the time to take notice of the popcorn vendors, shoe-shine boys, and Mr. Podbielski's famous barbershop where five barbers were always busy cutting hair. Today was different. She was on her way to New York City for a glorious few days with Larry before they sent him to God knows where.

Once aboard the train, she folded her heavy overcoat and laid it with scarf and gloves on an empty seat directly across from her, then sat down to undo her boots. She wiggled her frozen toes and waited for the feeling to return. She glanced over at her companions, Angie Volpicelli and Angie's mother-in-law, Alvina Volpicelli, who had insisted on going along to insure their safety.

Alvina toted a large shopping bag overflowing with boodle for son John that included salami, cheese, wine, and other spicy foods. The smells wafting from her bag filled the entire compartment, reminding Azelia of the Italian marketplace in Boston's North End where her mother would take her shopping once a year.

The Volpicelli women piled their heavy coats on hers and settled down, Angie beside her and Alvina across from them. Once the locomotive picked up steam and the train began to sway gently in rhythm with the clickety-clack of its wheels, most passengers, including Azelia's two companions, began to doze. She closed her eyes but could not sleep because of a nagging premonition that something was terribly wrong.

There was no reason for it. Larry was already at Camp Shanks in Rockland County, Orangeburg, a staging area for troops headed overseas from New York ports of embarkation. He had been promised a three-day pass. This would be their last time together for a while, and they were both looking forward to it.

While reading an article in Photoplay about a famous movie actor suspected of being a Nazi sympathizer, she slowly succumbed to the motion of the train, falling in and out of sleep - until being jolted awake when the train lurched to a sudden stop in New York City.

The scent of spring filled the air as the three women stood outside hailing a cab that took them to the Claridge Hotel in the heart of New York's Times Square. They checked into a room that was neat and clean, though poorly lit. As evening approached, the room grew steadily darker. The halls were dimmer still as they made their way to the elevator and down to the lobby to ask the concierge for places to eat. A block away they found the delicatessen he had recommended.

No word from the men that night.

The following morning they ate breakfast in the hotel and waited four hours in the lobby, but neither Larry nor John arrived. There were no messages. There was absolutely no way to reach the men. At noon, Mrs. Volpicelli insisted the girls grab some lunch and bring her back a sandwich while she held court in the lobby.

"I'm sorry, Cpl. Heron, but like I told you, all furloughs have been canceled," said Sgt. Julian Brunt, from Mississippi.

"But my wife is waiting at the Claridge right now sergeant. I was guaranteed this pass."

"There are no guarantees in war time, corporal. Colonel's orders have changed. Nothing I can do about it."

"But my wife!"

He shook his head. "Sorry."

"Let me at least call the hotel to let her know."

"Can't do that."

"Why not?"

"No one can call out. The base is locked down and everyone in it is secured."

"What about the guys still out on leave?"

"They've all been ordered to return immediately. That's all they know."

He labored until he felt his lungs would burst. His joints flashed fatigue alerts. Instead of stopping, he turned up the heat, increasing his speed, running as fast as his body would allow, pushing harder than ever before in his life. It was as though he were punishing himself for not finding a way to get out to meet Azelia, or sneaking off to locate a phone just to tell her he was sorry and how much he loved her. But that would be impossible. Making such a call might lead to his confinement for the next six months.

Sgt. Brunt had warned, "If anyone breaches security, I will make it my life's work to see that he ends up in the stockades surrounded by barbed wire - with a shotgun up his ass."

Besides letting off steam, the running helped rid his body of empty beer calories. Sweat stung his eyes, blurring his vision. He sucked air in through his nostrils and let it out through his mouth in harsh, shrill tones. His heart and legs pumped in unison as he bested all prior running speeds and levels of endurance.

Showered and dressed, he was headed for the recreation room when Staff Sgt. David Thomas stopped him. "Lt. Bonafin wants to see you right away."

Something had happened to Azelia. No. Can't be. Word doesn't travel that fast. Perhaps his orders had changed and he'd been granted a weekend pass after all.

He followed the sergeant to a small building, drab and poorly lit. The lieutenant was smiling when Heron entered his temporary office. He was offered a cigar and told to have a seat.

Heron took the cigar, thanked him, and then slipped it into his shirt pocket. Next, he drew up a metal folding chair and looked from the lieutenant to Sgt. Thomas who was grinning at him.

"Congratulations!" said the lieutenant. He hesitated then finished, "*Sergeant* Heron." Hearing that he had just made sergeant gave Heron a momentary lift, but his heart remained heavy with concerns for Azelia's well-being.

Sergeant Thomas was a likeable fellow, a New Yorker who was always ribbing Roger Burt about the Yankees beating the Red Sox. Heron admired him for his street smarts. Like John Sears, whatever the battalion needed, Thomas had a way of coming up with it on demand. Like the time Lt. Bonafin needed paint and brushes to fix up the interior of the barracks. Thomas "requisitioned" ten gallons of paint and a dozen brushes. No one knew from where, and no one dared ask.

After leaving the lieutenant, Sgt. Thomas invited Heron and Roger Burt to the NCO club where he bought the first round. Heron smoked the cigar and then attempted to drown himself in beer. His fellow noncoms attributed the excess beer consumption to his joy at being promoted.

Sgt. Robert "Red" Meyers shook his hand and ordered another round. The sergeant seemed nervous. "Have you ever been to sea?" he asked.

"My father used to take me fishing in Quincy Harbor and York, Maine," Heron replied.

"Ever get seasick?"

"No. Been in some rough situations but it never seemed to bother me."

"The mere mention of the ocean makes me sick. I'm not looking forward to a long boat ride," Meyers groaned. The sergeant had a faraway look in his eyes and his face looked as tormented as any Heron had ever encountered.

"Mind over matter," he offered. "It won't be so bad on a large ship."

Meyers' face seemed to turn more ashen at the mention of the word "ship." Heron thought it best to change the subject.

"Where are you from?" he asked.

A few minutes past six p.m., the hotel desk clerk approached the three women sitting in the lobby, politely asking if he could be of assistance.

"No thank you," Azelia smiled. "We're waiting for our husbands."

At seven p.m., Angie told the desk clerk that if anyone came looking for them, they'd be back by nine. Then they left to dine at the Waldorf Cafeteria.

At nine-thirty they were back in the hotel lobby. No one had come looking for them and there were no messages. The women waited until 11:30 before returning to their room for the night, leaving a message at the desk that they should be notified immediately if anyone should call.

The next morning after breakfast there was still no word. People passing by a third or fourth time began to stare.

"What should we do?" Angie asked.

"We'll wait." Azelia answered quickly. She hadn't come all this way to return home without seeing Larry.

At four that afternoon, a man wearing a dark blue suit and a gray fedora approached. There was an intensity about him that immediately caught Azelia's attention. He could have stepped out of a G-man movie. Cop was written all over him. He removed his hat and took a seat in the wing-backed chair directly across the coffee table from them.

"Excuse me ladies," he said. "I am Philip Rothman, the hotel detective." He cleared his throat. "I could not help but notice you've been waiting in this lobby for several days. Do you mind if I ask why? Who is it you are waiting for?"

"Our husbands. One is her son," Azelia said, nodding at Mrs. Volpicelli. "They're in the service – at Camp Shanks."

"They were supposed to be here by yesterday morning but haven't shown up or called," Angie added anxiously, hoping the detective could help.

"What do you suppose has happened," Mrs. Volpicelli asked.

"I'm afraid it means they're not coming," he answered truthfully. "I've seen it before. My advice to you ladies is to go home – wherever that may be." He sighed and leaned forward with a frown on his face. "If they haven't called in the past few days, it means that they are already out on the ocean somewhere."

"Wouldn't they leave word?" Mrs. Volpicelli asked.

"That's the way it works sometimes, Ma'am. Top secret. You could be here for the duration. They will not show and you won't hear anything. The Army brings 'em to Shanks for one purpose, get 'em aboard and ship 'em out. You had best head for home ladies."

Reluctantly, the three women boarded a train the next morning for Worcester, Azelia teary-eyed most of the trip. Larry was headed into harm's way without so much as a final embrace or a goodbye kiss from her. She wanted to tell him just one more time how much she loved him. All she could do now was pray for his safe return.

He woke with a start and rolled to one side of his cramped bunk, peering into the darkness. Was he really awake, or was one foot still in the dream with her smooth, naked body curled against him? Her soft smile lingered like the afterglow of a flashbulb in a dark room. He closed his eyes with the hope of reentering the dream but it had already faded into an abyss of reality. It took a moment to realize that he was aboard the Queen Elizabeth as it plowed through a roiling sea, transporting him closer to his appointment with destiny.

7

Utah Beach

On Thursday afternoon, April 6, the Queen Elizabeth steamed up the Firth of Clyde and dropped anchor off Geenock, Scotland. Cheering British subjects and a band of Scottish pipers dressed in kilts were on hand to greet them with cheers and stirring music. At 0800 the men climbed aboard a train that took them to Tiverton station in Devon County.

The next two months were taken up with training exercises and battle preparations. On weekends the men would be invited into British homes as welcomed guests. They soon learned to enjoy fish and chip dinners rolled in newspapers sprinkled with vinegar, as well as visits to the local pubs. And just as abruptly, their training came to an end.

At 0830 on June 3, they were issued Hershey bars, extra cartons of cigarettes, a French-English phrase book, and special French franks. The carbines in their hands held real bullets this time. No more games played with empty weapons on friendly fields.

They were bounced roughly over British cobblestones in the back of two-and-a-half-ton trucks, American soldiers traveling in convoy south from Tiverton to Torquay Bay. Half the members of Company A were ferried to a marshalling area to participate in Overlord, the invasion of Europe, code-named Operation Neptune.

England had become a vast ordnance dump overnight. Roads were clogged with trucks, ambulances, tanks, armored cars, jeeps, bulldozers, and every type vehicle imaginable. Mountains of stores were piled everywhere.

The rusty soil and barren fields were corrugated with chevrons of tire and tractor treads.

Roger Burt gripped his French phrase book tightly in both hands as their truck negotiated sharp curves and steep inclines. To pass the time, he began practicing on his good friend, Francis Healy, who rode opposite him in the rear. "Parlez-vous Français?" Burt shouted above the cacophony of grinding engine and metallic groans from beneath the truck bed. His voice rattled and he sounded out of breath.

"Voulez vous couche avec mois? That's all the French you need to know," Healy chuckled.

"Wants put to bed you with months? That'll get him far," Heron admonished.

"Ha, ha. Funny Heron."

"How does an Irishman come to know French?" Fiske asked him.

"One-quarter Irish," he corrected. "I studied it in high school."

"Is that what they teach you in Catholic schools, how to negotiate your way into bed?" Burt joked.

Heron smiled over at him, creases forming in the corners of his eyes. Burt and Healy struck him as bookends, a matched pair. Both short, rugged, and wiry. If God had made them six feet tall, together they could have whipped the entire German army.

The men may have been laughing outwardly during the verbal exchange, but the undercurrent of fear was ever present and building. After seven intensive weeks of preparation in Tiverton, the four hundred-forty officers and men and sixty-seven vehicles comprising the 87th's assault wave were headed into harm's way.

The truck stopped abruptly, shaking Heron from his reverie and catapulting him roughly forward. He grappled for a handhold on the mountain of gear piled in front of him. Each haversack held a raincoat, shelter half, mess kit, utensils, toiletries, and cigarettes. Inside each blanket roll were cotton drawers, handkerchiefs, service shoes, socks, undershirts, blankets, clothing, half a two-man tent, and poles with ropes for assembling the halves. Piled up too were cartridge belts, canteens, first-aid pouches, bayonets, and entrenching tools.

From behind the truck, Lt. Bonafin's voice cut through the stillness like a bayonet through warm butter, "This is it, men. Welcome to Plymouth." The soldiers felt their knees buckle as they hit the ground under heavy loads.

The Plymouth-Devon area presented a pleasant view of the sound, but it was soon obscured by a blanket of fog that issued in like a dark shroud from Dartmouth Bay. An eerie quiet settled over the waterfront as the line of men, bent under heavy gear, paraded like weary Jonahs into an LCT (landing craft, tank) with its ramp hanging open like the mouth of a giant whale.

The LCT ferried them out to the U.S.S. Bayfield anchored a short distance from shore. As the craft drew close to the gunmetal gray transport, Heron spotted rope ladders like those they had practiced with on dry land. Boarding was much more difficult under the weight of full battle gear.

The Battalion Commander and his party, as well as the Commanding Officer of the 8th Infantry Regiment and his landing team, were already aboard.

It seemed that no sooner had Heron's gear hit the deck than the ship weighed anchor and stood out to sea. After the breakwater was crossed, Colonel Van Fleet announced D-Day would commence on June 5th, H-Hour at 0630. The path was forward – destination Utah Beach.

Heron sat quietly beside his gear, his Garand rifle in the crook of his arm and an elephant condom of thin plastic Pliofilm draped over the barrel to protect it from the water.

After two days aboard the vessel, the men were mostly lost in thought or dozing from nervous fear and exhaustion. It had been said that those going in on the first wave were expendable, chilling words that now came back to haunt them.

Sgt. Heron was sitting on the deck wondering if he would ever see Azelia again, when someone suddenly stopped before him. In an instant he recognized Brigadier General Teddy Roosevelt, Jr. He leapt to his feet and started to salute but the general waved it off. "At ease, son. What outfit you with?" He spoke softly.

"Company A of the 87th Chemical Weapons Battalion, sir."

"I watched you men in practice. You're damn good with those mortars. We will be relying on your speed and mobility." The tone of his voice was calm and reassuring. He wished Heron luck and moved on, leaving him feeling more at ease than he had scant moments ago.

The general was wearing a knit cap, walked with a limp, and carried a cane, having sustained a leg wound in World War I. Despite a bad heart he had begged General Raymond O. Barton to permit him to go ashore with the first wave. He felt it would demonstrate to the troops that they were not alone.

Moments later, Roosevelt began leading the men in singing the *Battle Hymn of the Republic*. Heron joined them, his eyes growing moist with the words, "As He died to make men holy, let us die to make men free".

"Here's your helmet, Larry." Sgt. Meyers had offered to camouflage Heron's helmet using a net garnished with strips of burlap. The only part left exposed was a horizontal white stripe on the back, as required by regulations. By contrast, officer's helmets bore a four-inch vertical white stripe.

Meyers face was ashen. He had been popping motion sickness pills like candy but apparently they weren't helping. Heron's hand inadvertently went to his shirt pocket to feel for his own six-pack of Dramamine. "Better go easy with those pills, Sergeant," he offered.

Meyers seemed lost as he staggered away looking like a man who had just polished off a quart of bourbon, his hands searching his pockets for more Dramamine.

At a meeting at 0415 hours on June 4, RAF meteorologist and Group Captain John Stagg convinced General Eisenhower that the weather would be too stormy for the planned June 5th assault. True to his predictions, the weather increased its fury, hell bent on driving the armada from the sea, and D-Day was postponed for 25 hours.

The delay left Heron with more time to contemplate what lay ahead and wondering how he would react under real fire. He felt somewhat as he did just prior to the annual football game with Northbridge High, except that now the stakes were higher. He glanced at the faces surrounding him wondering how many would be maimed or killed and caught their eyes doing the same. *I'll make it. I promised Azelia.* He had always kept his promises to her. *Just for you!*

Two hundred forty-five minesweepers covered the area from the Isle of Wight through the Channel to the transport anchor line off the French coast, where mines were the greatest naval threat from the Germans. Next came LCTs loaded with jeeps and tanks towing trailers filled with ammunition. Rigged with floatation devices, the tanks were to land at H-Hour minus five minutes in support of the infantry.

Behind them came six battleships, twenty cruisers, and sixty-eight destroyers. The mission of the battleships was to go against the heavy concentration of German batteries, a hundred-twenty guns ranging from 75 to 210mm. The *Nevada* had the distinction of having been the only battleship that had managed to get underway during the attack on Pearl Harbor.

At two o'clock on the morning of June 6, the wind was high and the channel choppy with winds exceeding fifteen knots. After fifty-two hours at sea Heron was anxious to plant his feet on solid ground again, despite the enemy threat. Ten miles from shore, he saw flashes of *ack-ack*, and viewed the silhouettes of small boats groping against the waves.

Then came the sudden *pow, pow, pow* of the Navy's big guns, like the bowels of hell erupting. The resulting concussions passed thunderous shockwaves through every part of his body. He felt as though his brains had been jarred loose and were rattling around in his skull.

Elsewhere, things weren't going as planned. The 82nd Airborne had yet to secure the town of Ste. Mère Eglise, where half the 507th and 508th Parachute Infantry Regiments were landing in areas flooded by the Germans, many drowning under the heavy weight of their equipment. The Air Force's bombing of coastal defenses was failing miserably due to overcast skies and a combination of bad luck and misjudgments. At 0330 an NCDU team (Naval Combat Demolition Unit), armed with a ton of explosives, timed their landing to fall within an hour and a half of low-tide to clear exposed obstacles from the beaches.

Seventeen hundred feet from land, the Battalion Commander's party, the Regimental Landing Team, and the men of the 87th began descending into landing crafts lined up alongside the ship. Just as during Operation Tiger on April 27, Heron swung over the side and labored down a cargo net. Only this time the sea was rougher, the sky darker, and the ropes wetter and slipperier.

The seas roared, engines revved, and officers shouted commands. Waves churned up snow-capped mountains that lifted the LCVP (landing craft, vehicle and personnel) half way to the ship's rail before plunging it down once more into the next trough. The men had been warned to keep helmets unbuckled, for if anyone were to fall, the force of its rim hitting the water was enough to break a neck.

Just as Heron dropped into the craft it pitched wildly, throwing him against the gunwale and drenching him with seawater. Rubbing his hip, he adjusted his haversack and made himself as comfortable as possible in the standing-room-only vessel.

Waves chopped the rails, washing down the men closest to the sides and spilling onto the deck so that there was consistently an inch or more of water underfoot. First one man, then another began to retch until every burp-bag had been filled and thrown overboard. The smell wafted to the pit of Heron's stomach.

To take his mind off the stench, he struck up a conversation with the coxswain and was pleased to discover that he was from Medway, a town in Massachusetts adjacent to Milford. They promised to look one another up if both made it safely home. Heron admired the courage of the grim-faced coxswain as he guided their craft as close to shore as possible - without ramming it so far aground that it could not exit.

The thirty-six men on Heron's craft waded ashore with shells exploding all around them, and spewing geysers of muddy water into the air. It was impossible to make swift progress with the weight of both water and backpacks dragging them down. Fortunately, the Germans had failed to complete the fabrication of water barriers and fewer mines were being set off than expected. The NCDU teams had successfully cleared paths by now, and naval bombardment had punched holes in defenses. Even the German shelling had inadvertently assisted by opening craters for foot soldiers to use as cover.

Heron found a shell crater and dove headlong into it, spinning around just as Sgt. Volcjak came sailing through the air and landed with a thump beside him. "Damn. My men are all over the place and we have no equipment," Volcjak shouted.

"What happened?"

"Our mortars and ammunition went to the bottom of the channel with our LCA (landing craft, assault). My squad got picked up and we were dumped ashore. Gotta find the lieutenant." With that, the sergeant climbed out of the crater and disappeared.

Heron moved fifty yards further along a causeway where he collapsed into another shell hole. Along the way he passed a few dead and several wounded being attended by medics. Another hundred yards brought him to a seawall where men were moving past a lively General Roosevelt wielding his cane as though directing traffic.

The Utah landing was a mile off-course due to unexpected currents. Instead of panicking, the general kept his cool and uttered the immortalized words, "We'll start the war from right here." The general would later receive the Medal of Honor for his courage, gallantry and leadership on this day. He stopped leading only when he heard the piercing whine of a screaming German ME 109 sweeping in at a low level, spitting death and destruction. He dove for cover just as the plane strafed the beach, kicking holes in the sand where he had been standing a moment ago. Just as suddenly, a British Spitfire swept the German plane with bursts of machinegun fire, breaking it into pieces that slammed into the sea.

The General was immediately back on his feet, waving men forward with his cane with movements stiff from a severe case of arthritis. Before the invasion, it had been rumored that he would be sidelined with pneumonia. Though the ravages of sickness were clearly evident in his face and bearing, he was now moving and shouting as though energized by a bolt of lightning.

As Heron rose to his feet, a deafening blast knocked him sideways, his helmet slamming into a concrete piling. Ears ringing and head shaken, Heron scanned the area for signs of his squad. Miraculously, all were within a hundred feet of his position.

Branson was crouched a few feet to his right, talking into a radio. "Camel Green! Camel Green! This is Camel Red!" He turned to Heron and shouted, "Set up your mortars behind that tetrahedron." Then he was back on the radio. "Camel Green..."

Heron's Company A was code-named *Camel Red,* battalion headquarters *Camel Green*, and companies B, C, and D *Camel Purple, Blue*, and *Orange*, respectively. The helmets of the men of the 87th bore a camel the size of a half-dollar stenciled on the left side in a color that matched their respective codenames.

Lieutenants Bonafin and Cable, Sergeants Burt and Faber, and Cpl. Trant, acting as forward observers, had landed at H-Hour with the 8th Infantry Regiment of the 4th Division, in the wake of the NCDU teams.

Companies A and B arrived with the first wave at H plus 50 minutes in support of the 1st and 2nd Infantry Battalions respectively. C and D landed forty minutes later in support of the 3rd Infantry Battalion and the 22nd Infantry Regiment.

Fiske placed the distant aiming point 200 meters from the mortar and leveled the elevation bubbles. Sgt. Heron set the mortar sight deflection and elevation. After Shanahan added the boresight to the mortar and leveled its bubbles, Heron adjusted the elevation knob and set the deflection, ensuring the proper sight setting on the fixed deflection scale.

As if on cue, a Weasel (M-29 cargo carrier) pulled up with hundreds of mortar rounds aboard. Soon the entire company was firing in response to directions from their forward observers.

For the next six hours, the 87th was the 4th Division's sole artillery support, firing at enemy strong points, machinegun nests, pillboxes, and concrete emplacements. This marked the first time the battalion had ever fired over the heads of its own troops against an armed enemy.

No sooner had Heron's squad fired its first forty rounds than the earth erupted in smoke and flame all around. German counterfire. Violent explosions. The thunder and fury of dozens of lightning bolts spewing earth and fire. Shrapnel and debris whistled past their ears. The men quickly dismantled their mortars and ran for cover, carrying mortar parts with them.

German artillery batteries and mortar units honeycombed in the vicinity of Pointe du Hoc had been pounding the beach with heavy shells throughout the landing. The Airborne Rangers' plan had failed to neutralize them. The rattle of machine guns could be heard amid the din of an infinite variety of weapons, from small arms to 88s. Everything that could be scrounged from the German's own arsenals and even some from captured stores once belonging to the Allies were coming at them.

Despite this wall of resistance, the 87th suffered few casualties. A post-landing inventory showed that two of the battalion's mortars and two vehicles had gone down with a pair of LCVPs. Pfc. Smith of Company C had been killed by a direct hit on his foxhole. Lt. Cooper stepped on a mine and lay for a time in the middle of a minefield with both legs ripped apart. He continued to direct his men past mines while everything leaked from his lower extremities onto the ground.

Fletcher reached him first. By then, the lieutenant's eyes were glazing over. "Lieutenant," he cried.

"Yes, I'm here." But a moment later he was not. He had died.

Overdosed on Dramamine, Sgt. Red Meyers attacked the beach like a drunken sailor. Later he would not be able to recall a single event that took place that day on Utah Beach. Of the 23,000 men who landed, only 197 would become casualties, much fewer than the 749 lost during training exercises in England, and far less than the 2,400 being slaughtered over on Omaha Beach.

Company A, moving inland with the 1st Infantry Battalion, 8th Regiment, set up its mortars in the vicinity of La Madeleine. Meanwhile, battalion headquarters passed through Ste. Marie-du-Mont and set up in the vicinity of Les Forge. The men would get no sleep that night. From a position concealed between hedgerows, Heron's platoon rained high explosives and white phosphorous on Turqueville, setting the village on fire and eventually destroying it.

The following day, the infantry swept through the town with Company A right behind. The 1st Platoon was led by Lt. Branson and S/Sgt Julian Brunt, the 2nd Platoon by Lt. Lesh and S/Sgt. David Thomas, and the 3rd Platoon by Lt. Bonafin and Sgt. Heron.

Early on the morning of June 8, the company was reattached to the 12th Infantry Regiment of the 4th Division, which made its assault generally along the main road connecting Ste. Mere Eglise and Montebourg. Company A set up its mortars south of Emmondville around noon to cover the attacking infantry. With just two members of the 87th Battalion wounded in action, the attack was deemed very successful. Mortars had taken out three German 88s and four machinegun nests. No one had had any sleep for hours on end and the men were now so hungry that they didn't even mind eating food from "golden cans," a.k.a. the much-maligned Army C-rations.

On the morning of June 11, the final push to take Montebourg was underway with Company A firing from a position north of Joganville. Late that evening under heavy enemy bombardment, Cpl. Wilkevich was killed and 1st Lt. Leah received shrapnel wounds.

Early on June 12 Company A was reassigned to the 3rd Battalion, 22 Infantry Regiment, attacking the town of Ozville. Sgt. Harry Faber was wounded by shrapnel and Pvt. James O'Donnell received severe burns on both hands when powder charges accidentally exploded.

As the infantry stormed city after city, the 87th, working in tandem, continued delivering murderous firepower onto enemy positions. And all the while, each platoon found itself being detached from one outfit only to be reattached to another; moving from one strange-sounding town to the next: Quinville, Ste. Colombe, Orglandes, Hauteville-Bocage, Valgnes, Delasse, the latter two towns scant miles from Cherbourg.

The second phase of Eisenhower's plan had two major objectives, capture Cherbourg and amass sufficient forces and materials to break out toward Germany. Cherbourg was a major port located at the tip of the Cotentin Peninsula. Cherbourg and the port of Le Havre were both deemed necessary for the buildup of personnel and supplies to support twenty-nine combat divisions. Original plans were to take Cherbourg by June 21. The push was on to make it happen as close to that date as possible.

On June 19, he turned twenty-four. That morning, he opened a letter from Azelia and withdrew a string of black rosary beads with a solid silver crucifix that she had included for his birthday. He counted his prayers on it, kissed the crucifix, and slipped it into his left breast pocket.

June 21 found Company A consolidating its position in preparation for the attack on Cherbourg by the VII Corps. Ammunition convoys from Utah Beach were encountering great difficulty in keeping up with the voracious demands of the infantry, now totally dependent on the "mortar men" for support.

On June 22, the rear echelon of Company A stopped northwest of Valognes to sidestep a 9th Air Force attack on Cherbourg's high ground, then moved to a position northwest of Delasser. Three days later, Company A was within 4000 yards of Cherbourg. On that day, General Omar Bradley ordered a naval bombardment on German batteries located in the city. Three U.S. ships entered into a three-hour duel with German gun batteries off Cherbourg's coast that took the lives of 52 sailors, and inflicted damages to the battleship *Texas* and the cruiser *Glasgow*.

Four more days remained before Heron's life would be changed forever.

8

The Suicide Mission

In the early morning hours of June 26 the VII Corp tightened its circle around Cherbourg. Advance units of the 9th Division halted before the dockyard and Company A took up a position behind the 39th Regiment in the vicinity of St. Sauveur-le-Vicomte, about 2000 yards outside the city. During this advance, 1000 Germans were taken prisoner, including garrison commander General Schoieken and Naval Commandant Admiral Hennecke, the man who had ordered the harbor destroyed to keep the Allies from using it, for which Hitler would award him the Iron Cross.

At this time, the 87th Battalion's ammunition dump took a direct hit from German artillery that destroyed all accumulated mortar rounds. It would take days for supplies to be replenished.

At 1800 hours, Company A was down to its last twenty rounds. A desperate call went out for volunteers to retrieve hundreds of shells from the back of a disabled two-and-a-half ton truck a hundred yards toward enemy lines. A mine had blown its engine, popped its hood, and flattened both front tires.

"We need volunteers," Lt, Bonafin told Heron. "The third infantry battalion is pinned down and screaming for mortar fire." Bonafin's voice was barely audible above the terrifying cacophony of heavy artillery, tank fire, and the din from engines revving and tank treads grinding over waxen terrain – all sounds that turn a soldier's blood to ice and ratchets his pulse rate up several notches.

When he returned to where his men were dug in, Sgt. Heron relayed the lieutenant's message, and watched as each man averted his eyes like a school kid hoping the teacher wouldn't single him out - but not before he caught sight of naked fear reflecting off soulful eyes with the intensity of sunlight off the Star of Africa.

"It's suicide," Cpl. Bartosiewicz said, the perspiration beading his mud-streaked face like rain on a waxed Cadillac. "There are snipers out there."

In that moment, Heron made the costliest decision of his life. He would go it alone rather than risk the lives of the men in his squad. He told Cpl. Madeiros, "Give me ten minutes. If nothing happens bring up the squad." To Cpl. Fiske he added, "Fire at anything that moves."

"You don't have to do this." Madeiros pleaded. "You're the Sergeant."

Three thousand five hundred and forty-two miles away, Azelia awoke with a start, her nightgown damp with cold sweat. She vaguely recalled the dream that began with Larry as a young boy then shifted to the present. Dressed in his army uniform, he stood wearing a sad expression. Though she had been sobbing prodigally in her dream, her eyes had opened as dry as an Oklahoma dust bowl, but not for long. Moments later, she stumbled bleary-eyed into the bathroom, stopped up the drain, and turned on the hot water. Then she stared into the large mirror above the sink while the tub filled. The eyes that looked back exuded disconsolate terror. She watched the ripples spread to the sides of the tub then kneeled to swish her hand in the water to test the temperature. After adding cold water, she stepped into the tub and for the first time that morning felt her muscles slacken and inexplicably the tears began to flow.

An alarm sounds at the nurse's station in the Milford Hospital. Lights flash. It's the old woman in Room 201. In seconds the nurse is at her bedside. Azelia is having grave difficulty breathing. It's OK this time though, just the IVAC machine warning that the fluid is running low. The nurse checks the monitor. Azelia's pulse rate is a bit high but not enough for alarm.

When Azelia is alone once again, she notes that the moon has advanced a quarter of the way across the hospital window. There is no panic over what had just happened with the alarm, no fear of death. Larry had faced it many times in his life. The first time was on that fateful day that he made his costly decision to rescue the mortar rounds from the truck. At the time, she had had no idea that he was in any trouble. How could she from thousands of miles away? But it would not be long thereafter that she would receive a strange and baffling omen.

9

The Direful Prediction

Friday afternoon found Azelia pacing in her kitchen awaiting the second arrival of the mailman. Mail was being delivered twice a day in Hopedale, and she had not received a letter from Larry for the past three weeks.

A fan on the kitchen table droned monotonously, lifting white-lace curtains that danced gracefully above the sill. Growing restless, she almost welcomed the sound of the phone when it began to ring at two o'clock. It was Amelia. She wanted to know if Azelia would like to go shopping in Milford with her and sisters Olga and Vera the next morning. They would visit Virginia, Amelia's neighbor, around noon to have their fortunes read.

Why not? It might take her mind off things.

At 2:30 PM the mailman arrived with a copy of *Life* and the usual bills, but nothing from Larry. "Perhaps his letters are queued in a central repository and will arrive in one huge bundle," the postman suggested. "Just give it time."

The sisters arrived at Virginia's precisely at noon. Wonderful aromas greeted them as the front door opened. Virginia was a marvelous cook and a wonderful hostess. Her husband worked on Saturdays, so she was alone. She worked two jobs during the week and looked forward to weekends when she could cook and play hostess, which was her favorite means of relaxation.

Before the door could be closed, a low rumble was heard from somewhere up the road that quickly became a loud roar, and moments later an army convoy pulled to a stop directly before the house. An officer leapt from the lead jeep and began barking orders. Soldiers disembarked the trucks and grouped into teams that entered the woods in orderly fashion. Soon fifty-caliber machineguns and small artillery pieces were set up and concealed under camouflaged cloth, brush, and broken branches. Some of the men carried bazookas, others rifles. It all had taken but a few moments.

Azelia immediately thought of Larry and hoped he would never have to fight. The others found these maneuvers chilling but not unusual, for the country was at war and Ft. Devens was only forty miles to the north. Virginia ushered her guests to a country kitchen in the rear of the house where the view through thin-laced curtains was of a huge garden overflowing with an abundance of hearty vegetables. To help with the war effort, nearly every family in America owned a small "victory garden." This one took up a full acre.

"Coffee's ready," Virginia announced as a small brass ibrik began to froth noisily and threatened to overflow. She poured a demitasse for each of her guests and they made small talk while sipping the strong coffee. After the cups were drained, each was inverted over a saucer to allow the fine grounds to assume a telltale shape. Before coming to America from Armenia at age twelve, Virginia had already developed the art of reading fortunes with uncanny accuracy.

When enough time had been allowed to pass, Virginia reached for Amelia's cup but her neighbor held up a hand in protest. "Azelia first," she said. "She hasn't heard from Larry and is dying for some good news."

"News isn't always good," Virginia said, stolidly. A wisp of cool air sweeping down from Montreal gently raised the translucent white curtains, as she lifted Azelia's cup and turned it slowly in her hands, gazing intently at what was a clear and meaningful picture to her practiced eyes.

Azelia leaned forward expectantly, hoping to hear that the war would soon be at an end and that Larry would be coming home.

Virginia's gaze slowly turned into a frown that broadened deeply then spread across her brows.

"What is it," Azelia asked. "Is it about Larry?"

Virginia hesitated.

"What do you see?" she repeated. Her heart raced and her fingers absentmindedly tapped the edge of the table.

Virginia made eye contact above the rim of the cup at last. "He's in a place where people wear crowns." Then she hesitated. Clearly, she was holding something back.

"Crowns? Like kings?" Vera asked. "Like in France and England?"

Virginia, suddenly reticent, said, "Yes. A place where they wear crowns."

"If it's England, then he must be OK," Olga said, with an encouraging glance at Azelia.

Virginia's face was ashen. "No. He's not. Not OK, I mean. Larry is..." After searching for the right words and finding none, she settled for, "It's not good." She placed the cup on the table and reached for Amelia's.

"Wait. What does it mean?" Azelia pleaded.

"Maybe he's just sick or something," Vera offered.

"It's worse," Azelia said, resignedly. Virginia had said "not good" but the dire look on her face was more revealing. "Tell me."

"He's in a building and he's in...not in good shape. I'm so sorry, but that's what I see." Virginia tried but failed to mask the horror lodged in her eyes. And in the past, she had predicted the future with unsettling accuracy.

In these past few moments, despair had swept into the kitchen like a dark cloud, crowding out everything that moments ago had been bright and cheerful. And it was obvious that Virginia had "seen" much more than she cared to reveal.

That night, Azelia told Emma, "Tomorrow, I'm going to apply for a driver's license." It hadn't made sense until now because everything she needed, including her workplace, was just a few short blocks from home. And she had been counting on Larry returning safely to do all the driving. But now she could no longer be sure.

On July 16th she toweled off following a hot bath and added skin lotion to dry areas. Then she threw on a sweatshirt and a pair of slacks and treaded barefoot down to the kitchen to start a pot of water for tea. This was her place of solace. The room had pale yellow walls, white moldings, a sturdy wooden drop-leaf table, and bucolic pictures artfully framed and hung with an artful eye. Nothing too extravagant or overbearing but everything just right for its place.

She poured herself a steaming cup of the tea and sat down at the kitchen table to begin reading the paper. Before she could take a first sip, the doorbell rang with such urgency that even before opening it she was certain that bad news awaited her on the other side of the door. When the door swung aside, a boy she did not recognize stood before her holding a yellow envelope. Then he said the words everyone in America dreaded to hear, "Telegram for Mrs. Heron."

Words formed a logjam in her throat. "I...I'm Mrs. Heron," she uttered mechanically.

"Sign here please." Her hand trembled as she scrawled out her name. *Please God! No!*

She would remember this day and everything she did from the moment she set eyes on the boy with the telegram. Her heart skipped then she felt faint. She sat down at the dining room table and laid the telegram before her.

Emma suddenly appeared from the kitchen. "Aren't you going to open it?" she anxiously asked.

Azelia did not respond. Until she opened the letter and read the contents, he would remain alive. Not until she read the words, "killed in action," would he truly be gone.

"Maybe it's not bad news. Perhaps he's on his way home," Emma said. Her terrified eyes belied her words.

Azelia felt that somehow his life depended on her not reading the telegram. Perhaps that would seem solipsistic and irrational to someone else, but it made a warped sort of sense to her. "Go on," Emma urged. Then with shaking hands, she tore open the envelope and removed the telegram. "Here," she said, handing it to Emma. "You read it." She closed her eyes in silent prayer and listened.

Emma read aloud: "REGRET TO INFORM YOU..." Azelia's heart leapt. "HUSBAND SERGEANT LAWRENCE J HERON WAS..." She grew lightheaded and found it difficult to breathe. "SERIOUSLY WOUNDED IN ACTION TWENTY SIXTH JUNE IN FRANCE." Emma dropped the telegram on the table in front of her and collapsed into a chair. The bad news had fallen on both women like a sudden downpour, drenching them in despair and sudden fatigue. It weighed down not only their spirits, but their bodies as well. "At least he's alive," sighed Emma.

"It said serious. How serious?"

"Any serious is bad enough."

Azelia heard Virginia's voice: *It's not good.* Her head was spinning. *You can't die, Larry Heron. Don't leave me. Dear God, please don't take him.*

"We must hope for the best," Emma declared.

Azelia laughed bitterly, without mirth. Nothing in her well-ordered life made sense any longer. "It's all so relative, isn't it? What makes sense and what doesn't, I mean." Yesterday she was smiling, happy, anticipating the day he'd return. And now...

"Don't worry," Emma said, unconvincingly. "He's strong. If anyone can make it, he will."

"Why didn't they tell us the extent of his injuries or where he is?"

Emma steeled herself. "All we can do is wait and pray for the best, dear," she said.

Azelia clung to the hope that whatever the extent of his injuries, he would recover. Pick up any newspaper practically any day of the week over the last two years and there would always be articles about soldiers missing in action, injured, or killed. Though no consolation, she was sure that thousands of similar telegrams were being sent out every day.

That night Azelia pushed the food around on her plate, tidied the kitchen and retired to her room early where she dragged out the photo albums. All the pictures of him were in black and white except for their large wedding picture hanging on the bedroom wall. Larry looked so handsome in all of his pictures – so virile, so full of energy. That night, she cried herself into a fitful sleep.

She sat wistfully at breakfast the next day, looking at her food and wanting to throw up. It was Monday. The thought occurred to call in sick but Emma convinced her that it would be better to keep busy. Later that night she called best friend Lt. Norma Ripanti, home on leave from the army. Norma concealed her shock well. "It'll be all right," she said. You won't know the full extent of his injuries until you see him, so don't think the worst. I'm sure it's not as bad as it seems."

If only.

The Milford News carried an old picture of Heron in uniform, describing that he'd been seriously wounded. The news sent shockwaves reverberating throughout New England, where Heron was regarded as a sports legend with a promising career.

On her way home from the grocery store, Azelia paused before a wall in the center of town. Across the top was an eagle crest separating the words: TOWN OF HOPEDALE ROLL OF HONOR. Below was a row of flowers behind a low white picket fence. The wall contained more than three hundred fifty names. A star beside two of the names signified that they had been killed in action. One of the men listed had been taken prisoner by the Japanese on the island of Bataan. Still others were in hospitals.

Every town in America had its honor roll. A black star on a white background graced the front windows of many homes to proudly signify that a family member was serving in a branch of the armed forces. A gold star indicated that a member had been killed. Whenever she stood looking at those names, she felt as though she was standing inside a church. The feelings of reverence toward those protecting the freedoms of their loved ones, and of the nation, were that profound.

The moon has reached the halfway point in the window in Room 201. She recalls a discussion following the war during which each had confessed to having whispered 'I love you' to the moon while half the world away from one another. She thinks perhaps millions of lovers have been doing the same since the beginning of time. Is it so surprising then that the moon should be regarded as a symbol of love?

The last time they had the opportunity to view it in one another's company was while seated on a bench by Hopedale Pond. It was just before he had left for war. Hopedale was the only place on earth where they had been able to look up at it together, because that is where she had spent almost her entire life. How fortunate was that? If one had to spend her entire life in just one town, then Hopedale was not such a bad choice, she decided.

Hopedale was an idyllic town with a rich and unique history. Elsewhere the sun may rise, but in Hopedale it steals from behind the hills with a whisper, and gently bathes the valley with rays of love, hope, and peace.

In 1841, Universalist Reverend Adin Ballou and forty-five followers invested in communal stock to fund the purchase of a 600-acre farm on the Mill River, a parcel of land belonging to Milford and known as the "Dale." Ballou's blueprint for communal living was shared by close friends Henry David Thoreau and William Lloyd Garrison, and admired by Leo Tolstoy who predicted Ballou would one day be "acknowledged as one of the great benefactors of mankind."

But a series of financial and political disasters bankrupted the Dale, and in 1856 Ebenezer Draper, a machine shop owner, purchased all stock certificates and took ownership. Fortified with several key patents for loom parts, he and his brother George grew their tiny business into an industrial empire that soon led the world in the production of textile looms and equipment.

In 1886, after a long and bitter struggle, the brothers forced a break from Milford and founded the town of Hopedale. For decades the company flourished, as did Draper wealth. The Drapers used a good deal of their wealth to develop what would become "America's model company town," where residents never felt compelled to attend town meetings because everything was done on their behalf.

The Drapers paid well and provided outstanding medical benefits. They built award-winning homes, which were rented to employees for practically nothing. Repairs were made to homes as needed. Draper craftsmen paid annual visits to spruce up each home at no charge. The town boasted the state's finest educational system, recreational areas, and award-winning civic buildings.

Since the early 1800s all company homes were on sewer systems and Draper-made sprinkler systems protected the factory as well as every town building, features unheard of in small towns at the time.

There were other benefits, like Draper-sponsored Fourth of July Field Days that included tennis, racing, the long jump, logrolling contests, and other sporting events.

In 1892, Eben Summer Draper was elected lieutenant governor, and in 1909 he served two one-year terms as governor of Massachusetts. He used his power to benefit Hopedale in every way possible. The Drapers and Hopedale continued to prosper for many years, as did the residents of the town.

The loud closing of elevator doors outside Room 201 interrupts her journey back in time. Seconds later, she slides back on her bed and props herself up on her pillows, thinking she had been fortunate to have had so much support from close relatives, friends, and neighbors through that awful period of her life.

On July 17, 1944, Azelia received a brief letter Heron had dictated to a nurse simply informing her that he'd been hospitalized. Three days later a letter arrived from the War Department: *Dear Mrs. Heron, This is to confirm your husband, Sergeant Lawrence J. Heron, was seriously wounded in action on 26 June 1944, in France.*

Theater commanders submit periodic reports of progress and accordingly you will be kept informed as these reports are received. Such reports must of necessity be brief and will not include information concerning the nature of his injuries.

I assure you our hospitalized soldiers are receiving the very best medical care and attention and it is hoped that a favorable report in his case will be received in the near future. The letter ended with Heron's temporary APO address and bore the signature of the adjutant general.

The phrase that struck her was "a favorable report."

Then on August 11, she heard the doorbell and went to the door expecting to find Vera, who had promised to drop off a stew pot she'd borrowed for a baby shower. Instead, there stood the young man whose presence she had come to dread. "Telegram for you, Mrs. Heron," he said flatly. "Sign here please."

With heart pounding, she tore open the telegram and read, MY THOUGHTS ARE WITH YOU ALL WELL AND SAFE LOVE AND KISSES=LAWRENCE HERON. Nothing about his injuries. She rushed to find Emma and share what appeared to be some very good news.

No family was immune to the horrors of war. Every day the newspapers carried articles and displayed pictures of area men who had been killed, wounded, or missing in action. On August 19, 1944, Azelia read that Peter Saltonstall, the twenty-three year old son of Massachusetts Governor Leverett Saltonstall had been killed in action. Her heart went out to him and his family.

On the morning of August 23, 1944, with war, death, and injury flooding the newspapers, Azelia turned to Emma. "When do you think we'll get more details of his injuries and learn when he might be coming home?" she asked.

"No news is good news," Emma replied.

The next day, Azelia went with Amelia to pay another visit to Mrs. Kalpagian. This time, Virginia was reluctant to read their fortunes. She had been visibly upset by what she had seen regarding Larry on their last visit, so much so that she vowed never again. But Azelia could be quite persuasive. "Just one more time. You were the only one who had it right. Besides, it can't get any worse."

Holding the cup to the light, Virginia said, "I see a huge building with a large flag flying from a tall pole out front. When you enter, you will be greeted by three gray ladies. They will leave you with three large bundles."

The call came at six o'clock that evening. Azelia answered the phone and a woman on the other end identified herself as a nun.

"Mrs. Heron? I'm at the Municipal Airport in New York with…a man who loves you very much."

"Oh, thank God. Is he all right?" Larry was on his way home at last. Soon she would learn the truth about his injuries. "Can I speak with him?"

"He's not able to come to the phone, I'm afraid."

"How badly is he injured?"

"You'll have to ask his doctor."

"When can I see him?"

"I don't know."

After a moment of silence, the nun said, "Like I told him, you really shouldn't see him this way."

A pencil fell from Azelia's hand onto the hardwood floor and rolled noisily to a stop.

The nun added, "But he told me that you will insist on it, that you love each other that much."

"Yes, sister. I do. I love him and I want to see him as soon as possible. Where are you taking him?"

"We're on our way to Framingham." The nun gave her the address of the Framingham Cushing Hospital, a 1,750-bed hospital fifteen miles east of Hopedale. Azelia lifted another pencil from the holder and jotted the address down on a notepad. The nun added, "Many injured soldiers are arriving there daily from overseas."

"Tomorrow then," Azelia said resignedly, knowing that was all she was going to extract from the nun regarding his condition. Slowly, she lowered the receiver to its cradle while she brushed away the tears. The telegram sat on the table, right where she had left it. She looked at it again then tried to piece together what she knew. Larry had been wounded in action then sent to a hospital in England, a *place where people wear crowns*. His injuries were severe enough that he couldn't come to the phone. The nun wasn't talking. Just as Virginia had predicted. *It's not good.* Azelia felt like she was trapped in quicksand. All the news she had been receiving was skimpy at best. Perhaps tomorrow she'd learn something new.

The next day was Saturday. She phoned the hospital early that morning, hoping that by then Larry was settled in and that she'd be allowed to see him. The nurse would not discuss his condition over the phone. Sergeant Heron needed rest after his cross-Atlantic trip and would not be allowed any visitors until Monday. "Call back on Monday," she heard the nurse say.

10

The Painful Truth

Azelia's driver's license had arrived a week ago Friday. On Monday, with Emma in the passenger seat beside her, she drove to the Draper office building to pick up a ration book then headed for the Draper gas station to fill up. She'd been issued "A" coupons, and on her windshield was an "A" sticker limiting her to 150 miles of driving each month. "B" coupons went to people with jobs far from home, and "C" to doctors, ministers, farmers, and people directly connected with the war effort. Politicians and congressmen were allowed unlimited gasoline access.

Gas rationing, which began in May 1942 when rubber had fallen into short supply, was a hardship that served as a constant reminder of the war effort underway. Since ninety percent of the nation's crude rubber originated in the Far East and most was being consumed on the roads, it had been reasoned that gas rationing was the simplest way of conserving rubber. Soon sugar, meat, coffee, fuel oil, automobiles, and specific items such as shoes and typewriters would be added to the list.

After stopping to pick up Heron's sister, Ethel, she turned her car onto Route 16 and headed the vehicle east toward Framingham. Thanks to rationing there were fewer cars on the road these days. People not only walked more, they stretched meals, planted victory gardens, and stayed at home to listen to the radio.

When the women reached Framingham, Emma read from the directions Azelia had written, "Follow Winter Street to Mount Wayte Road, which should be around this next corner."

First a row of army barracks appeared, then a large building with an American flag fluttering from a tall pole. *I see a huge building with a large flag flying from a tall pole out front.*

"There it is!" said Emma. "That's the hospital."

Azelia was glad she was driving. It kept her mind off what may lay ahead. Her heart was in her throat and her stomach kept doing somersaults. She turned onto the property, located between Dudley Road and Winter Street. The facility had been constructed in 1943 for wounded soldiers returning from World War II and had been named for Harvey Cushing, a World War I doctor.

When they entered the building, Ethel, who hadn't spoken much during the drive, suddenly exclaimed, "Oh my!"

Azelia spotted them at the same time, seated behind a table the length of an aircraft carrier - three nuns dressed in gray who were all nodding and smiling at them. She returned the favor. *When you enter, you will be greeted by three gray ladies.*

The reception desk was adorned with a spray of roses and a bowl of pale out-of-season apples. A neat young woman looked up at them from behind the desk. "Can I help you?" she asked.

"We're here to see my husband, Sgt. Larry Heron."

"We've been expecting you, Mrs. Heron."

The receptionist was an olive-skinned woman with delicate features and a strikingly attractive face. Her hairstyle reminded Azelia of movie actor Dorothy Lamour. "Please wait here a moment," she said in a business-like tone. She motioned to the three nuns who rose in unison and began digging through some large boxes stored under a table. They each retrieved a large package, then all three came forward like the procession of the Magi to begin stacking their packages on a corner of the desk. *They will leave you with three large bundles.*

The closest nun introduced herself as Sister Elizabeth and the others as Sisters Mary and Alice. Gesturing toward the packages, she said, "Volunteers knitted these afghans as a token of appreciation."

"It's not nearly enough," added Sister Mary. "They are meant to express our nation's heartfelt gratitude. If there is anything more we can do to help, please let us know."

Sister Elizabeth smiled and said, "God be with you."

They thanked the three nuns who proceeded down the corridor with gray gowns flowing then vanished around a corner like ghostly apparitions.

In response to the questions posed on each of their faces, the receptionist said, "They are called the Gray Nuns, Sisters of Charity. Volunteers in gray habits, who nurse the sick, read and write letters for the war-wounded, sew on buttons, or just talk and listen."

"You can leave your afghans with me until you are ready to leave," she added. "Here comes the nurse to take you to see Sergeant Heron."

Azelia felt a rush like on the first day of school, anticipation mixed with fear of the unknown. The nurse identified herself as Frances Reid, a short, stout woman with graying hair, heavily bagged brown eyes, and skin as pale as the white outfit she wore. "Please follow me," she said, and led them down a dimly lit corridor to an equally dim elevator from the days of Edison. The flexible brass-colored gate clacked shut like the door of a cattle-car then the elevator creaked and groaned as it slowly lifted them to the second floor.

The procession moved off the elevator, down a vomit green corridor on vomit green linoleum squares that gleamed under infinite layers of wax. They rounded a corner and suddenly the color schemes switched to variations of institutional drab, beiges with pink undertones and washed-out blues. Azelia wondered how a new hospital could be made to look so old. They came to a stop before Room 207. Thus far, she felt as though she were walking on air. Emma took her hand and a nurse held her other arm. Azelia's face smiled ruefully while her eyes displayed the terror that was locked inside.

The nurse pushed the door open slowly to a dimly lit room with only daylight leaking in through partially closed blinds. A man dressed in white with a stethoscope dangling from a pocket stood on the opposite side of a bed above a body wrapped like a mummy. Her knees buckled and she would have slumped to the floor but for hands reaching out to take her full weight, her strength draining from her like water from a crushed sponge. She felt herself being lowered into a chair beside the bed where the powerful smell of antiseptic seized her.

"What's going on?" Heron asked softly.

"Are you all right Mrs. Heron?" the nurse asked.

No! I'm not all right! She wanted to scream. "Yes. I...I'm fine."

This was not Larry. It could not be him. Gauze covered everything except for two holes, one for his mouth and another where his nose should have been. Something white protruded there that looked too much to her like bone matter. A tube dangled from that same opening, through which she could hear labored breathing. His eyes were completely covered. The scene was like a gathering around a cadaver in a morgue. It could have been anyone under the layers of gauze. There were no soft eyes looking back at her.

She closed her eyes and wished she would wake up in bed and find that this was all a bad dream. But when she opened them again, she was still in the hospital and everything was all too real.

"Oh Larry!" Gently she touched his arm, the only contact she dared, not knowing the full extent of his injuries. "Honey I love you so much. I'm so glad to have you home." The words sounded hollow even to her, like talking to someone through a door, not able to look into his eyes or read his expression.

His mother said, "We're here, Larry. "Your sister and I will take care of you."

Emma's words cut through Azelia's heart like a serrated blade. *Your sister and I?* Had Emma interpreted her fainting spell as a sign of revulsion? Anger seized her. She smiled at Emma, reproachfully. "I love you, Larry," she repeated. Calmer now, she leaned forward. "Everything will be all right. *I* will take care of you."

This reunion of husband and wife proceeded with all the makings of a wake. Azelia's mind was in a whirl. When visiting hours finally ended, she said, "We'll be back tomorrow, darling. I love you."

After everyone had exited the room, she turned and said to him, "One more thing. We're all so proud of you. Everyone in town wants you to know that you are in their prayers."

She wiped tears from her cheeks and looked for a place to kiss him. No bare spots were visible so she pulled back the covers. To her horror, she found that his chest was also bandaged. Finally, she lifted a sleeve and touched her lips to a clear spot of skin on his forearm.

There was a knock and the door opened. It was the nurse who entered and said, "Sorry Mrs. Heron, but visiting hours ended long ago."

"Yes. Yes. I'll be back tomorrow, hon" she repeated to Larry. "I love you," she said again.

"Me too," he murmured, drowsily. He felt relaxed from a recent shot of morphine and the past hour had drained him. Soon he'd be fast asleep.

"How much were you told?" Dr. Saenz asked the three women as he ushered them into his office.

"Nothing really," said Azelia. "The telegram indicated he'd been wounded in action. It did not elaborate."

The doctor's eyes moved over her admiringly. She was a woman of great beauty and he sensed an inner strength and determination. Emma and Ethel leaned forward expectantly, leaving little doubt that they were every bit as strong. They would need to be for what he was about to tell them.

When they departed the hospital rain was falling hard. She became drenched by the time she reached her car but didn't care. She even welcomed the chill that passed through her as darkness fell. It fit her mood perfectly.

On the drive home, she was plagued with a sinking feeling in the pit of her stomach. The only sound came from the wiper blades marking time like a metronome, not quite cleaning the glass and leaving streaks that created a distorted rendering of the outside world. Her thoughts journeyed to distant places. Her palms felt clammy and her body feverish.

Mesmerized by the multicolored blurs from street lamps crossing her windshield, she listened to the muffled drumbeat of the wipers. Outside, water splashed over the hood and rushed gutters in search of unclogged drains. The few pedestrians she passed were vague shadows rushing by.

In the rearview mirror, she could see that Ethel had fallen asleep. She looked over at Emma who also had her eyes closed and her head resting against the window. She had proven to be a rock, the one person who truly shared her torment. Perhaps with luck and determination they would find a way to restore quality to his shattered life and even some of the joy that had been wrenched from his heart. But after what they had just learned, she wasn't at all sure it would be possible, not without some sort of divine intervention.

Heron awoke six hours after Azelia's departure. He lay still as a rock but his mind was wide-awake and rambling. The soft chime of a clock from somewhere in the hall let him know it was three in the morning. Everything was pin-drop still. He knew he would not fall asleep again until his next morphine shot, which was five hours away.

He tried to form a mental picture of Azelia but failed. The horror of his dilemma caused him to panic. For all intents and purposes, he had died out there on the battlefield. His life had been removed and it could never be restored. His wife had just been to see him and he couldn't even look into her eyes or kiss her on the lips. Thank God he could still recall the luminous clarity in her eyes – deep blue like reservoirs of pure spring water, trusting eyes that saw equal trust in the eyes of everyone she met. He took a deep breath then exhaled slowly, calming himself. There had to be a way to bring her face into focus.

Nothing he tried would work. Her face flashed through his mind one piece at a time. He finally forced a shot of her flashing a smile but couldn't hold it. Suddenly, he recalled the black and white picture that he had kept in his locker. This time her image entered his mind in black and white and he was able to hang on. Just long enough. Perhaps it worked because it was a still photo. Next, he switched to the wedding picture on the wall of their bedroom. It was in color. This time she came in clearly. He held on to her image for as long as he could.

"Since you are still awake, let's have another look at your blood pressure, Mrs. Heron."

"Let me know if you find any," Azelia jokes.

After the nurse leaves, she lies wondering how she had reached eighty years of age so quickly. Wasn't it just a few short years ago that she had been young and energetic? My God, she thinks, I am an old lady. My children are all grown and I have grandchildren in college. And he's been gone, what is it, five years now?

The details of the horrors her husband had endured on the battlefield had been parsed to her over a period of years from various sources, with very little coming from Larry, who rarely spoke on the subject for fear of reliving it. The ongoing operations throughout his life had been enough of a reminder.

During the time she had worked at the library to supplement their income, she had borrowed every book on the war that she could find, supplementing what she learned from returning veterans who had fought alongside Larry. Two key sources had been his friends before the war: Fr. Edward T. Connors, and another of Milford's sons, Dr. Joseph E. Murray. Both men's lives had crossed paths with Larry's during the most critical periods of his life.

And then there was John Sears, God bless his heart. John had made it his life's work to chronicle the history of the 87th, supplementing it with daily journals and other materials that he'd collected from various sources.

Many years would pass before she was finally able to piece together the exact details of her husband's brave actions on that fateful day. He had saved an infantry battalion at the cost of his future and everything that was meaningful in his own life.

Almost frantically, she searched until the moon slowly reappeared from behind a cloud. She felt the need to complete the recall of their lives before it could move beyond the window and vanish from sight. There was no rational explanation for why she felt that way, but now that it was back in sight, she let her thoughts return to Normandy and that awful day, June 26, 1944.

11

Handshake with Death

"You don't have to do this." Madeiros pleaded. "You're the Sergeant." But they all knew that Sergeant Lawrence J. Heron was the one man in the outfit with even the remotest chance of reaching the mortar rounds trapped in the rear of a disabled truck. Before being drafted, he had established himself in the sports world as one of the fastest running backs ever to play high school football. He had set new records for stolen bases and home runs, not just in high school, but also while playing for the American Legion, and later for Draper's semi-pro baseball team.

He was, without a doubt, the fastest man around.

Whoosh! A single artillery shell sailed overhead and exploded a hundred yards to the rear, shaking the earth to its core. Each man hugged the ground or mindlessly assumed the fetal position, though all knew it's the ones they didn't hear that would get them.

Pvt. Williamson, his face caked with sweat, blood, and grime said, "If you go, I go." Terror flashed in his eyes belying his brave words.

"If there's a sniper, I will draw him out. Just keep your eyes open." With that, Sergeant Heron swung into action with explosive intensity, like carrying a football, only this time the field was uneven. There was no protection. The penalty for error was death.

He zigzagged forward, diving for cover every twenty yards. His legs felt like lead when an eternity later he reached the rear of the truck and disappeared behind a canvas curtain.

Several hundred meters to the north, a sniper lay frozen under the ruins of a farmhouse. He was following the movement of the man charging with rifle held loosely in hand, hips swiveling, changing direction in an instant, moving too fast for him to get off an accurate shot. From his vantage point he watched as the soldier dragged a crate to the rear of the truck.

Heron pried off the lid and removed first one shell then a second, laying both rounds gently on the bed. Then he leapt to the ground and carried them one-by-one to the M-29, out of the sniper's view behind the truck.

The sights of the Browning in Fiske's hands passed directly over the farmhouse detritus, ready to sweep it with .30 caliber bullets at the slightest movement or the glimmer of a weapon.

Heron was drenched with sweat from both physical exertion and extreme fear. He had seen men's bodies jerk from the impact of a sniper's bullet even before the sound of the exploding cartridge had reached his ears. He could be dead in the next instant and never hear it coming.

The sniper guided his crosshairs to the center of the soldier's head, his finger poised so that the slightest caress would dispatch a bullet spiraling through the air and blow out the top of his skull. *Movement.* He eased his finger off the trigger. Other soldiers were joining him. *Wait until they cluster then go for a shell shot.* He had done it before, setting off high explosive rounds that killed five men.

A moment longer...

Fatigue was taking its toll as Heron stopped to wipe the sweat from his brow with the back of a sleeve.

Six men were closing in to lend a hand.

The sniper moved his crosshairs to the crate at the soldier's feet, his trigger finger delicately poised.

As Heron reached down to lift the top round from the crate, sweat beaded his face like condensation on a cold bottle of Coke on a hot summer's afternoon. He wished he had one at that moment.

The sniper centered his crosshairs on the shell, drew a breath and exhaled half. Then he squeezed the trigger. The bullet hit the shell in Heron's hand, unleashing the fury of seven pounds of chemicals inside the twenty-five pound shell. That blast set off a second shell in the crate below. The intensity of both blasts sent shell fragments smashing through his body and carried him twenty feet to where he landed on his back with gray smoke billowing from his flesh and clothing.

His head felt as though it had been stuck in a blast furnace and his eyes hit with twenty thousand volts of electricity. The excruciating pain was palpable, so intense that he didn't realize he was bleeding from multiple shrapnel wounds.

Fiske caught sight of the muzzle flash and began raking the debris with bursts of .30 caliber bullets, shattering glass, ripping wood into fragments, and turning stone to dust. The first burst removed the top of the sniper's skull. He was already dead when a second entered his left shoulder leaving a gaping exit hole behind and below the right armpit. Fiske kept firing until his weapon had emptied.

Heron was barely conscious, approaching a state of shutdown, the point where cognitive thought ceases and defense mechanisms kick in. Circuits overheated and synapses fired. Thoughts careened around in his brain like a flock of startled pigeons, then fragmented into packets of pain slicing through his brain. His fingers clawed viscerally at his face where fiery nuggets of white phosphorous adhered to burning flesh. There was no merciful unconsciousness, no single ray of hope – only unfathomable pain.

Divine providence had deserted him.

His lungs pumped like organ bellows attempting to re-inflate, squeezed by the force of the concussion. His heart was clunking like an off-balance washer on spin cycle.

Cpl. James N. Madeiros, Cpl. Edmond S. Bartosiewicz, Pvt. Michael A. Valette, Pvt. Arthur Almeida, and Pvt. Robert L. Williamson picked themselves up slowly from where they had been knocked to the ground. None suffered more than minor burns and superficial wounds. Williamson felt something foreign stuck between his lips and spit it into his hand. To his horror, he recognized part of an ear and flung it away.

When the shock of the explosion abated, all thoughts centered on Heron. No one expected to find him alive. Blood soaked his clothing. His face, or what was left of it, was a mess. Each man looked down at him. Some turned away to vomit. An ordinary man would have died instantly. They all left his side knowing that his fate had been sealed. No one could survive two shells exploding in his face, not even Larry Heron.

He heard voices.

"We'd be doing him a favor," someone suggested.

Dear God! They want to put a bullet in my head. Never in his wildest dreams had he ever imagined it would end like this. He had always been sure he could survive any catastrophe no matter how grim the circumstances. The notion of his own mortality seized him. "No!" he cried. "My wife! She'll take care of me." His mouth was stuck dry and the words adhered to the back of his throat. *They can't hear me. Please God. Azelia...*

Fiske jabbed at the sniper's body with his rifle like a cat poking a dead mouse. The one eye remaining in his head was open and the mouth already had a fly in it.

The men were drawing straws when Lt. Bonafin rushed forward, a path opening for him. "Hold on." The lieutenant felt for a pulse. "Jesus Christ, he's still alive." Heron's face was like an oozing sponge, eye sockets dark wells of pulp, and the nose and most of both ears were gone. His life's blood poured from multiple wounds, soaking the ground. "For Christ's sake get a medic over here!" Bonafin shouted.

"Medic!"

Heron was sure that the chemicals had eaten through his nerve endings, for he could no longer feel his face.

"Medic! Get a fucking Medic over here!"

Bonafin listened to the sounds of battle coming from where the infantry was dug in and fighting to survive. "Madeiros," he ordered, "get the men to gather up these shells. Take them over to the mortars and commence firing."

"Yes sir!" Madeiros shouted. Ignoring the ringing in his ears, Madeiros rounded up the remainder of the squad. Minutes later Company A was delivering punishing fire on enemy positions and laying down a barrage that allowed the trapped infantry to break free.

Cpl. Fiske was out of breath as he addressed the lieutenant. "I got him, sir. I found the body of a German sniper in the remains of the farmhouse."

Bonafin cocked an eye. "Fucking snipers. We're a half-mile behind front lines." He took a step toward Fiske and patted him on the back. "Good work, Fiske. You sure he's dead?"

Nearly an hour had elapsed between the time of the explosion and the arrival of a medic who took one look at Heron and turned toward the lieutenant, "There's nothing I can do for him, sir. Better I help those who can survive."

"Get your ass back over there and do whatever you can for that man," Bonafin barked with asperity. "He just saved an entire infantry battalion."

The medic turned back to Heron. There was no nose. The eyelids resembled torn lace. There was no left ear and only portions of the right. Pieces of the forehead, lips, cheeks, and jaw were gone as well. Blood oozed from shrapnel wounds like ketchup through a caldron. The medic dosed him with sulfa, applied compresses, and hooked up an IV.

"What else can you do for him?" Bonafin asked.

"I'm doing everything I can think of," the medic responded. "He's not going to make it anyway." He groped Heron's pack for morphine, tugged on a sleeve, then pierced his arm with a needle his patient did not feel. Normally, he'd have used Heron's own blood to mark an "M" on his forehead to prevent someone from inadvertently giving him a second shot that would prove lethal, but the forehead was too badly burned and bloodied. He wondered how Heron could still be alive, why he hadn't at least passed out.

"What's he saying?" Bonafin asked.

"I don't know. He's incoherent." If he had been following prescribed procedures, the medic would have scraped the raw and bleeding phosphorous burns with a brush. But he had never done that to a raw face and could not bring himself to do it now. Neither was there a large body of water handy to flush the burned areas, so he decided to simply cover them with wet gauze.

He unsnapped Heron's canteen, unscrewed the top, removed a roll of gauze from his backpack and soaked it with water. Then he lifted the injured man's head gently and began wrapping it. This would help smother the chemical, cutting the supply of oxygen. "Someone should have done this sooner. Most of the particles have already burned themselves out."

He examined the dog tags, noting that Heron was Catholic. "It's no use," he said to Bonafin at last. "Better get a Catholic chaplain to read him the last rites."

Bonafin could hear the mortars coughing in the background as he mouthed a silent prayer.

Twenty minutes after the call went out for a chaplain, a jeep pulled to a stop nearby. Painted on its side were the words *CONNORS COFFEE SHOP*. A soldier with a chaplain's cross painted on his helmet stepped briskly from the jeep and rushed to Heron's side. Whether the dying man was Catholic or not made absolutely no difference to Fr. Edward T. Connors, who had volunteered to be here. A friend to enlisted men and officers alike, he had become a living legend and a war hero. Men of the 9th Division of every faith referred to him as the "Great Chaplain," the "Soldier's Chaplain," and "Our Chaplain."

Connors Coffee Shop had become a 9th Division tradition. In his tent, one would always find a caldron of coffee atop a kerosene-heated ration-can. Whenever it ran low, he simply added coffee and water.

Connors fell to his knees beside the wounded man. He'd already witnessed more deaths than any man should in one lifetime. Death had become as much a part of the landscape as trees, rocks, farmyards, fields, and streams. He had given last rites to men who had stepped on landmines or fallen on grenades, men whose bodies had been ripped apart with no chance to survive.

The Chaplain examined the dog tags then froze in horror as he read the name. "Dearest God!" he uttered aloud.

"What?" Bonafin asked. "What is it Father?"

"I know this man," said Fr. Connors. "I...I can't believe it's him!"

"Before joining up, I was the athletic director of a school in Fitchburg, Massachusetts. He played for St. Mary's, and they always beat us whenever he played. He's the fastest and most powerful back I've ever seen play the game."

"Larry, Larry Heron. Can you hear me?"

Heron's head rolled from side to side. His lips moved but nothing could be heard.

"It's Father Connors. Ed Connors from Fitchburg, Massachusetts. St. Bernard's."

If there was recognition, Connors could not be certain. He placed a gentle hand on Heron's shoulder to calm him. Then, slowly, hesitantly, he produced a bottle containing the "oil of the sick," wet his hand and began anointing: "In nominee Pa tris, et Fi lii, et Spiritus Sancti." In the name of the Father, and of the Son, and of the Holy Spirit. He followed a field form of the ritual aimed at destroying any power the devil has over a dying man, then anointed his eyes, ears, nose, lips, hands, and feet in that order, each time praying forgiveness for their wrongful use.

There was not much left for him to do now but wait for his young friend to embrace death, and meanwhile continue to pray that his soul would find the right door.

12
Black 4ᵗʰ of July

Late in the evening of June 26, a jeep rigged with four stretchers attached to metal brackets delivered Heron and three other wounded to a clearing beside a temporary hospital. Each of the injured was covered with a blanket to prevent the shock that accompanies blood loss and severe burns. Three of the men were carried inside the hospital tent where they were greeted with the lusty smells and noises peculiar to hospital surroundings.

Heron's stretcher was left outside on the ground with him still in it. The battlefield "triage process" called for the dying to be left outside because of the shortage of beds, medicines, and hospital staff. Studies had shown that patients burned as badly as Heron usually survive only for a period of minutes, suggesting that he would be dead by morning no matter what was being done for him.

Heron kept slipping in and out of consciousness, the trip having weakened him considerably. Fortunately, an orderly had the presence of mind to continuously administer fluids. Despite this, his body experienced rapid dehydration, and lack of saliva prevented him from being able to speak.

The fact that he remained alive two days later was a marvel attributable to his superb strength and stamina. Having beaten the odds, he was finally taken inside the hospital and placed on one of three beds that had suddenly become available. The tent was packed with the severely wounded, a place of shadows congruent with Heron's world of darkness.

It seemed to Heron that with this temporary loss of sight, his hearing

92

had become much more acute. Or was it simply the result of straining harder to pick up every piece of sound: the cacophony of wails, moans, and screams, the incongruous jolts of laughter, and the associated noises unique to a field hospital on the battlefield?

A nurse began carefully unwrapping the outer gauze from his face. "Oh my God!" she gasped. She left Heron's side to go in search of Lt. Leonard B. Bristle.

"This one's real bad, doctor," she whispered to him.

"They're all real bad," he replied, with mild distain. "Eighteen year-old amputees, paraplegics, stomach wounds so huge we can't stretch the skin far enough to cover them. Tomorrow they'll be hundreds more for whom we can do little more than ease the pain."

The doctor's hair was mussed. A stethoscope swung like a pendulum from the pocket of his white jacket. His eyes flashed fatigue and his face was lined with stress. He tore off his bloodstained coat and began washing his hands. After slipping on a clean jacket he grabbed for the stethoscope. "He can't be any worse off than the others," he said on the fly. "Last night, or was it this morning, I excised the legs of a young man of eighteen. Told another he'd never use his arms or legs."

He reached Heron's side then turned abruptly to the nurse and whispered, "Holy shit! This *is* bad!"

He relived the events over and over, trying to piece things together, groping for a handhold on an icy slope and finding none. A flashbulb of comprehension and a wave of monumental stress engulfed him, the impact of the explosion hurling him through the air, the shrapnel ripping through his body, the white phosphorus burning his flesh, searing it to the bone. The experience was engraved in his brain like a cancer. It would revisit him in his sleep, and register again and again in sudden uninvited replays in the weeks and months to follow.

The pain was unrelenting. Besides physical injuries, he wondered about the damage to his mind and, worst of all was the blackness with only occasional sparks of light.

"You don't have to do this," Madeiros had argued. But it had to be done. The odds had simply gone against him.

What about Azelia? What will she do? Twenty-four years old and at the peak of her beauty, the long hair, bottomless blue eyes, exquisite bone structure, delicate skin, and a smile that crushed all barriers. She drew people to her, greeting everyone like a lost friend. An angelic aura surrounded her. Women wanted to be her friend. Men wanted to protect her. *She could have her pick of any man.*

Suddenly, he felt a presence. "Who's there?" he asked. His voice was feeble. The priest could barely make out his words.

"Father Connors, son. How are you feeling?"

"Father Connors? From Fitchburg?" He recognized the steadfast voice.

"The same. Feeling any better?"

"When I regain my eyesight, perhaps." Momentary flashes of light had given rise to the hope of regaining some of his sight. His heart swelled at the thought, ushering in a flood of dreams for a brighter future.

"What have they been doing for you, Larry? How are they treating your injuries?"

"They give me morphine when I scream, then it begins to wear off and they give me more. But how did you...where did you come from?"

"It's a miracle. I just happened to be in the vicinity. I'll speak to the doctor, Larry. See what else can be done."

Connors soon learned that besides morphine, penicillin and sulfa the doctors had been giving him whole blood. And that he had been incoherent the past few days – barely conscious.

Later, Connors asked the doctor, "What's the prognosis?"

"Not good, Father. He's lost so much blood that it's a wonder he's still alive. He's in terrible shape."

"He seems no better than when I saw him in the field, but no worse either," Fr. Connors whispered. "What does it mean?"

"I don't want to shatter your hopes, but I'd say he has no more than twenty-four hours. Severe burns and blood loss initially sent him into mild shock," the doctor said in a low voice. "But the long-range prognosis is not good."

Connors fixed Dr. Bristle with tired eyes. The priest was near exhaustion and out of breath, as though he hadn't slept for a week. The fact was that for weeks now, he had been sleeping for only a few hours each night. "I'd like to pray for him. Give him last rites one more time, if that's the case."

"Be my guest. Does it matter that he's not awake? I sedated him."

After performing the ritual one more time, Connors located the doctor. "What happens next?" he asked.

"Tremendous fluid loss and physiological shock. The exterior surface of his face, especially the right cheek, has been eaten down to the subcutaneous tissues causing edema."

"These aren't like the usual burns you treat. I mean this was not caused by fire."

"There are similarities. White phosphorous burns in the presence of air, and since no one took immediate action to smother the burned areas with mud or water, the damage went deep and was quite considerable."

"He has a lot going against him. Plasma leakage, decrease in blood mass, lowered circulation, and a number of subsequent metabolic disturbances. Tissues and red corpuscles will likely release liquids into his circulatory system, introducing anemia and hypertension which could lead to cerebral and pulmonary edema."

"English please."

"A build up of fluids and toxic products from destroyed tissues is being re-absorbed into his blood stream. This could bring on liver and kidney damage. If he were to survive another ten days, he'll drop about ten or twelve pounds from fluid loss alone."

"There's also the danger of infection which could inhibit nutrition and block healing – and lead to death. So you see, he likely won't make it."

Fr. Connors approached the bed and stared down at Heron, who was sleeping restlessly. He picked up his chart and surveyed the damage. *Severe burns of the cheeks, eyes, nose, a good part of both ears, and lower lip. Burns on forehead, neck, and shoulder. Shrapnel wounds over his entire body.*

Connors planned to say some very special prayers that night in the hopes of shifting the odds in Heron's favor. He was not only a dedicated priest, but also a caring man who had been in the thick of fighting in North Africa, Tunisia, and Sicily. Even before landing on Utah Beach with the 9th Infantry, he had given last rites to so many fine young men that he'd lost count. Larry Heron was as bad as off as anyone he'd seen.

After the chaplain departed, a medic came by to change his dressings and tend to his medications.

Connors lay on his cot that night but could not fall asleep so he reached for his mug, the one with CONNORS COFFEE SHOP painted on it. He tipped the pot more than forty-five degrees to eek out a full cup. It was blacker than night but still plenty hot. He went outside his tent and stared up at the stars.

Luxuriating in the warmth of the mug, he lifted it to his lips with both hands and sipped the strong blend, remembering the way things had been in the 1930s – the way things would never be again.

On his first night in the field hospital, he woke up screaming. It felt as though a fifty-gallon drum had been dropped over his head with someone pounding on it with a sledgehammer. The white phosphorous dream. The classic flashback. "A common experience of survivors following extreme trauma, particularly burn victims," the doctor had explained. "It will go away in time." Amazingly, the dreams were always in color, which the doctor claimed was unusual.

He drifted off but awoke an hour later with searing, burning chemicals eating his face and shrapnel tearing through his body. He was sweating and staring into darkness. *This had better end soon,* he thought. *If only the pain would ease.* Moments later the nurse was by his side with a welcomed shot of morphine.

Fr. Connors dropped by the following morning prepared to pray for his friend's departed soul. Heron was in a corner of the tent, his face wrapped in heavy bandages as well as his shoulders, chest, arms, and legs. Perhaps he would pull through, but if so, what kind of life was ahead for this once proud athlete?

Connors had come to regard "field" hospitals and "transit" hospitals as unnecessary delay points in the evacuation process. So-called "transportable" patients were being evacuated as quickly as possible while dying patients like Heron, classed as "non-transportable," were being held until they either died or showed strong signs of recovery. Connors located Dr. Bristle to ask why more wasn't being done for his patient.

"Frankly, we don't think he has any chance of survival, and even so, we are under strict orders to give first aid care only in this hospital."

"What?" The chaplain asked incredulously. The doctor's words came as a shock.

"There are thousands of wounded men who have a much better chance of survival. Frankly, that's where we must focus limited resources like penicillin - where they will do the most good, which forces us to take Heron off penicillin.

"What's the problem with penicillin?" Fr. Connors asked.

"The fifty billion units ordered for June did not arrive. There were only 600 million units on hand during the assault phase of the invasion. Half made it to the beaches and the rest were loaded onto LSTs (landing ship, tank) destined for hospitals in England. For patients in transit we're under orders to apply standard operating procedures only, which equates to first aid care only. Keep the ones alive we think can make it, load them on a ship, then send them to England where they receive proper care." His face was flushed. "You think I like it? Those are my orders, for Christ's sake! Oops – sorry Father."

Connors didn't stay around to argue. Instead, he rounded up a jeep and paid a visit to General Manton S. Eddy, the 9th Infantry Division commander. Connors had been with the 9th Division since October 1942 and was close to all its officers and men, especially Eddy. He had been in the front lines with the troops when they saw their first combat in North Africa on November 8, 1942, and again when they launched their attack in southern Tunisia on March 28, 1943. And when they drove to Bizerte on May 7, he had shared their foxholes. In August, when the 9th landed at Palermo to participate in the taking of Randazzo and Messina, he had been a great source of comfort to every soldier. He had trained with the men in England and was with them when they landed on Utah Beach on June 10.

When Fr. Connors related Heron's story to General Eddy and asked why the wounded weren't receiving the care they deserved, the general became furious. He sent word to General Paul R. Hawley, the Army's Chief Surgeon. Hawley blew his stack when he read the message. "That's a gross misinterpretation of my order. SOP does not mean neglect." That very morning he had responded to a similar complaint from Colonel Cutler.

General Eddy received an immediate response from Hawley: *Orders misinterpreted. New orders cut today. Every effort will be made to save every injured man. Enclosed is (1) a copy of my order and (2) a personal message on its way to Lt. Bristle.*

The next day, Dr. Bristle informed Heron that he was to be evacuated by hospital ship to Salisbury, which was equipped and staffed with highly trained personnel to begin the process of reconstructive surgery.

"Will I be able to see again?" he asked.

"I don't know," was all the doctor would volunteer.

On July 2, 1944, Heron spent long hours on a stretcher in a location reminiscent of a scene from *Gone With The Wind* where the wounded were stretched side-by-side on the streets of Atlanta for as far as the eye could see.

He reached up and felt his shirt pocket for his rosary beads. They were gone. "My rosaries!" he cried out. "Where are my rosaries? They were in my pocket."

"We didn't find anything like that," a deep male voice answered. "I'll look around. Is there something special about them? Perhaps you can replace them."

"These cannot be replaced," he said.

The orderly spent a half-hour searching through his clothing but did not find the string of beads. "I'll get word back to the field hospital and see if they can come up with them." He feared though, that they probably had removed his shirt and thrown them away. It was doubtful that they would ever be found.

Heron viewed the loss of the rosaries as a bad omen.

Several hours later, he was carried aboard an LCT filled with dozens more casualties and taken to a hospital ship lying off the coast, an LST. The LST would not leave for England until fully loaded, which ended up taking another twenty-four hours.

After it docked in England, eight more hours passed before he was finally taken ashore and transported overland to #158 General Hospital in Salisbury, a complex containing 2000 beds that were distributed throughout clapboard buildings set in neat rows, more like an Alaskan mining town than a hospital.

The town of Salisbury was best known for its Salisbury Cathedral, the mother church of the Salisbury Diocese. A glory to God in stone and glass, this majestic and awe-inspiring cathedral had been the setting for many great occasions. Slender columns and sculptured busts of dark Purbeck marble were set in a sparse, barren interior of understated beauty. Its 13th century cloisters were magnificent. The spire rose to 404 feet, the tallest in the world in its day. One of the four original copies of the Magna Carta was still on display in its 13th century Chapter House, along with a stone-carved frieze of Old Testament Bible stories.

None of this was of any consequence to the heavily sedated man being transported into Building #28. Upon Heron's arrival, Lt. Vance Bradford started his examination and was horrified by what he found. Third degree burns to the eyes, lids, face, forehead, neck, shoulders, and hands. Missing tissue, dead tissue, and festered cells. Multiple shrapnel wounds.

By now Heron's condition had weakened considerably. His immune system was losing the battle against infection and he'd lost his appetite. "I want him on a liquid high-protein diet, immediately." The doctor continued to write in his chart as he spoke. "Get me a blood count. Continue the penicillin, 20,000 units every four hours," he ordered. "And start him on sulfadiazine every four hours."

Dr. Bradford reapplied fine mesh gauze soaked in petroleum jelly to the burned areas then added a bandage, a treatment that had been developed at Mass General Hospital in the early forties by a doctor named Bradford Cannon.

As the medications began to take effect, Heron's senses became more acute and he began to grow restless, occasionally screaming in pain. Dr. Bradford administered a shot of morphine and prescribed additional doses four times a day. "Let's get some head X-rays," he told the nurse, while jotting more findings on Heron's chart

After re-examining the shrapnel wounds, the doctor ordered saline sulfa dressings bound to his right shoulder. That evening, in addition to morphine, Heron's dressings were changed and he received a 500 cc blood transfusion.

He dreamed she was standing beside him in a large room overlooking a river of black blood. Azelia gasped as she pointed to a dark silhouette approaching their window, an evil being who wanted them dead. All he could do was close the blinds so they didn't have to look, and as he did a hand closed over his mouth and he began to suffocate.

Suddenly, he tried to rise to a sitting position and to pry open his eyes but nothing happened. Vertigo seized him as hands grasped his arms and a gentle voice said, "It's all right. One of the pillows covered your face and stifled your breathing. Anyway, it's time for some breakfast, if you feel up to it."

Heron moaned at the thought of food. Instead he asked for and received a shot of morphine followed by sulfadiazine. The doctor ordered another blood workup.

As the drugs began to take effect, Heron asked an orderly, "What day is this?"

"The 4th of July," the orderly answered. He wondered if his comrades were faring any better.

Several years would pass before the woman in Room 201 would learn of what had happened to David Rubenstein and some of the others whose names she'd come to know.

A tray crashed to the floor somewhere down the hall, the sound jolting her from her reverie. Then a door closed and all was silent once again. Where was the moon? Still there. Where was she? Oh yes. He had been worrying about his comrades – rightfully so. That 4th of July had turned into one of the worst tragedies.

On July 4, Company A operated in support of the 2nd Battalion of the 330th Infantry Regiment. Not long after Heron had been knocked out of action, Cherbourg fell to the Americans – but not without a price. Six officers and 88 enlisted men of the 87th were killed during the assault. Since then, Company A had been fighting non-stop through towns that read like a French tour guide.

Thus far in the campaign, the company had fired 32,000 mortar rounds, and following a lengthy barrage on Greville, 150 Germans came forward to surrender. Then it was on to Carentan, with forward observers from the 87th operating side-by-side with their field artillery counterparts, each supplying direction to their own and the other's firing batteries as well.

Following a 200-round volley in the early morning hours, there came a lull that provided time for a well-earned breakfast. Most gravitated to fox-holes dug under tall trees for protection where they broke out their mess gear.

Roger Burt was sipping coffee when Francis Healy leapt to his feet and challenged him to a wrestling match. Healy danced around jabbing the air like a prizefighter. "Come on. Let's go a few rounds." The two men had taken to wrestling between engagements to help ease tension and keep in shape.

"Are you nuts?" Burt asked. "I haven't finished my coffee."

"Afraid?"

"Of you? You're crazy. Let's go. But remember, no gouging, kicking, biting, stomping, or pulling of hair."

"What do you think I am, an animal?"

"A sissy."

"You're begging for it."

They moved off to a clearing about fifty feet from their foxholes, circling one another like angry cats, eager to slough off pent up energy. "Gotcha," Healy boasted triumphantly, as he clamped his hands around the back of Burt's neck. But the wiry Burt grabbed a handful of shirt and fell backward pulling Healy with him and using leverage to flip them both, with him landing on top. He began counting, "One, two, thre..."

Kaboom! An enormous explosion shattered the air as an enemy shell exploded in a tree above where the men were dug in. Their foxholes offered no protection against the downpour of shrapnel from above. *Kaboom! Kaboom!* Instead of protecting their heads, helmets sat turtle-like on the ground or inverted in laps to hold rations or water for washing.

"Tree bursts," Healy shouted. The two wrestlers covered their ears and hugged the ground as several more shells hit nearby trees. It grew ominously quiet for a few seconds then they heard screams and knew immediately that the Germans had scored deadly hits. They rose to their feet and ran to see what could be done for the injured.

Pfc. Sheffield lay on the ground, crying, "I've been hit. Oh God. I'm bleeding."

"Jesus!" Burt exclaimed. Sheffield's arm was bleeding all right, but when he wiped away the blood he could see that it was just a scratch. He turned away and sank to his knees beside Staff Sergeant David Thomas, his close friend. "Oh no. Not you," he said. One look told him that Thomas was dead. His friend sat Buddha-like, mess gear in his lap, a spoon in his hand. The only indication that he'd been hit was the single pinprick of blood oozing from the side of his head. Burt took him gently by the shoulders and lowered him to the ground. Then he reached over to close his eyelids. When he did, his tear-filled eyes were drawn straight ahead to where Thomas' dark lifeless eyes had been staring a moment ago. For the first time, he noted the bodies of Sgt. Volcjak and 1st Lt. Arthur L. Gump lying in one tangled heap, like a pair of discarded puppets. He could tell without further examination that both were dead.

Cpl. David Rubenstein was slumped over in his foxhole. The top of his head had been sheared off while he was opening a can of rations. Pvt. Leslie S. Kolman's crumpled body lay beside him, a pool of blood outlining his head.

Sheffield continued to sob, "Help me! Oh God, help me!"

Burt decided he'd better take a closer look at Sheffield's wound. "It's just a scratch," he said, dispassionately. "A million dollar scratch."

Sheffield believed he had suffered a life-threatening wound and continued to moan and wail.

Burt and Healy split up and went in search of help. Burt soon located a handful of medics and some chaplains eating breakfast in a barn. "Come quickly," he said. "They need help."

Heads turned. They read the terror in his eyes and followed him wordlessly. Five were dead, seven wounded. Art Fertitta had been wounded, as was William S. Collins, who would later succumb to his wounds and be interred in France until 1947 when his body would finally make it home.

"How's Sheffield doing," someone asked Healy.

"Shove a lump of coal up his butt; he'll squeeze you out a diamond. That's how tight he's wound. But he'll be fine."

The next afternoon did not fare much better for Company A. The 3rd Battalion of the 329th Infantry Regiment led an attack south of Piereres at 0700, with Company A getting off 300 rounds of supporting fire before moving to a position south of Le Culet.

Lt. Branson and Lt. Moore went out as forward observers to relieve Lieutenants DeWitt and Berry. Lt. Branson, the third officer selected for forward observer duty, located Fiske. "Cpl. Fiske, grab your Browning and follow me. You too Shanahan, we need a good radioman." Shanahan smiled and eagerly bent to the task of adjusting the gain and squelch, then hefted the radio pack onto his back and followed.

The three men moved forward about a thousand yards to the base of a hill that appeared to be a perfect spot for an observation post from which to direct fire on enemy positions and report back on results.

A German machinegun team, concealed behind a copse, spotted the men as they started up the hill. "Was uns hier haben?" said a German soldier peering through binoculars at the approaching men.

The gunner, looking through his own binoculars, responded, "Amerikaner!"

The Americans were on the move, spaced about ten yards apart.

"Kommen Sie hier!" The gunner whispered, coaxing them closer.

"Hold up. Something's not right," the lieutenant said. "Too quiet."

At his signal the three men dropped to their knees to listen.

"Call for fire on that hill," Branson said.

"Roger." Shanahan rose to his feet to slip the radio off his back. That's when the machine gunner raked a path across his chest that coughed holes in the radio. His hands flew out to his sides like a chicken flapping its wings. His body danced grotesquely. Mini-geysers of red sprang from his chest and soaked into his clothing. If he was screaming, it was inaudible above the clatter of the machinegun as his body smacked the ground like a lead-stuffed doll.

"Shit!" cried the lieutenant, diving for cover behind a small rise. Fiske made a running dive into a crater on his left as bullets kicked up sand at his heels.

The German gunner focused on the mound that afforded Branson minimal cover. The machine gun coughed and the lieutenant felt an immediate stab of pain in his upper left leg and a burn in his left shoulder. He knew he'd been hit.

A smile creased the gunner's face as he continued to squeeze off rounds. Bullets kicked at the mound protecting the lieutenant, chewing it slowly to dust. Branson was powerless to do more than pray and count down what appeared to be the remaining seconds of his life.

Left alone, Fiske rolled to a kneeling position and laid down a withering fire with the Browning, catching the enemy off guard. An expert rifleman, he had hunted often with his dad. Before the Germans could respond, he was on his feet, advancing as he laid down rapid fire, the rifle pinned against his side by his powerful forearm.

John M. Browning had designed the weapon for trench warfare. And that's exactly how Fiske employed it – firing with such deadly accuracy and rapidity that the Germans could only duck for cover. A bullet struck the gunner in the forehead, sending brain matter spewing out the back of his skull. The second German frantically pushed his comrade aside and took up the gun but it jammed. Panicking, he lifted his rifle and fired blindly.

Fiske was hit. Blood gushed from his left shoulder. As he fell to his knees, he removed a grenade dangling from his chest, yanked the pin and lobbed it toward the machinegun emplacement. As the grenade sailed through the air, another bullet caught Fiske in the throat. The last thing he heard as he pitched forward toward the ground was the sound of the grenade exploding.

Lt. Branson, only slightly wounded, ran to Fiske's side firing his pistol. He picked up the Browning but all activity in the machinegun nest had ceased. Both Germans were dead.

Branson felt sick to his stomach when he couldn't get a pulse. Hoisting Fiske over his shoulder, he limped down the hill and laid his body behind a clump of trees, then returned for Shanahan. As Shanahan's limp body rolled next to Fiske's, Branson sensed activity and glanced up the hill to where a large number of Germans were advancing toward his position. There was nothing to do but get the hell out and live to fight another day.

The clock beside her bed reads 3 a.m., and the moon has almost reached the three-quarter point in its trek across the window. Suddenly a strange feeling passes over her and she feels her body growing weaker. It's as though everything inside her wants to shut down; her body is telling her to let go. But her mind will not allow it. Not now. She must not doze, not before she can complete her thoughts. If she does, she fears she will never wake up. She must hang on long enough to finish the story of his...their lives. It has become a challenge for her to finish it before the moon disappears, for a voice inside tells her that the end is near. Where was she? Oh, yes.

Every time Heron learned something new about what had happened to one his comrades, it had taken many days for him to get over it. Though she had never met many of his friends, she felt as though she had come to know them all. She had gathered details about them purposely, the ones that made it home, and the ones that did not. And it was not always the lower ranks that death chose to visit.

On July 12, 1944, while all the fighting and dying was taking place on the battlefield, Brigadier General Teddy Roosevelt, Jr. was felled by a heart attack while serving as the military governor of Cherbourg. He left behind his wife, Eleanor, nicknamed Bunny, and their four children. Azelia had read how the couple's marriage had been built on a firm foundation of trust and deep love, not unlike her relationship with Larry.

Not long before he died, Teddy had sent his wife a letter summing up their "grand life" together, how they had packed enough into the years "for ten ordinary lives." He wrote of their happiness. "I pray we may be together again," he wrote. He was only 56 years old when he died.

The dying didn't stop there.

On July 13, Lt. Bonafin called down to the battalion commander of the infantry unit for which he was directing fire on enemy positions in the vicinity of Bois Gommet. "It looks to me like a rattrap, sir," he warned. "They're making it look too easy." The commander disagreed. "We have them on the run, is all," he replied. Sometime later, Bonafin heard the dreaded squeaks and clanks of tank treads. Mark VI tanks suddenly burst into view one-by-one from behind camouflaged positions. The infantry battalion was encircled. Bonafin was caught in the rattrap along with the unit he had been trying to defend. He was cut down in a hail of bullets from a machine gun mounted on one of the tanks and died instantly.

"They were all so young," she whispers to herself. "Like my Larry."

13

There's No Going Back

Each morning, Heron was being fed a light breakfast. On most days, he was taken to the operating room to have his burns bathed and scraped, a process called debridement or enucleation, an extremely painful method of removing dead tissue by brushing or peeling. His shrapnel wounds were also being treated and dressed regularly.

On July 14, Dr. Vance Bradford visited his bedside. His heart was heavy, his voice gentle. This was not what he had signed up for. He wanted to save lives, help patients to heal, cheer them, not bring them bad news. "Sergeant," he whispered.

"Yes."

"It's time we discussed your eyes."

"Did the nurse tell you? I think my eyesight is returning!"

The doctor took a deep breath. "You told her that you see flashes."

"Yes. Doesn't that mean I'll see again?"

"I'm afraid it's not possible."

"What?" The voice suddenly grew feeble, weighed down with shock and disbelief.

"You see," the doctor said, quickly regretting his poor choice of words. "They were destroyed by the intense heat. There's no way of saving them."

"But the flashes?"

"A sporadic residual retinal reaction. Electrical impulses from the optic nerve. Nothing more."

It could not be true. Any minute he would awaken from this nightmare. It could not really be happening. "Can't you fix them?" Desperation had seeped into his voice.

"Your eyes were completely destroyed. They're dead tissue that must be removed before infection sets in."

Heron's sigh reflected an overwhelming hopelessness. "When?" he asked, as if it made any difference.

"The sooner the better. "Tomorrow morning."

This was it then. Nothing would ever efface the darkness. Hope had vanished. All along he had been holding on to the belief that his blindness might be a temporary state. Whenever a doubt had crept in, he refused to accept it. But now it was final.

When he was alone, he wept, but no tears fell from his eyes.

At 0730, Heron was returned to the operating table where his back, buttocks, thighs, and abdomen were prepped as donor sites. At 0900 he underwent eight-hours of surgery to remove what remained of his eyeballs. The empty eye sockets were covered with split skin grafts, as were his forehead, face, ears, and neck.

The doctor checked in later that night to find his patient lying on his right side. His left side, the donor site, was also bandaged. Heron woke up and soon complained of severe eye pain. The doctor increased his morphine.

"Keep him on a liquid diet – whatever he can tolerate," he ordered. Soon after the doctor had left, two units of plasma and 500 cc of blood were administered and his blood pressure was taken every fifteen minutes for the next three hours.

The next day, the doctor found Heron awake and quite lucid. "You're a very brave man," he told his patient. "I grafted the soft defects in your right cheek and lower lip. The wounds will soon heal but you'll need many more operations before things begin to look normal. That will take place back in the states where we have our best plastic surgeons."

"In a few weeks time, after you've healed, we'll send you on your way. Meanwhile, I'll introduce you to some Red Cross workers who will teach you how to read Braille."

"Oh. By the way," the doctor added, "This arrived for you today." He put something in Heron's hand.

"My rosary beads? They found my rosary beads?"

"Appears so."

"Will you describe them to me doctor?"

"Sure. Black beads with a solid silver crucifix."

Heron tried to smile but his face was as tight as a snare drum.

"There's a note that came with them." Dr. Bradford read it to him. *I'm the orderly who searched for your rosary beads. I finally tracked them down in a pile of clothing headed for the incinerators. Hope they bring you luck.*

"I don't even know his name so I can thank him."

Bradford said, "It's signed by a Ronald Williams. You can dictate a thank you note to the nurse. We'd be glad to forward it to him for you."

"I can't believe he found them."

How awful it must have been for him in #158 General Hospital, though he never complained to her about it. She learned later that he had spent his time practicing Braille and reminiscing about his "first life," a life that almost always included her. She recalled some of those days now, the Friday night dates that invariably ended with watching a movie at the State Theater. After the movie, they would cross the street to Nolan's drugstore. She could almost recall the apothecary odors emanating from the drugstore half. The other half held a soda fountain with a granite counter and marble-topped tables surrounded by hourglass chairs. They'd sit at one of the tables and eat hamburgers or fried chicken and follow it with a slice of homemade apple pie or a banana split.

On Saturdays they might go to the park and play tennis all afternoon on the well-maintained clay courts. On rainy Sundays they would often be invited to someone's house to play Monopoly. And in the dead of winter, after the pond had frozen over, town plows would be dispatched to clear away the snow for skating.

Life in Hopedale was simple then. It was a time when a dollar bill would buy enough meat to feed a small family. Just one dollar would also buy four large potatoes, a pound of green beans, a head of lettuce, a large tomato, and four dinner rolls, with five cents left over for a Coke or Pepsi. It was a safe and comfortable existence.

Then came the awful war and he was sent away to foreign shores. And just like that, he was severely injured. She cried now as she pictured him alone in his tomb of darkness, lying in his bed, knowing he could never pick up life where he'd left off before the war, knowing he could never return to the sports he loved. How frightened and alone he must have been, though the doctor's report she obtained years later indicated that he had handled it pretty well.

Pursuant to orders that he be "remanded to the Zone of the Interior" (Continental U.S.) on August 15, 1944, Lawrence J. Heron was taken aboard a ship that transported him to New York. Before his departure, Dr. Vance Bradford wrote the following summary into his records: *At 1830 hours on 26 June, 1944, at the battle for Cherbourg, France, Heron was unloading phosphorous bombs and was severely injured when enemy fire hit and exploded a bomb he was carrying.*

The day after admission to #158 General Hospital in England, on 3 July 1944, I had him in surgery without anesthesia to deride necrotic burn tissue from his face and neck. His eyelids were practically destroyed and his eyeballs were without color, resembling rotten grapes. It was my unpleasant duty to tell him that his vision was gone. He told me that he could see some flashes, but of course what he thought was some vision was only sporadic residual retinal or optic nerve reactions.

At the 8-hour operation on 15 July 1944, what remained of his eyeballs was removed and the whole forehead, face, ears, and neck were covered with split skin grafts. One strip of skin graft covered the empty eye sockets.

The grafts healed well without complications. Although only 24 years of age, Heron accepted his blindness with exceptional serenity.

While waiting for transportation to the Zone of the Interior, Heron was already being rehabilitated. With a cane and a guide, he walked about the hospital grounds, visited Col. Graham, our commanding officer, and was coached in Braille by the Red Cross women.

Heron has soft defects in his right cheek and lower lip. The wounds were grafted and healed but he will need more plastic surgery to restore these defects. Although regulations permitted us to do any cosmetic surgery that could be accomplished within_180 days, our basic mission was to get the wounds healed and preserve function.

Heron is quite a stark contrast to another burn victim with severe disfigurement of his face and eyelids. The other man repeatedly tried to commit suicide, even though he had not lost his vision.

The war had affected their lives in so many ways. It would never be the same for any of them after the war. Roger Burt had since told her how his whole life had been altered and how his faith and belief in God had only been strengthened by it all.

14

The True Test of Love

Burt watched as wave after wave of fighter-bombers dropped their loads just ahead of him, so close that it raised the hackles on the back of his neck. The planes had been at it all day, cutting a wide path through the countryside for the infantry. This would eventually go down as the operation that preceded the Saint Lo breakthrough, one of the most bloody and difficult phases of the Normandy campaign.

As he entered the small village, he saw a child who couldn't have been more than eight years old coming toward him with something held in her hand. As she drew closer, he could make out a small gold cross. It was obvious that she wanted him to have it. He reached out and took it from her. "Merci," he said. Then he pulled out his phrase book. "Quel est votre nom?" he asked.

"Michelle," she responded.

"Mon nom est Roger," he said. "Roger Burt." He squatted down so that their faces would be at the same level.

She smiled and kissed him on the cheek. Then without another word, she turned and walked briskly away.

He held the cross for a long while, turning it to catch the light. Then he slid it into a compartment of his wallet, in front of a booklet of prayers that had been given to him by the nuns of St. Joseph, prayers that whenever read would continue protecting him from harm for the next thirty days. With these two precious items in his wallet, he felt safe. They would go with him everywhere for the remainder of his life.

On the morning of September 12, Company A was in Koul supporting the 1st Battalion, 16th Infantry of the 1st Division, dropping twenty-five rounds on an enemy convoy and causing the Germans to flee in panic. As they moved through the Aachen forest, they came upon the first of a series of fortifications guarding the approaches to Germany, hills and ridges marked by marble blocks, wire fences, and blazed trees. A network of roads followed the valley floor, connecting several towns and villages to the industrial mining centers of Forbach, Stiring-Wendel, and Saarbruecken, the southern gateway to Germany's Sarre basin, the fortress city of the Siegfried Line. The men were in a state of exhaustion as they dug into their new position. Resistance being light, they took few precautions, unaware of the horrors awaiting them after midnight.

At 0200 hours on Wednesday, German 88's and flak guns broke the silence, catching them completely by surprise. The horrific shelling that ensued ran non-stop through the night and did not end until ten o'clock the next morning.

In the midst of this violent enemy firestorm, a dozen successive shells hit Company A's gun emplacements, resulting in heavy casualties. The wounded were everywhere. With shells whooshing overhead, Pfc. Angelo Bastoni zigzagged to the side of 1st Lieutenant Doug Peterson, who was bleeding profusely from a shoulder wound. Bastoni did what he could for the lieutenant, covering the wound with a compress. Then he looked to his other fallen comrades.

Ten yards away, he found Sgt. Chuck Learned writhing on the ground. Not far from him, Pvt. Almeida had also fallen. He was badly wounded and losing copious amounts of blood. Scanning the area, he spotted more of his comrades who all appeared to be in a bad way. He knew he must act quickly to get them out before the shelling finished them off or they bled to death.

He dashed across an open field with shells bursting all around with just one thought - find a way to evacuate the wounded. He found the answer parked under a tree about a hundred yards away, the lieutenant's jeep.

Five-foot-eight Pvt. Bob Williamson recalled General Roosevelt's words back at the landing. "Why are you men wasting your energy digging fox-holes?" he had asked. "If one's going to get you, it's going to get you. Just keep moving!" And then it happened. An eighty-eight shell exploded a few yards behind and lifted him off the ground as shell fragments knifed through his body.

I'm going to die, Roger Burt was thinking, as German artillery contin-ued to rain in around him. At that very moment, he saw young Williamson fall, blood pouring from his wounds like wine from a barrel shot full of holes. As he made his way toward his fallen comrade, he heard a jeep pull up beside him with Bastoni at the wheel. Bastoni had already evacuated Peter-son, Learned, and Almeida, and was returning to pick up more wounded. "Come on, get in," Bastoni shouted.

Burt leapt into the passenger seat and they headed for Williamson. Without a word, both men jumped out to drag the man onto a raincoat and lift his limp body into the back of the jeep, both thankful that he was uncon-scious and feeling no pain. Despite Burt's frantic efforts to plug the wounds, by the time they reached the aid station, a gallon of blood had pooled in the folds of the raincoat and Williamson was dead.

Bastoni had made four roundtrips through a raging hell storm to remove a total of ten wounded men. Pvt. Williamson was the only one of the wounded that he didn't save. For his heroic deeds that day, Bastoni would be awarded the Bronze Star. Roger Burt's bronze star and promotion to Staff Sergeant would come later for numerous acts of courage under fire.

Williamson's death that day did not surprise Burt, who the night before had sensed his young friend's impending doom. It happened that same way with several others just before they had died. This power of presentiment frightened the hell out of him.

As happens to soldiers who have faced death repeatedly, Roger Burt had grown more religious and also quite superstitious. Some of them made sense like "never three men on a match." By the time it reaches the third cigarette a sniper will have had time to zero in on the light. Also, he discovered, as did many of his comrades, that soldiers were often killed soon after taking a memento from a dead German. For that reason, he had seen many of his comrades walk right past a coveted Luger without giving it so much as a glance.

The battlefield was a robust environment where emotions ran high. It was also a place where men of reason and intellect found religion. The prayer-lines were always overloaded before battle. Whenever a chaplain appeared, it didn't matter which faith, soldiers would gather round him to pray. The man who drew the largest crowds was Fr. Edward T. Connors. Soldiers and local townspeople flocked to his Masses, en mass.

Fr. Connors sent the following letter to Bishop O'Leary on September 14, 1944: *The people are happy to see us. Occasionally, I hold Mass in a church for my units. When I do, the whole town turns out, though the only warning is the ringing of the bell before Mass. The Nazi's have spread false propaganda that the American army is filled with Communists. But that perception is changing and we are drawing larger crowds at Mass and Holy Communion.*

In one town we entered, the people were in a turmoil of bitterness and grief. The Germans had departed a few hours earlier - after setting fire to many homes. When some men tried to extinguish the flames, they were shot down then butchered. I counted fourteen bodies – a horrible sight. The next morning I offered Mass in their parish church for the victims and those of my men stationed nearby attended, as did the entire town. The SS troops had murdered fourteen men. American troops prayed for the men.

Azelia hears footsteps coming down the hall and hopes it isn't the nurse heading for her room again. She hears a door open and close then footsteps leading away. Good, she can get on with her thoughts while everything is still fresh in her mind. The men returning from the war all had stories to tell her, but none with injuries nearly as bad as his. One newspaper even listed him as "World War II's most severely wounded soldier," as she was to learn for herself on that dreary day in August. Everything looked so hopeless for him then that she never suspected what was to take place next.

Framingham was only eighteen miles away, about a half hour drive, so she visited him every day. She would walk everywhere around town to conserve gas, and her sisters and friends contributed portions of their ration stamps to further the cause. Her daily routine included a trip to the hospital in time for evening visiting hours.

As she entered his room one night in September, he felt a breeze and smelled the first cool air of fall gusting through his open window. Her fragrance reached him before she planted a kiss and squeezed his hand. She could hardly wait to say, "I have something for you, sweetheart."

"What is it?" he asked.

Instead of answering, she plugged in the combination radio/record player and dialed a local music station. "I thought you might like listening to some of your favorite programs."

"Also, I picked up a few records."

"Thanks, sweetheart." Heron was truly grateful. It was a thoughtful gift that would help take his mind off blindness and chronic pain.

The next morning, after his dressings had been changed, he told the nurse that he was feeling fine. In truth, he was in agony because he had asked the doctors to cut back on the morphine. The pain was becoming so unbearable that he wanted to scream. Instead, he turned the music louder and began singing along with a Frank Sinatra recording of *I'll Be Seeing You.*

The louder he sang, the better he felt. Remarkably, singing took the place of screaming in terms of easing pain. *I'll Be Seeing You* sat atop the "Hit Parade" and played every few hours. Days later, Heron had the words down cold. In the past, he neither had the time nor the inclination to sing, but now he found that it lifted his spirits and exercised his lungs. His doctor claimed that it would even speed his healing.

On her next visit, Azelia brought more records. Soon, he knew the words to *Danny Boy, Irish Lullaby*, and *I'll Take You Home Again Kathleen.* On a Friday night, at the conclusion of singing *Danny Boy,* applause and cheers broke out amongst the several nurses and orderlies gathered outside his door to listen.

"You have a gorgeous voice," Nurse Barsanti told him. "How about *Black is the Color?* I heard you singing it the other day and loved it."

Why not? He began: *But Black is the color of my true love's hair...* Not being able to see helped stave off an attack of nerves. When he had finished, there was only silence. *No one likes my singing.* He felt his face flush with embarrassment. If he could see, he'd know that there was not a dry eye within hearing range. Suddenly Nurse Barsanti began clapping. Then everyone joined in with applause and cheers. From then on, Heron would be flooded with requests. And with each song he grew bolder and his voice much stronger.

Word of his talent spread and soon large groups of patients and staff gathered in the rec room to listen to his singing. His strength was coming back a little more every day and by the time his stay at Framingham came to an end, Heron had developed a repertoire, and had taken an important step toward recovery.

When Azelia came by on his last day at Framingham, he turned his head toward her and reached out. She took his hand in both hers then held it to her lips. "This whole thing must be an enormous shock to you," he said. "I'm sorry for coming home such a mess."

"Sorry? You have nothing to apologize for." There was so much she was longing to tell him, to help him understand how her heart ached for him.

"I know I'll never look like I once did and that I'll be blind for the rest of my life," he said. "When these bandages come off, you'll see you're married to a monster."

"You'll look just fine."

"No. Wait. I've been doing a lot of thinking and we have to talk about this." His voice had taken on a pleading tone, as gentle as a violin concerto, stopping her next protest in its tracks.

"You could have any man you want. If you decide to leave me, I...I will understand. Before going blind, I would have had to be blind not to have noticed how other men look at you." She was so beautiful. Only twenty-four years old. If she decided to stay with him, it must be without pity. If he were to get through the awful months ahead, there could be no doubts. Once the operations started, he could not survive losing her.

"Leave you? Why on earth...?"

"The doctors warned that reconstructive surgery... Well, I don't want to travel that road if there's even the slightest chance that when the going gets rough you'll..."

She finished for him. "Leave you?"

"I'm not the man you married, Sweetheart. No one will blame you. This is not what you bargained for."

"Neither did you. And I don't care what other people think. You're the only man I've ever wanted and I've got you. I love you more now than ever. So let's get you through this and home where you belong!"

He drew a deep breath. "When you see my face, you'll be repulsed. You won't want to hold me close or kiss me, let alone make love to me." He hesitated. "Don't make this any harder than it already is."

Azelia's heart was aching. "A Greek poet once wrote, 'Love built on beauty, soon as beauty – dies.' Our love has a strong foundation and will endure."

"There's a rough road ahead. The pressures will be enormous."

"For better or worse. In sickness and in health."

"Sweetheart, there are going to be an ungodly number of painful operations, just to make me presentable – not to restore my looks, not even to make me look normal. If you should change your mind and quit part way through, it would be much worse than if you just walked away right now." *I won't face years of operations without you, because without you nothing matters.*

She played her words in her head before speaking, like swishing a fine wine around in her mouth to sense the flavor and aroma before swallowing. "If you were to decide against the operations, if you want to stay looking just as you do right now, it won't matter. It was never just your looks that attracted me. It's what's inside. Can't you see that? I want to grow old with you, Larry Heron. That's all I've ever wanted. I've loved you since I was six years old, wanted your children."

She pulled a tissue from beside his bed to wipe her tears. "You're stuck with me and that's that!" She leaned forward and rested her hands lightly on his shoulders wishing she could embrace him.

"I love you, dearest," he whispered. "Always have, always will. It was you who kept me alive. I just want to spare you from a life of misery." She paused. "Oh Larry. I love you so much. I would die without you." It was impossible for her to hold back the tears cascading down her cheeks. She wiped her eyes again and pressed herself against him, careful not to hurt him.

"You make me so happy. Because of you, I am the luckiest man alive," Heron said tenderly.

There was a knock and the door opened. It was the nurse.

"Just a little longer," Azelia pleaded before the nurse could ask her to leave. "Please?"

The nurse knew she had interrupted something important. "Certainly," she said, "another few minutes won't hurt anybody." She promptly left them alone.

15

The Doctors at Valley Forge General Hospital

On Monday, November 6, Heron was transferred to Valley Forge General Hospital in Phoenixville, Pennsylvania, three hundred miles further away from Azelia. VFGH was a large facility, an order of magnitude greater than the Cushing Hospital where he knew his way around and had become familiar with much of the staff and many other patients.

Ten days later, he was deeply depressed when a nurse announced, "There's someone here to see you, Sgt. Heron."

A familiar voice said, "Hello, sweetheart."

"Azelia?"

"I decided to surprise you. I've booked a hotel room for the weekend."

"Why didn't you tell me you were coming?"

"Frankly, I thought you might protest. I didn't want to give you the chance to tell me not to come."

Heron was delighted. Only she was wrong. He would not have discouraged her from coming.

She took his hand and leaned in close. "Can you sit up?" she asked.

"Yes. And walk around. Anything but see."

"No, I mean will you sit up for me right now?"

"Sure. What's up?"

Without answering, she helped him to a sitting position and started untying his hospital gown.

"The nurses," he protested.

"They won't come in here unless you push the alarm button. They promised me an hour so we'd better get started. She carefully helped him get undressed and then slipped under the covers with him. He felt her naked body press against his and let out an audible sigh. "This beats the hell out of submersion in a saline bath," he exclaimed.

"Let's not waste time talking," she whispered.

On November 8, 1944, Chaplain Edward T. Connors wrote Bishop Thomas M. O'Leary from somewhere in Germany: *In this region, we find a multitude of devout Catholics. In a number of towns, I was the first American priest that the parish priests had ever met. They have all been very kind and their people faithful. Evidently Hitler failed in rooting out the Catholic faith.*

The commander of the 9th Division is a devout Catholic, General Louis A. Craig. He always receives Holy Communion and is a fine example to the men.

I recently began to instruct one of the battery commanders. He is from the south and had met few Catholics before the Army. He has been impressed by the strong hold the religion has on the men and has asked to be received into the church. "Veritas impellit."

This is something of a consolation to a priest. We do get weary after two years, mostly in combat. A bit weary but never lonesome or discouraged – and I would never think of leaving.

It was a blustery day outside Valley Forge General Hospital on Wednesday, November 8, 1944, with a cold wind blowing down from the north. 1st Lt. Joseph E. Murray removed his Harvard Medical School ring and the watch his wife had given him a year ago, right after his graduation. He placed the items in his suit jacket, draped the jacket over a hangar and hung it in his locker.

Just then Col. Bradford Cannon entered. "Good morning," he said. He took a final sip of his coffee before placing his mug on a table beside Murray's.

"And a good morning to you. I hope we can make it a good one for this patient."

Dr. Cannon began taking off his jacket and tie then dropped his ring and watch into an inner jacket pocket. "Yes, another sad burn case," he said. "The patient's burned over so much of his body that we've run out of healthy tissue and have to use cadaver skin as a temporary surface."

Scrubs were donned. Loose hair was shoved under caps. Masks were slipped on. Knee controls were pushed to turn on water and foot controls to pump drops of antimicrobial solution onto palms. There came the sound of vigorous brushing as they started with their nails.

"If only we could get past rejection," Murray said, as he worked up a lather on his arms. "Think what we could do for this patient." Murray had a habit of spending the majority of his time probing the mysteries of science, delving into patient's charts and files, running lab experiments, and relentlessly dogging for answers to questions that had been baffling the world's best doctors and scientists for generations.

"That's all I think about," Cannon responded. "I wish we could figure a way around it."

The slow rejection of foreign bodies had been weighing heavily on Murray. "How does the host distinguish another person's skin from his own?" he wanted to know.

After a thorough lathering and vigorous brushing, the doctors rinsed off, taking care to keep their elbows low.

"Let's not forget Brown's success with the twins," Cannon said. In 1937, Dr. James Barrett Brown, chief of plastic surgery at Valley Forge, experimentally cross-skin grafted a pair of identical twins.

"Yes. He established that the closer the genetic relationship between donor and recipient, the slower the dissolution of the graft." Gowned and gloved scrub nurses held out towels for the doctors who followed the prescribed method of drying each arm.

Dr. Murray then pushed open the OR doors with his backside and felt the hissing air escaping the pressurized operating room. He continued holding it open while Dr. Cannon slipped through.

"That was a first step. A transplant between people immunologically close – and it worked." That thought would occupy Murray's mind, forming the impetus of future study and dramatic breakthroughs.

"I'm afraid the new discoveries and innovations are going to have to come from brilliant minds like yours," said Cannon. "It's all I can do to keep up with the flood of patients waiting to get into the OR."

"I'm flattered, but I also don't believe it for a minute. You're always breaking new ground."

The scrub nurses held out sterile gowns for each of the doctors. Then they offered a glove with the cuff stretched open. As a hand was slipped into each glove, the nurse gave a firm downward thrust and let the cuff clamp down on the wristlet with a characteristic snap. Meanwhile, the circulating nurse was tying the backs of their gowns.

"I'm just grateful to be able to work with a living legend," Murray added.

"Ha! I wish I were that good, Doctor!"

"You are that good, Doctor!"

"The patient is ready," said the OR nurse.

Dr. Cannon began prepping the patient's skin for surgery, arranging sterile drapes to confine the incision site.

That evening Dr. Murray entered Room 330 and picked up the new patient's chart. Everything about the young doctor exuded confidence. He was tall, lean, and handsome, with diamond-edged eyes that took in everything. The plastic surgery wards were always jammed with patients and he devoted every spare moment circulating amongst them, observing the results of the most imaginative reconstructive surgical procedures.

That's where he could be found night or day - in the wards, talking to patients, helping with dressings, and picking up valuable bits of information. Born with an extreme curiosity, he questioned everything, then questioned the answers, and when he received new answers, questioned them further. Absolutely nothing would be taken for granted.

Murray took one look at the chart, then at the patient and gasped, "Good

Lord! Are you *the* Larry Heron that played for St. Mary's in Milford?" He silently prayed that the answer would be no.

"That's me," Heron replied. "You sound like...Joe Murray?"

"How in hell did you know?"

"Some people never forget a face. I never forget a voice. You played first base for Milford High. You were quite the competitor."

"So were you. I will never forget my last game against St. Mary's," Murray said.

"That was in 1936," Heron said quickly. "You were the team captain."

"You have a fantastic memory."

"I will never forget that day. The papers called it a slugfest."

The four thousand fans overflowing bleachers and jamming the sidelines watched Murray drive in three runs in the first inning with a single and a stolen base. Heron answered with a bases-loaded homer in the second. Murray hit one out of the park in the third to tie the game then followed with a triple in the fifth to put Milford ahead. He would have scored again from third base on a hot grounder, except for a perfect throw to home plate by St. Mary's shortstop, Dave Tredeau. The catcher put the tag on Murray's toe as he slid wide, thus ending the inning.

In the seventh, Heron hit a home run with a man on base and two outs. St. Mary's held a six to five lead going into the final inning. That's when Murray came to bat with two out and no one on base.

A hush fell over the stadium as the pitcher wound up. Then a single fan yelled, "Come on Murray. Hit one out of the park." St. Mary's catcher signaled low and inside. The pitch came in slightly outside. He stepped into the ball with a solid *crack* that was heard downtown. Murray's homer tied it, six apiece.

Heron's turn came in the bottom of the ninth with two outs. Azelia bit her lip and watched his fingers dance on his cap in a familiar pattern – so quick and subtle that few would recognize the sign of the cross.

"Steer-ike one," the Umpire yelled. Heron swung hard at the next pitch for strike two. Tense moments slipped by as the next three balls in succession passed just outside the strike zone. With a full count, the pitcher sent one down the middle. Heron hit the ball solidly but the bat broke. What should easily have been a homerun fell between right and centerfield and rolled toward the fence with both fielders in hot pursuit.

Heron crossed second base as the right fielder reached the ball. He rounded third as the ball was fired in a low trajectory toward home plate. Tearing up the turf in long strides as the ball sailed home, he slid wide of the plate, barely tagging it with a toe as the catcher swiped at him with the glove but missed cleanly.

As Heron raised his arms triumphantly toward the admiring St. Mary's crowd, the Milford High catcher walked forlornly behind him and swiped the folds of his shirt in frustration, but Heron never felt it. As far as he was concerned, he had scored and the game was won.

Then why hadn't the umpire signaled him safe?

Heron felt compelled to do something he would later regret. He ambled back and tagged home plate a second time. With all the dust and dirt blowing around, perhaps the umpire hadn't seen him tag it the first time.

"Yerrr out!" the umpire shouted, jerking his arm and pointing his thumb to punctuate the call.

The St. Mary's fans showered the umpire with boos and blasphemies. The Milford fans, many of whom had been stunned into silence, started a belatedly low cheer that grew louder as the realization sunk in that their apparent loss was now a tie. The umpire headed for the sidelines. The game had ended.

Dr. Murray's tone turned somber as he asked, "What did you do to yourself?"

Heron gave him a summary of his misadventures: a shell exploded in his hands, he'd gone for days without treatment, and had lost his eyes in England.

Murray choked back tears. "It's time to change your dressings, so let's get started."

"I'm going to give you something to make you comfortable." He swabbed Heron's arm. Taking the IV needle from the nurse, he administered a general anesthetic to prepare Heron for the painful process of removing the gauze. He gently peeled away the greased up gauze soaked with Heron's body fluids and was startled by what he saw. Heron's face had been chemically erased, the eyes sockets covered over with skin grafts.

His badly scarred face and feral display of teeth formed an incongruous smirk, like some creature from the lowest depths of the ocean. At least the teeth were perfect. The surgeon in England had done a fair job of covering the empty sockets with split-thickness grafts. But his ears! The only unaltered feature, it seemed, was a healthy crop of brown hair.

The following was in his chart:

Diagnosis:

1. *Burn (white phosphorous) face, forehead, eyes and lids, neck, and patchy areas of shoulders and hands, third degree, with loss of large amounts of tissue.*
2. *Laceration Wound, severe, multiple, involving lower lip, right cheek, right anterior shoulder, palms of hands, left knee.*
3. *Nasal bones, maxilla, right. A.I. when two phosphorous bombs exploded in his face as he was loading them.*

Operations:

3 July 1944 - Debridement of burns. No anesthesia.

15 July 1944 - Dermatome grafts of face, forehead, jaws, neck, ears, and enucleation of eyes bilateral. Anes. Endotracheal 10 hours duration.

3 Aug 1944 - Repair of lip defect. Skin grafts to orbits, nose & chin. Anesthesia, local procaine.

Murray could not stop the flow of compassion for this virile athlete, a legend in his hometown. With the loss of both eyes, a flame had been extinguished, a bright light dimmed.

"I can't believe you're my doctor," said Heron.

"Well actually I'm not. You are fortunate to have one of the best plastic surgeons in the business, Dr. Bradford Cannon."

"Good?"

"None better."

"What's he like? I'd like to know something about the man who is going to reconstruct my face."

"Sure. I've finished my rounds for the day." Murray began to brief him on Cannon, hoping to put his mind at rest.

"Ever hear of Dr. Walter Cannon, the man who proved how the esophagus really works? He also showed us how the body secretes adrenaline in response to emergency situations and provides athletes a second wind - you know, the fight or flight theory."

"It seems I've heard of him."

"Well Bradford is his son. After graduating from Harvard Medical School, he did his residency at a major plastic surgery center, the Barnes Hospital in St. Louis, where he first met Vilray Blair and James Barrett Brown."

"The two doctors that head up this hospital."

"Correct. Seven years later he was a surgeon at Mass General's plastic surgery clinic, and a protégé of the world-famous Dr. Varaztad Kazanjian, the man who made plastic surgery a specialty."

"Before I met Bradford in the early 1940's, he and Dr. Oliver Cope had designed a new treatment for burns. The old method began with a harsh and very painful scrubbing to remove destroyed tissue, which was followed by a spray of tannic acid solution to form a protective membrane. The doctors found that the membrane forestalled healing and led to infections. Their method, now used everywhere, involves covering the wound with fine mesh gauze impregnated with petroleum jelly. It is far less painful, prevents infections, and aids healing. Their findings came out just prior to the Coconut Grove fire."

"Were you practicing then?"

"I was still in grad school, but I remember it as though it happened yesterday. November 28, 1942. That night football games were being played to decide championships. I remember Holy Cross upsetting Boston College. Dr. Cannon was called away from his turkey dinner. A hundred and fourteen of the most severely injured were brought to Mass General. All but thirty-nine died within a few hours. Thirty-six of the hundred thirty-two taken to Boston City Hospital died as well. The number of dead would have been far greater had it not been for those two doctors." He drew a breath. "Enough about doctors. Let's hear about you. I don't know how anyone could have survived what you went through."

"I had to get back to my wife. I love Azelia too much to leave her," Heron replied.

"I know exactly what you mean. I feel the same way about my fiancée."

"Fiancée? Who would that be? How'd you meet her?"

"My last year in med school, I attended a Boston Symphony Orchestra concert with several classmates and spotted this incredibly lovely young lady. I told my friends that she was far too nice for the fellow she was with."

Heron laughed.

"At intermission, I made it a point to run into her in the corridor. She was alone so I introduced myself. Her name was Bobby Link, a music student majoring in voice and piano. By the time intermission ended, I knew we were destined to marry."

"That's nice. When's the big day?"

"This June."

"Congratulations. Sounds like we were both lucky in love."

Murray stopped by to visit with his old friend as often as time allowed and Heron was grateful for the attention. The doctor took a personal interest in his progress, and it elevated his spirits whenever they found time to reflect back on better times.

Dr. Cannon also dropped by often to check on his new patient. "I hear you and Murray were baseball rivals," he said one day.

"Yes. He was quite a player – good enough to have played professionally, but being a top surgeon was his first priority."

"And he succeeded. The man's brilliant. One of only two from his class at Holy Cross that made it to Harvard Med School."

The two doctors obviously had great respect and admiration for one another. And without a doubt, both were tops in their fields. Heron felt fortunate to be at Valley Forge.

On Monday, November 13, 1944, the outside temperature was 40 degrees in Phoenixville, where Heron underwent his first surgery under the capable hands of Dr. Bradford Cannon. First, the doctor released some scars around the corners of his mouth to enlarge the surface area of the skin covering his face. This would allow the underlying muscles and nerves to function so that Heron could open and close his mouth with relative ease.

This procedure would be repeated in stages during subsequent operations. Since burn scaring contracts the skin in every direction, Cannon had to incise the scars on both sides of his face from the corners of his mouth upward towards his ears. Cutting through scars was like cutting an elastic band. The freed ends retracted leaving craters of raw tissue, which he then had to fill with skin from Heron's flank and thighs. Then he placed skin grafts over burned areas of the face and lips.

That night Heron lay swathed in bandages. His world had been reduced to a small bed in the corner of a tiny room, under a shroud of darkness as black as the center of a Pharaoh's tomb.

Everything went exactly as Dr. Cannon had described. First the burned areas were prepared by scraping them raw in preparation for the new skin grafts - a painful procedure that had Heron on the verge of screaming. The next step was to cover the areas with matching skin from healthy parts of his body. The new skin would require dressings that would have to be replaced daily until new growth would appear and the danger of infection had passed.

On the morning of November 16, an orderly stopped by to read parts of the newspaper to Heron. He preferred to listen to the headlines first to keep up with what was happening on the front. Next came the news from the sports pages.

After listening to the war news, Heron said, wistfully, "I'll bet the 87th is in the thick of things. They'd be right up there in front with the infantry."

16

A Not So Merry Christmas

At that precise moment Company A was attached to the 331st Infantry, 83rd Division. Heron's platoon, in the hands of Sgt. Nicola, was located in the vicinity of Birgel. Their morning started off with the firing of high explosive and white phosphorous rounds at enemy positions near Krauthausen.

During a lull in the action, John Sears pulled up in a jeep and immediately searched out Cookie for some coffee and snacks. Prior to the landing, he'd been transferred to Battalion Headquarters and reassigned as Brigadier General Barber's driver. The jeep bore a plate on the front with one star. Upon taking on his new assignment, his first order of business was to remove the jeep's canvas top to improve peripheral visibility, and to take out the windshield so as not to reflect the sun.

"So what's new," Cookie inquired. Somehow, Army cooks always manage to insert themselves as intricate cogs in the rumor mill.

"All hell broke loose in the Ardennes," Sears replied. "The bloody Krauts are pouring through by the tens of thousands in a straight line toward Paris."

"Where in hell's-name is Ar-dens?"

"A huge forest in eastern Belgium and northern Luxembourg."

"Geez, the man's a geography whiz as well as a historian," one of the chefs piped up.

"Yeah? Well when they reach the Siegfried Line, they're going to get their butts kicked," Cookie admonished. The chef added, "News coming in with the reserve troops is that the war in Europe is as good as over."

"Tell that to the Krauts," Sears stated flatly. "Not only are they on the offensive, I hear they plan to drop paratroopers behind our lines. Hitler's hell-bent on retaking Aachen."

"Shit. You're Barber's driver aren't you? You must be in the know."

"I didn't get this from him. They could be headed this way is all I'm saying. It's just good to be on the lookout."

"They've got to go through us to get to Aachen," one of the helpers speculated.

"You got that right," Sears shot back.

Sears' remarks would later prove accurate. On December 16, Hitler's Belgium troops crossed the Meuse River where he unleashed his Fifteenth Army to take Aachen. The Germans followed up with a massive offensive against a weakly defended American line in the Ardennes, catching the Americans by surprise and smashing a forty-five mile hole through their lines. German armored columns then swept through the hole and attacked supply dumps located along the Meuse River.

On December 17, in the vicinity of Kufferath, Germany, with the temperature below freezing and an icy wind gusting to over seventy-five miles per hour, Pvt. Angelo Bastoni and First Lieutenant Marvin J. Dewitt were directing fire on enemy positions from a house on the high ground in Burzbuin, about 2000 meters northeast of Gey.

Bastoni held his nose to ward off the acrid smell of rotting flesh wafting from piles of dead horses, the German army's principal means of transportation. As pungent as acid and as thick as smoke, the stench could not be blocked by a sleeve or a rag clamped over the nose. Suddenly he heard the dreaded grinding of tractor treads. Worse still, the noise abruptly ended. Had they been spotted? Was the tank about to fire at them?

The answer came a second later with a "*whump*" that separated Bastoni from the ground and rattled his brain. *Whump! Whump! Whump!* Three more explosions followed. Marvin Dewitt was thrown twenty feet to where he lay with blood pouring from his nose, ears, and mouth. Bastoni knew before he reached the lieutenant that he was dead but he checked for a pulse nonetheless. There were no external wounds so he supposed the concussion had killed him. Time to get the hell out of there. *Whump!_Whump! Whump! Whump!*

The building was in a small glen, hidden by a thicket about a mile from where he had left the lieutenant's body. He would have to remember the way back in order to retrieve it later. Windows had been blasted out and doors blown away, but the structure remained intact. He strained to listen until he was certain that no one was inside. Then he cautiously entered through a side door. The brick walls blocked out the wind but not the cold.

Suddenly his body reminded him that it had been over seventy-two hours since he'd slept or had anything to eat. Darkness was falling and it was extremely quiet. He located a corner in a small bedroom and curled into a fetal position behind an old wardrobe closet lying on its side. The next thing he remembered was waking from a dream in which he was back home on Christmas Day. His mother was standing by a Christmas tree looking at him with tears in her eyes.

As he awakened, his eyes were blinking involuntarily, trying to dispel a gritty substance. It felt as though an elephant were squatting on his chest. He tried to move but was locked in place.

Where was the bright sunlight coming from?

He heard them speaking German before he spotted them gathered where an entrance had been the night before. There were three of them standing twenty feet away. Two looked to be much younger than he, lacking enough whiskers between them to make one penciled mustache. Their leader moved like a man of forty but looked over at him with the tired eyes of a man twice as old. He had iron gray hair and a splotchy beard.

Sometime during the night the Germans must have brought up tanks. The building had taken several direct hits and crumbled around him. He'd slept right through it. Now that it was daylight, they were here to investigate. Still groggy, he had yet to move a muscle - thank God. His head was tilted back at an angle that allowed him to see through his lashes without appearing to be awake.

The tip of his rifle poked out from under the ruble. His hand was touching the stock. By the time he could free it they'd have pumped him full of lead. Fine dirt particles lay like snowflakes over the surface of the jagged detritus, some in his nose so that he wanted to sneeze. Each of the Germans gave him a cursory glance but seem unconcerned. Who would have lain still through the night with dirt and bricks piled up on him if he were still alive?

Then he heard a noise from somewhere behind him. They heard it too. Six eyes focused on him like gun barrels. Rifles were being aimed. He prepared to die. Suddenly, the Germans broke into nervous laughter as one of the younger men made his way toward Bastoni. *Are they laughing at me?* Just when he thought the jig was up, the German vanished from his peripheral vision. Sweat made a path down his neck. When the German came back into view, he was carrying a scrawny kitten and scratching it behind the ears. Bastoni could hear it purring like a motor, which seemed to put the Germans completely at ease.

Moments later they cleared out, taking the kitten with them. He waited another ten minutes then freed himself and his weapon from the pile and shook off the dust. An hour later he was back in friendly lines, a half-hour after that he was leading a search party to retrieve Dewitt's body.

Thus began a turning point in the war. General Von Rundstedt's forces had launched a counter-offensive that broke through a weak spot in the American lines to start the campaign that would go down in the history books as the *Battle of the Bulge.* Deep snow, severe cold, and intermittent rain would render this one of the toughest campaigns of the war, with Company A right in the thick of things.

Sometime later, the entire battalion pulled out of Germany and headed into Belgium to take part in a stand that would turn the German tide. One section of Company A moved from Schleckheim at 0900 hours, arriving in Havelange at 1400. The main body jumped off from Ober Forstbach and bivouacked in a small town near Marche.

Christmas Eve fell quiet. On December 25, the men sat down to their first Christmas dinner overseas. The depression that had been building with the approach of Christmas was somewhat offset by a splendid dinner prepared by a hard-working kitchen staff. The menu included turkey, potatoes, vegetables, cranberry sauce, pies, candy, fruit, and a few rounds of confiscated liquor.

17
Reconstruction and Rehabilitation

Azelia took a plane to Philadelphia and a room at a nearby hotel so that she could spend the holidays with her husband. They enjoyed sleigh rides and dances, and joined in singing Christmas carols. A concert was held on Sunday, December 17 at which Heron sang *White Christmas, Silent Night*, and *What Child is This* to a packed house.

His voice was soft yet riveting, powerful yet rich, but not as shrill as an Irish tenor's. The audience was captivated by more than just his voice. Standing ramrod straight with his cane characteristically held at a slight angle from the ground, he appeared much taller than his six-foot one. He finished to a standing ovation, with the crowd expressing admiration, not pity, though there were enough tears shed to fill Lake Erie.

Later, a fellow patient asked him, "How can you be so elated? Every Sunday when you show up at Mass and sing in the choir, you lift my spirits and make me ashamed for feeling sorry for myself. Don't you feel any bitterness and anger towards God for what you've endured?"

To that he replied, "Lots of good people died in this war. I'm one of the lucky ones. The only thing I regret is not being able to be with the Fighting 87th."

On the 25th, the Herons sat down to Christmas dinner at Valley Forge. Surprisingly, the food was quite good. The meal included a rich mélange of turkey, mashed potatoes, gravy, butternut squash, corn, and cranberry sauce. After he finished everything on his plate, he patted his swollen stomach. Azelia's presence had him in a good frame of mind.

"Like another helping?" she asked.

"Soon as I burp."

"Larry!" she scolded.

"Well, I've got to make room for seconds."

After dinner, they sat drinking hot-mulled cider as Azelia filled Heron in on the news back home. She read the names of locals listed as killed, wounded, or missing in action from back issues of the Milford Daily News and the Worcester Gazette. The end of the war could not come soon enough.

On Monday, January 22, 1945, Dr. Cannon grafted more skin to Heron's face and chin. On March 6, he added grafts to his cheeks and neck with skin tissue taken from his back, buttocks, thighs and abdomen, once again precluding his finding a comfortable position to lie in.

On April 16, the doctor explained what was to happen next, "We'll smooth out your face a bit and rebuild your left ear with cartilage from your rib cage. At the same time, we'll prepare a tissue flap roughly four by seven inches long from your upper arm, which is called a pedicle graft."

How interesting. The bile rose in his stomach at the thought of yet another portion of his body being mutilated.

"Why the arm?"

The doctor explained how one end of the flap must remain connected to his arm until the nose hookup could be established. After it had built up its own independent vascular system, the flap could be permanently disconnected from the arm.

"Is this a new technique?"

"Italian rhinoplasty has been around since 1597."

"A nose from arm muscle."

Suddenly, the door swung open and a nurse entered carrying a tray.

"Oh. Sorry doctor," she exclaimed. "I didn't mean to interrupt."

"No problem," Dr. Cannon said. "Continue with whatever you have to do."

"I'll be out of here in a second." Her shoes made a light *clop, clop, clop* as she approached the opposite side of Heron's bed from the doctor.

"Hello, Jane," Heron said.

"Good morning." She was used to being identified by her voice, or the sound of her walk.

Heron heard pills falling into a small container, the container being placed on the tray, water spilling into a glass, and the occasional clunk of ice. "You need to take these pills now," Jane Barsanti said.

After she left, Dr. Cannon asked, "Where was I? Oh yes. Preparing the flap. We have to set a proper thickness, de-bulk certain areas, and plan ahead for contraction. Therefore, the flap must be cut larger than the area it's to cover to compensate for shrinkage during healing, and for the later effects of atrophy and gravity."

"How long before you detach the flap from my arm?"

"It usually takes about three weeks. Your arm will be strapped to your head and braced against the headboard to keep it from being detached prematurely. During this period, the wound-bed must be irrigated to keep it from drying out, and suction applied to evacuate the fluids that will accumulate and to keep the flap firmly pressed against the wound-bed."

Heron thought of the prospect of having his arm locked in one position for such a length of time. He would have to rely on the nurses for everything: bedpans, baths, clothing changes, even scratching. "How will you know when the flap has its own blood supply?"

"We'll test for it with a flourescein dye introduced into the bloodstream intravenously."

"OK doc." He had heard enough. From the day of the injury, he had known nothing but pain. Circles of pain. Ripples of pain. Unrelenting pain. Every night he drifted to sleep with it, dreamed of pain, and then woke up with it. What he just heard was that he must look forward to an extended period of prolonged pain and discomfort. But he must not give up. He had promised her he'd see it through. He'd given his word. Perhaps after another year or more of operations, he would wake up one day with a real face, one that Azelia could stand to look at. She deserved that much.

On May 8, 1945, Azelia sat in the VFGH waiting room with newspapers piled beside her. Bold headlines declared Victory in Europe - VE Day. Thank God. But for Larry, the battle to get his life back was just beginning. He'd been under the knife since early morning.

Dr. Cannon came out to see her at noon looking like a man in need of a good night's rest. He was still dressed in scrubs and had what appeared to be a spot of blood near his lapel. "The operation went well," he said with a smile. "The skin grafts and cartilage transfer to the ear went exactly as planned. Also, the arm flap has been prepared to make improvements to his nose."

"Flap?"

Just as he had done with Heron, he gave her a quick overview on rhinoplasty. When he was through, she pictured the arm muscle carved like a turkey breast, one end of the slice left attached to the arm to keep it 'alive.' Her knees grew weak and her stomach queasy. But she was elated when she saw Heron up and moving about later in the day. His face was completely bandaged, as was his left arm. And there were more bandages on his hip and thigh areas where tissue had been harvested.

Heavy bandages covered his eyes and lengths of cloth crisscrossed his chest and back like bandoliers. His bare arms showed scars from shrapnel wounds.

Heron asked her to slip on his sunglasses. When she complied he asked, "How do I look?"

"You don't really want to know," she laughed.

"Funny? Do I look funny?"

"The opposite. Remember the H.G. Wells movie we saw years ago, *The Invisible Man?*"

"Like Claude Rains? Everybody was afraid of him and obeyed his every command. Are you afraid of me?"

"That'll be the day," she laughed, sardonically. Then she asked, "Do you know what they plan to do next?"

"Yeah," he said blithely. "Build me a new nose."

By June 5, the grafts had healed and Dr. Cannon placed new grafts on both ears. At the same time he shaped the arm flap for later nose reconstruction.

From the beginning Heron had been fighting to avoid becoming an addict. Now he limited himself to no more than four shots of morphine a day, two less than his caregivers would have administered, although it caused him to suffer more pain.

By June 15, he was sufficiently healthy to proceed with skills training in anticipation of being sent home for a short spell in just a few more weeks. Though the wounds to his face no longer required bandages, reconstruction was far from complete. His face remained a patchwork of scars and craters, his ears still horribly deformed. The arm flap had healed but would remain bandaged to protect it from damage. He was still missing most of his nose, and his left cheek held a depression where a huge chunk had been gouged out. To his sensitive hands his face felt like a living portrait of Dorian Gray. To others, it resembled a face of wax that had been left too long under a hot sun.

"You'll be going home next week," Nurse Barsanti told him.

"I don't want to," he said. "I prefer to stay here until this is over."

"What on earth do you mean? I thought you'd be thrilled to be with friends in familiar surroundings." She knew what he was feeling. She had experienced it with other patients many times before. They would balk at leaving their comfort zones and go home to shock people with their appearance. They felt ashamed. Going home was a terrifying prospect.

As if to confirm her thoughts, he said, "I'm too ugly and scary. I'd rather wait until the operations are complete."

"Nonsense," she said, knowing he would like to put it off indefinitely.

"I am ugly."

"OK. Let's say you haven't quite reached the handsome prince stage as yet. I know just the thing that'll solve your problem."

"What would that be?"

Just then an alarm sounded.

Jane almost sighed with relief. "Emergency!" she shouted heading for the door. "Gotta go. I'll have it for you on Monday."

Two small boys were tossing a baseball back and forth on the Community House lawn when they saw him coming. "Yikes! Look at that!" one said. They stopped their playing and slowly backed away as he approached them. The *Invisible Man* and *Frankenstein* movies were being rerun at the State Theater and imaginations being what they were, this man in the black mask and the sunglasses was pretty scary.

"I know who that is," his small friend said. "He's that Heron guy, the one who threw himself on a grenade to save his buddies."

"Wow! I would never do anything like that."

"Me neither."

Every street and every building held a memory; every person he chanced upon had a story to recall. As he painstakingly mapped streets and key locations in his mind, he also unlocked a treasure-trove of memories. The years rolled back as he made his way through town, to a much kinder gentler time, with the most pleasant memories involving Azelia. He was alive because of her. She gave him his life back, or at least the most important aspects of it.

The town was as he had left it, the homes owned by the same people, who greeted him warmly. Though his closest male friends were still at war, nothing had been neglected in their absence. The sidewalks were clear of kid's toys, trash, or obstacles that might impair his progress. The smell of fresh-cut lawns and carefully tended flowers was proof of proper care. Despite the paucity of manpower, nothing had been ignored. The women and children continued to see to everything.

On Sundays, people still attended church. Those out for a stroll stopped to chat; others called out greetings from a porch swing or lawn. He astounded them by recognizing their voices. Wherever he walked tales of his heroics on the battlefield preceded him. "There goes the man who gave up his future to save the lives of others."

Not many in Hopedale and surrounding towns were unaware of his heroics and sacrifices, or the beautiful young wife that was so devoted to him. Plenty of men sought to test her resolve in subtle and not so subtle ways. Why would she want to spend her life tied to a blind man who would not be able to provide for her, when she could have a far easier life with someone in good health with a sound future? In short order, it soon became a known fact that Azelia was what was called "a one-man woman."

Most people knew their story and took the couple into their hearts. They admired Azelia for her loyalty and devotion. Rather than be repulsed by Heron's appearance, they seemed to gravitate toward him. The battlefield had been a sort of proving ground. Those who had fought were all affected by it, different in many respects from when they had left. Many who had managed to come home alive, without a physical wound, seemed both beaten down and thoroughly humbled, while others it seems had been reborn.

Heron had left home a sports figure with a brilliant future and returned a blind man who now found it a struggle just to safely walk across a street. But for all he had suffered, he still seemed to possess a strong sense of worth, and he certainly had maintained his sense of humor. He had not become reclusive, as some would have imagined. In fact, he was as outgoing as ever, shunning pity, even sympathy. He wanted to do everything for himself, asking nothing of anyone. He still commanded the same respect and admiration as when he could see. It was not long before people stopped looking at him as a blind man. They saw instead, a man who could match wits, a man who walked with a bearing and commanded total respect. Everyone wanted to be counted as his friend, and everyone wanted to know what was hidden behind the mask, but no one dared to ask.

He enjoyed his walks about town, a solitary figure stopping here and there to take in his surroundings by sound and smell, one sip at a time. Deprived of the pleasures of being able to look upon the exquisite beauty of the town, his mind would seek to recapture and play back old images.

One of those images was of the centrally located Bancroft Memorial Library at the corner of Freedom and Hopedale. Copied after the Merton College Chapel at Oxford University, it had been voted the state's most beautiful library in its day. Six cathedral-styled arches spanned the width of the main reading room and the walls were adorned with rich oak-paneled wainscoting and carved moldings. The paintings of Joseph and Silvia Bancroft were hung above a green-glazed tile fireplace and mantel of oak. Outside was a fountain of the Roman goddess, Hope, surrounded by Medusa, a dolphin, and a pair of eagles, all carved from Carrara marble, a symbol of eternal goodness and health.

He would walk out his front door along Hope Street and turn right onto Hopedale Street past the Draper factory, a brick building with ribbons of mullioned windows surrounding it. At the other end of the plant, where Hopedale crossed Freedom, the road left the factory behind and curved right by the pond, a source of hydroelectric power for Draper's hungry tool equipment. The pond was where he liked to fish. Continuing further along Hopedale Street would take him to the park where he could hear the voices of children playing games while the adults played tennis.

Another route would take him through the tiny business district, yet another past the cemetery, or along Adin Street, with its high-walled fortress surrounding the Draper mansions. And when he tired of Hopedale, he would make his way to Milford and back.

"I met Larry Heron at the Community House today," Bill Larson told his father. "As I opened the door on my way out, he was at the foot of the stairs. He froze in place when he heard me, as did I. He probably thought some idiot was standing there staring at him instead of holding the door."

"Go ahead," I said. "He didn't move. I knew then that he didn't want my help so I let the door close and continued down the stairs. When I looked back, he was proceeding on his own." Once he made it clear that he did not view himself as handicapped, the townspeople learned to treat him accordingly.

"There's plenty to watch out for," he told Azelia. "Vehicles moving at incredible speeds, kids whizzing by on bikes, cars not always parked where they are supposed to be. I feel vulnerable at times but I'll tell you, I am not afraid out there. Fear has no place in my world any longer." She resisted responding with, *you were never afraid of anything. Perhaps if you had been, you'd be fine today.*

He hadn't been away so long that he couldn't visualize the grandstand in the park where band concerts were held on Wednesday nights, the bench by the pond where he made up with Azelia after their one big spat, the sound of water lapping the shore by the pond. The memories were all there, yet it seemed strange to pass familiar places and not be able to view them ever again.

Whenever he left the house, he would wear the black mask that Nurse Barsanti had made and presented to him on that Monday. Not even Azelia had seen him without it. She detested the phantom aspects of it, claiming that people's minds would substitute images more dreadful, perhaps more despicable than reality.

"You have no clue as to what's under this mask," he told her. "If I remove it, you'll get a jolt of reality that will shock you."

"Do you really think your scars matter to me?" she asked.

"They will when you see them."

"Then you don't know the woman you married." No matter how bad his face, she knew she would eventually become inured. What bothered her more was that he had been injured at all and that there were many more painful operations ahead for him. How the explosions must have hurt and terrified him. Many were the nights when she would lie awake imagining him on the ground, screaming in pain, blinded and alone.

To help him get quickly through the healing process she knew that she had to first convince him that looks made absolutely no difference to her, that he was her perfect man. There was only one sure way to accomplish that goal. The answer had come to her, as did many good ideas and solutions to problems, while she was taking a bath.

When she finished her bath, she refilled the bathtub and led him to it. Then she lifted the mask high enough to slip him a warm kiss that elicited a gasp from him. "Meet me in the bedroom when you're finished, darling" she said.

When he finished his bath, she guided him to the bed and removed the towel wrapped around his waist. Then she propped him against a pillow and climbed in beside him.

"Now take off the mask," she commanded.

"You'll want me to put it back on the minute you see my face," he said self-deprecatingly.

Azelia remained silent.

Heron cleared his throat. "There's something I've been meaning to ask."

She closed the distance between them so that they were touching the length of their bodies. Her scent engulfed him and he trembled. She lifted his hand in both of hers and raised it to her lips to kiss first the back and then the palm.

It was as though the clock had been turned back and they were on their honeymoon once again. He pretended that instead of being blind, he had merely closed his eyes. She caressed him with fingertips that were warm, soft, and inviting. He touched her and the familiar stirrings began. It had been so long since they made love that his knees felt weak and there was an uneasiness he couldn't explain.

He swallowed hard. "Did you know that 1945 is going down as one of the best years for Bordeaux?" he asked.

"Is that what you wanted to ask me?" she laughed.

"Not exactly. I want to know how you feel about having a child. I mean...it might also be a good year to start a family."

Having children had always been in her long-term plans but today it was the furthest thing from her mind. Babies require constant attention. It would mean dividing her time between raising a child and caring for him. She might be forced to quit her job right when the need for extra cash was paramount. Of course they would still have Emma living with them. With her help Azelia could be back at her job within a few months.

And in his present state of mind, the slightest hint of rejection could be devastating. She hesitated a moment before answering. "Great minds think alike," she said at last. "Perhaps *one* child..."

Now that the commitment had been made, she felt a sense of relief. "Now take off the mask," she demanded.

"You shouldn't look at me. Might turn you off..."

"Just be quiet," she ordered. "Off with it!"

Gently, lovingly, she lifted off his sunglasses and placed them on the night table. He held her hands for a moment then passively removed them as she slowly lifted off the mask. At the sight of his face she bit down on her lip, stifling a gasp. Just as he had claimed, it was a monstrous patchwork to behold. She closed her eyes and tried to register a picture of him in her mind before the injury - without scars, missing pieces, and multiple skin grafts. She visualized his blue eyes first, then his jaunty chin, sensuous lips, and cocky grin. This was the first and last man she had ever been in love with. He could still jump-start her heart with his touch. Thank God he was back in her arms once more.

The whisper of an empty robe sliding off the bed and hitting the floor sent his pulse rate soaring.

"My God she said, touching him tenderly, you're more beautiful than I remembered." She bent forward to kiss him gently on the lips, forehead, and cheeks, taking in each scar on his neck, shoulders, forearms, hands, thighs, legs, and feet. She touched his chest with her lips and he shuddered involuntarily.

Rivers of emotion swelled inside his body spilling their banks - spreading, building, gathering momentum. Each kiss was delivered lovingly and with the utmost tenderness. He divined such bliss that tears, finding no outlet on his face, made a path down his nostrils and into his throat, and then he felt her tears.

She kissed his lips lightly at first then longer, deeper. When they finally made love, it was like a dream in which they melded - one body, one soul, one kernel of life suspended in time, neither uttering a sound. Just one word would have upset the balance, destroyed the mood - changed everything.

She wished her love could heal his wounds and restore his sight, that time could be reversed and he could be whole again. But she would settle for letting him know he was loved and by kindling the flames of his happiness. To that end, she would devote each day of her life.

18

The Lawrence J. Heron Post

On Monday, July 9, Azelia drove him to the Providence train station after a heated discussion. When she had finished her lengthy discourse on 101 ways something bad could happen to him, he took her in his arms and said, "Look. Sooner or later, I'm going to have to make my own way. You driving me to Philadelphia will only hold me back. I want to learn to travel to and from the hospital on my own."

"But you could get lost."

"Impossible. I get on the train in Providence and get off in Philadelphia. Ralph Davis will meet me at the station and take me to the hospital. Nothing could be simpler."

She guided him to an empty seat and placed his bag by his feet. "Call when you get there," she said through the tears streaming down her face.

"I will."

She gave him a long kiss goodbye then held a handkerchief to her eyes, as it was time for her to leave. Three soldiers boarding right behind them waited patiently for the aisle to clear. One of the men asked Heron, "Mind if we sit with you?"

"Not at all," he answered.

"Don't worry, ma'am," the soldier said with a friendly drawl, "We'll see that he gets to where he's going."

"You got somebody on the other end?" he asked Heron.

"Yes. An orderly will be waiting to take me to the Valley Forge Hospital."

"Shoot. That's where I'm headed. I work there. What's his name?"

"Ralph Davis."

"I know Ralphie. Ma'am, like I say, you don't have a thing to worry about."

Azelia felt a great sense of relief. These were obviously fine young men who would protect Larry. He would be safer with them than in her car.

On the day Azelia had accepted him without the mask, Heron had dispensed with it, though he was aware that people would stare. There followed gasps, even cries from frightened children, but it was something he could learn to live with. These soldiers worked at the hospital where they encountered many wounded men. His looks would not frighten them. He was in good hands.

She would not return to visit him until Labor Day, when she arrived wearing a bright smile and emitting a glow he could not see. But he did sense the happiness in her voice when she suggested, "It's such a gorgeous day. Why don't we go for a walk?"

She located a bench in the shade of a tall oak. Once they were seated, she gently took his hand in both of hers and placed it on her stomach. "Feel anything?" she asked.

"A lovely tummy."

"Anything else?"

Heron jumped to his feet. "Are you...are you telling me that I'm, that we're..."

"Going to have a baby," she finished.

Heron leaned forward and hugged her, then sat down and snuggled close to her. "You shouldn't have driven all this way by yourself. You should be at home resting." There was genuine concern in his voice. His mind's eye formed an image of her beatific face as she cradled their child lovingly in her arms.

"I'm not alone," she said. Your mom and Ethel are here. They decided to wait in the reception area until I had a chance to tell you."

The news was like an elixir from the gods. Suddenly he felt ready to face any amount of pain and suffering that multiple surgeries over the next few years were sure to bring.

During a lengthy operation on September 6, Dr. Cannon tied the loose end of the flap to the nose area, leaving the other end attached to Heron's arm. To maintain the integrity of the connection, the arm was then lashed to his head and his wrist to the headboard of his bed. This was the worst form of torture, like being buried alive. There are limits to the amount of pain and discomfort a person should be expected to endure. The pain was dulled with shots of morphine, but nothing short of death could bring his current misery to an end. And to top things off, he was experiencing throbbing headaches he never thought would end.

Nurses administered to his every need, for he was not allowed to move his head or arm independent of one another. After a week of torture, he asked Dr. Cannon, "How much longer?"

"Just a few more weeks," the doctor said stoically. "I wish I could say days, but time is a critical factor. It's taking nicely though, no infection. Other than the discomfort, how's everything else feeling?"

"It's a little tough to eat and breathe with an arm and bandages stuffed in my mouth. Other than that, I'm doing just fine." The voice was muffled.

"I'm glad to see you still have your sense of humor. You know, anyone else would be complaining endlessly."

"Just tell me when it's time to move again."

The doctor laughed. "That's not a complaint, is it?"

"Hey doc. How about a shot of Jack Daniels? That would help."

"Sure. With or without morphine?"

It would be two more weeks to the day, September 27, before the flap would finally be detached from his arm and Heron could at last boast a new nose. When he came out of the anesthesia he found that his arm had been detached from his face but it seemed to want to remain in the same position. "Nurse, I can't move my arm," he said to Barsanti.

"It's been immobilized for too long. Let me help you loosen it a bit."

She massaged his arm very gently at first, moving it a few degrees at a time. It took several days of therapy before his arm movement returned to normal.

But there was no respite from the pain, no end to the torture.

Dr. Carl Lisher painstakingly reshaped the left ear on October 25, at the same time adding new grafts to the right ear and revising the scars on his left cheek and arm.

Dr. Cannon finalized the shaping of the nose on November 1, 1945. When the bandages were removed, his face was beginning to show signs of improvement. But there was still a long twisting road ahead for Heron.

Thanksgiving Day fell on November 22. Azelia joined him at VFGH for a satisfying dinner that day, and told him of her plans to remain in Phoenixville through his next operation.

On the following Monday, Dr. Lisher refashioned and released Heron's left ear and reworked the mouth deformity.

Ripping his body apart had taken but a fraction of a second. The rebuilding process proved long and arduous. Azelia agonized each time he was to go under the knife, knowing that he was in much more pain than he would admit. Like Larry, she resolved to get past the operations - one at a time. She headed home on Saturday and returned to work the following Monday.

When he had first arrived at VFGH, his face looked like it belonged to a statue that a maniac had worked over with a ball peen hammer. But now, the slow, painstaking effort was beginning to show signs of a payoff. The craggy surfaces that once resembled the far side of the moon had been smoothed over and he now sported a well-shaped nose and rather normal-looking ears.

"My work is finished," Dr. Cannon told him one day. "The army thinks it is time for you to complete the rehab phase so you can be discharged." To Dr Cannon's trained eye, Heron's face still lacked the amount of elasticity he would have preferred. The face was waxen and his mouth slightly ajar. His sunken cheeks exaggerated the protrusion of the zygomatic bones, and only a faint delineation marked where the chin ended. But there comes a point where trade offs have to be made between the quality of life and cosmetic improvement. Each operation resulted in a slight improvement but each was also very painful and debilitating.

Overall there had been a marked improvement as revealed by photographs taken prior to the first operation compared with his most recent a year later. With a pair of sunglasses to conceal the sockets, he could now move about in public without appearing to be anything more than a blind man who had suffered a physical trauma. Heron could now go out and face the world. The hospital workers and staff all admired his great courage and lack of self-pity or complaint. He was very brave and very special. His head was always held high. He possessed charm, wit and humor, a high level of intelligence, and the courage of a lion. It was time for the next phase of his life to begin.

"That means you'll be leaving us soon," Dr. Cannon said, regretfully.

"Getting rid of me, doctor?"

"There's no sense keeping you here any longer. There are plenty of good doctors at the Veterans hospitals to handle further repair, many of whom were trained right here at Valley Forge. There are some very good ones at Jamaica Plain and West Roxbury so you won't have to travel far from home."

"Besides, your discharge will be coming through soon. You'll do much better at home with Azelia." That last statement held the most appeal for him.

"Good morning Larry," a familiar voice said on Monday morning, December 3, 1945.

"Good morning, Father." Heron recognized the voice of Father Thomas Carroll. Prior to his assignment as the chaplain responsible for training the blind at VFGH, he had been the Assistant Director of the Boston Catholic Guild for the Blind. Carroll was a pioneer extremely successful in applying the latest tools and research to serving the needs of the blind.

"Since I happened to be passing through, I thought I'd stop by to congratulate you for making history once again. Not only have you survived a shell exploding in your hands and been the subject of much advanced surgery, you are about to add a third historic achievement."

"What would that be?"

"The first living veteran to have a DAV chapter named for him."

"Oh, that."

"Don't be so modest. It has never happened before. There's never been a chapter dedicated to a live veteran."

"I guess I should be honored, Father."

"It's not trivial. I assure you it's not. It's a big deal. We're all proud of you."

"Thank you Father. I don't mean to sound ungrateful. Can't help thinking about those who gave much more than I - their lives. I often wonder why they were taken and I was left alive."

"God has a purpose."

"I wish I could figure that one out."

"I stopped by for another reason, to give you a heads up on Avon." Carroll's role as auxiliary chaplain of the U.S. Army's Experimental Rehabilitation Center at Valley Forge extended to Avon Old Farms Convalescent Hospital in Connecticut, where he divided his time.

"Father, I've been meaning to ask if you could explain the differences between these army hospitals, like this one, Letterman and Dibble General."

"Letterman General Hospital in San Francisco is the oldest. Been around since the Spanish American War. It was also the largest until Valley Forge was completed a year ago. But the injured have been pouring into both these hospitals faster than they can keep up, so construction began last year on Dibble General in Menlo Park, California to help alleviate the pressure."

"Where does Old Farms Hospital fit in?"

"Old Farms Convalescent Hospital is a misnomer. It's a school, not a hospital. On January 8 President Roosevelt signed an executive order declaring that no blinded serviceman would be sent home without proper training. That order exacerbated the overcrowding problem because the increasing numbers of blind servicemen ready for medical discharge could not be released without extensive survival training."

"The hospitals were offering only very basic introductory techniques in Braille, typing, writing, and orientation. Something had to be done about the rising numbers of blinded veterans, and done quickly."

"Old Farms happened to be readily available. It was quickly turned into a school for the blind with a specific curriculum to meet specific goals. Five months after the president's order, the school reopened as Avon Old Farms Convalescent Hospital."

"Only last June. That was quick."

"Yes. Made possible because of a personal friendship between Mrs. Theodate Pope Riddle and the President."

"Theo who?"

"She was born Effie Pope but changed it to Theodate, which literally means "God's gift. A graduate of Miss Porter's School in Farmington, Connecticut, her schoolgirl dream was to build an 'indestructible school for boys.' Don't ask why."

"It must have cost her a fortune."

"She came from money and gained more through marriage. She built her school in 1926 for eight million dollars and opened it a year later. Last year she had a nasty fight with the school's Provost. When they couldn't agree on a style of management, the entire faculty resigned and the school was forced to close."

"Roosevelt needed a location and Mrs. Riddle had an empty school. Old Farms satisfied a convergence of needs and an accommodation of mutual interests."

"What can they teach me?"

"All the fundamentals you'll need to cope with a lifetime of darkness in a sighted world. The 18-week program has four separate aspects: self-care and personal adjustment; physical activities, including many sports; social recreations like dancing, dinner parties, and movies; and finally a long list of elective courses such as Braille, typing, manual dexterity, English, music, public speaking, creative writing, and courses in industrial and commercial skills."

Heron suddenly felt like a child on his way to summer camp. Perhaps Avon could help restore the equilibrium and tranquility that blindness had taken. Fr. Carroll's presence would certainly help facilitate his transition to the school.

On the other hand, Heron was anxious to be in his own home with Aze-lia. "Is it really necessary for me to attend? I can get around quite nicely now with a cane."

"Without a doubt, you are doing quite remarkably. But there's a lot more you can learn, like how to get around *without* a cane. For example, you wouldn't want to be knocking about in your kitchen denting appliances, chipping furniture, or whacking your wife and friends with your cane."

Heron laughed.

"You have already mastered Braille. When you leave Avon you'll be a speed-reader by comparison. You'll know how to care for yourself, play sports, operate appliances, dance, take in movies, and enjoy many recreational activities. In fact, you'll learn to do just about anything you set your mind to."

"I want very much to drive a car again."

Fr. Carroll laughed aloud. It was a hearty, congenial laugh. "OK, with a few exceptions."

His voice grew serious. "I understand there's a job waiting at home for you."

"Yes. At the Draper Corporation as a quality control inspector. Imagine a blind person checking quality."

"Then you'll especially appreciate the final phase which includes vocational job training. It stresses the use of hands, sense of touch, manual dexterity, and coordination."

"I'm sure you'll do just fine from what I know of you. The program includes work with industrial machinery at one of the local factories. Or, if you prefer, you can choose to practice at a participating store, garage, filling station, or insurance company. These tryouts are the capstone of the program. Not only do they improve skills, but they also serve as important confidence builders."

Heron came away from the discussion with spirits elevated. He awakened the next morning with a resolve to expunge the loss of sight from his mind. Many people had been born blind, never having seen the light of day. At least he had enjoyed sight for the first twenty-three years of his life, and he knew what Azelia looked like.

Friday, December 7, 1945, was the anniversary of the bombing of Pearl Harbor. Hundreds of disabled American veterans gathered that day in Milford, Massachusetts for an unprecedented ceremony, dedication of the Lawrence J. Heron DAV Chapter #6 - the first and only chapter to be named for a living veteran.

Heron arrived at the ceremony amid a standing ovation, with Azelia and Emma at his side. They were led to the head table where he was seated between them. Blindness and disfigurement could not mask the raw power of the man who had left home a well-conditioned athlete headed for certain stardom. Larry Heron was a legend back then. Now he was a hero in another sense, one who had sacrificed his future for his country. He stood very tall, every bit the proud American. If he announced his intention to run for Congress at that very moment, he could have counted on the vote of every person there that night.

Peter Frascoti, retiring post commander addressed the crowd. "The remarkable rehabilitation of this man, against all odds, was the inspiration that led us to break a time-honored tradition. We had to secure permission from the Veterans Administration to name this chapter for a living American. This is the very first time in the long history of the DAV that a chapter has been dedicated to someone who has not made the supreme sacrifice."

"The pursuits of this fine athlete ended in the span of one fateful second. With no thought to himself, he single-handedly assumed the highest risk for comrades and country, and in so doing sacrificed a brilliant future. He was so badly injured that the men in his squad, men who loved him, were prepared to take his life. But he pleaded to be allowed to return to his lovely wife. Make no mistake she's as much responsible for his survival and rehabilitation as the doctors who worked on him."

A murmur passed through the crowd.

He turned to face Heron. "Larry, we owe you more than we can ever repay. Were it not for you, and men like you, we might not be standing here in a free society today. God bless you."

There was a standing ovation that did not let up until Heron rose to his feet and acknowledged their approval with nods and a wave of his hand. He felt embarrassed. All he did was follow his instincts, just as anyone in his place would have done.

As the room grew quiet, Frascoti continued. "And now it is my pleasure to announce that Mr. Heron has been selected the DAV Hero of the Month. This award is part of a national program that honors seriously disabled veterans who have shown great courage, ability, and initiative in rehabilitating themselves. In overcoming insurmountable obstacles, you have set high standards for yourself, even surpassed them on the road to becoming self-sustaining. One final note. We all wish to congratulate you and Mrs. Heron on the expected arrival of your first child."

Another standing ovation.

Asked later how he felt about having a chapter named for him, Heron answered, "I didn't particularly go for it, but they wanted it so I went along." He downplayed his heroism, referring to himself as "one of the lucky ones."

The next morning, Azelia awoke with a start. The silence in the house was palpable. Her husband was nowhere to be found. The sound of a snowplow reached a crescendo then diminished as she rushed to peer out an upstairs window. Snow was falling hard. Already a foot deep. The branches of tall trees drooped under heavy loads. From below came the sound of shoveling.

Grabbing her robe from a chair beside the bed, she slipped it on while descending to the first floor. Just as she thought. It was Larry. She refrained from calling out to him to come in and instead sat by the window watching him clear a path.

Already there was a white blanket covering the area he had just shoveled with drifts like desert sand. The front steps had turned to rows of white powder, mailboxes to mushroom caps, and bushes to soft white mounds. The branches of elms, maples and pines sagged to the breaking point. Heron kept at it until the falling snow had begun to diminish and he had at last gained an upper hand.

On Monday, he returned to VFGH by train for a final check up and received a clean bill of health. Two weeks later, he was discharged from the hospital and returned home in time for the start of the Christmas season. It would be a few weeks before he was to begin training at Old Farms in Avon. Azelia parked the car in their driveway and opened the trunk. Heron stepped out on the passenger side and came around to the rear where he handed her his cane. "You take this, I'll take the bags," he said emphatically.

Azelia decided not to argue. He had to explore and discover his own limitations. Yet she worried that he might slip and fall or otherwise hurt himself. She walked to the front steps. Heron followed, feeling for the snow bank with a foot until he made contact with the cement walk. When he located it, he turned and headed up the steps behind her.

When he reached the front door, he heard it open. Someone was blocking his way. If it had been his mother, she would have greeted him. Heron waited. Silence. He asked Azelia, "Who is it?"

"Let's go in and find out," she urged.

Heron followed her into the hall to a chorus of, "Welcome home!" The cheers came from relatives and a few close friends, mostly women whose men were still at war.

Later that evening, after everyone had departed, they went to the bedroom to finish unpacking his suitcase. "What's in this small box?" she asked. "Looks to be about the right size to hold a harmonica."

"Oh that. Better not open it."

"Why not?"

"It's a surprise."

Azelia smiled, her curiosity piqued. "When can I open it?"

"At the right moment."

Now she had to know what was in the box. She could peek now or come back and do it later, but that would spoil the surprise. Besides, it was important to maintain trust, especially now.

19

Avon Old Farms
Convalescent Hospital

His first Christmas at home served only to further his discomfort. Azelia was busy hanging Christmas decorations he would never see and placing colorfully wrapped gifts under a tree that he could only smell and feel, a sad reminder of happier times. Azelia tried to understand what he might be feeling and did what she could to make it a joyous time for him. She described each ornament as she hung it from a branch and when she had finished, directed his hand to the most meaningful, describing each in great detail.

The enormity of his handicap became even more apparent when he thought of what to buy for his wife. And what about her? What would she get for the blind man? Then what will he say when she hands it to him? *Oh what a lovely tie? Just my color?* More important, how does a blind man go about buying a gift for his wife?

Azelia's sister, Olga, came to his rescue by volunteering to take him Christmas shopping in Boston. "I shop downtown every year at this time. I'd be happy to help you pick out a nice dress for Azelia. I know that's what she wants."

Filene's Bargain Basement store, a Boston landmark, was located at the juncture of Washington and Summer Street, within walking distance of many historic sites like the Old State House, the Old Corner Bookstore, and Faneuil Hall.

This was 1946, when the area known as Scollay Square included the Government Center, Quincy Market, and parts of the North End. It was a raucous amalgam of burlesque theaters, vaudeville houses, hot dog stands, tattoo parlors, diners, and flophouses.

Going further back in time, the area marked the site of the lighting of the old North Church by Paul Revere, the house where Thomas Edison designed his first patented invention, and the building where Alexander Graham Bell invented the telephone. There was even an inn where George Washington had actually slept.

Parking was scarce so Olga left the car in a garage near the Common. They proceeded up Tremont past those great wrought iron fences and Bulfinch buildings. Larry kept a gentle grip on Olga's arm. "Let's stop here," she said suddenly. "We're standing beside the Granary Burying Grounds."

"I visited this cemetery in my younger days," Larry said. "It holds the remains of Paul Revere, Samuel Adams, and John Hancock."

"Wow. Gives me a chill," she said, reading the words on a small sign mounted on a post. "It says here that only parts of John Hancock's body remain. On the night he was interred in 1793, grave robbers removed the signing hand along with other body parts. How gross!"

"Gives *me* a chill."

They continued down Bromfield to a place that would one day be labeled as Downtown Crossing – America's original pedestrian mall, where department store giants Filene's and Jordan Marsh would compete on opposite sides of Summer Street. The area around Washington and Bromfield was teeming with jewelry stores, luggage and camera shops, stationary stores, liquor stores, joke shops, and music stores. Just about anything could be bought within a few short blocks.

Olga could not find much that appealed to her in Filene's basement, so they rode a creaky elevator to the third floor. The elevator operator was a short man wearing a bellhop uniform, reminding Olga of the Philip Morris man that appeared in all the ads.

"Here are some nice dresses," Olga said, after they had been searching for an hour without luck.

Larry felt the material. "Too coarse."

"Feel this one. It's black and quite sexy. Low back and scalloped front."

"Azelia will not wear anything low in the front."

"Better put it back then. It's a real cleavage number." She took down another. "Now here's a nice dress. It has three-quarter length sleeves and let's see. It's made of rayon."

"Feels clingy," he said.

"It is."

"What color?"

"Blue. A nice blue – on the dark side of navy blue."

"Do you like it?"

"I'd love it if Fred bought it for me. Rayon is really comfortable. It wears well and is easy to iron."

"I'll take it."

On Christmas Eve, Azelia was sleeping soundly when Heron stole downstairs to place his wrapped present under the tree. By now he was moving about the house with relative ease, counting paces in his head. Sitting down on a sofa close to the Christmas tree, he inhaled its familiar fragrance and was reminded of when he used to sit by the family tree in the dark at night, wondering about his future.

There are so many things he would never do again. Never more would he watch a summer sunset or gaze at foliage changing colors in the fall. He'd never view his lovely wife or drive a car. No more football, baseball, or reading books – except in Braille, or watching movies. How many times had he sat contemplating his losses?

A sigh escaped him. Minutes passed.

Finally, he lifted his head with resolve. His eyes, his looks may be gone forever, but never his pride and determination. He was not going to give up swimming, not even in the ocean with sharks. That's how he planned to live his life: without fear. His faith was stronger now than ever, for if God had wanted him dead, he surely would not be sitting here.

Something told him that when his time finally came, he would die of natural causes - probably heart failure like his dad. It was this sort of thinking that put him at ease with the world and helped him to deal with the cards he'd been dealt. He vowed to get on with his life, enjoy it as best he could, and not look back.

Heron was transported by bus to Avon Old Farms Convalescent Hospital on Monday afternoon, January 6, 1946. Doctors considered him a medical marvel. They had never seen anyone manage to survive with wounds this severe. Though his face was waxen, crated, and scarred, he had a mouth, ears, and nose. With a pair of sunglasses to mask his grafted-over eye sockets, his appearance was not all that shocking.

Four blind companions accompanied Heron on the bus ride. Three, like Heron, were sightless. The fourth was a man who had been injured when a mine exploded while he was on his knees clearing a place to lie down. He could make out dark forms and distinguish red and green traffic lights but his sight was continuing to deteriorate and eventually he'd be totally blind.

As Heron disembarked the bus, a guide took his arm and led him along a clear path and up a flight of granite steps to a grand foyer that echoed their footsteps. They proceeded to a large reception hall where Fr. Carroll was waiting to greet them. Heron could sense the majesty and beauty of his surroundings.

"The school was voted the most beautiful campus in America," Carroll informed them. "A world traveler, Mrs. Riddle loved the Tudor Cotswold style architecture and adopted it for her 3000-acre dream school. It has the quaint architectural style of centuries-old English schools like Eton and Oxford. Its massive walls are constructed of brownstone cut from local quarries. Its doors, woodwork, and sturdy beams were hand-hewn from massive trees grown on the property. The rooftops are of red slate that combines with the hand-wrought ironwork within and without to add color and beauty to its pageantry."

The irony of blind trainees touring the most beautiful school in the land was not lost on Heron, who could only imagine such splendor.

After being admitted, he was led to his room by an attendant. "Each door has a sliding wooden latch," he explained as they entered the building that housed his dormitory. About six paces from the door the guide halted him, warning, "In front of you are stone steps that curve up and to the right. It's the same in all the dorms, like stairs found in European castles."

"Why is that?"

"It stems from medieval times. Since most people were right-handed, they needed open space on their right to wield their swords. It's also why people drive on the left in England today."

They reached the second landing and walked twenty paces before stopping. "The door to your room is just to your left, and the doorknob is on the right side of the door. Go ahead and let yourself in." When they were inside, the guide described the room as small but efficient. It consisted of a wood-frame bed in one corner, a table and chair below a window, and a phone.

"Your suitcase is just to the right of the door," the attendant informed him. After a quick tour of the attached bathroom, he led Heron to a wardrobe closet and had him feel his shirts, pants, and jackets. "You can unpack the rest of your suitcase and put things in this drawer that pulls out from under your bed. That way, you'll be able to find them."

When Heron had everything put away, the attendant said, "Lose the cane. You won't be needing it until you leave the campus."

"But I depend on it for..."

"We're going to teach you how to get along without a cane. Especially indoors."

"I'm expected to go outdoors without one?"

"You'll use it only in town. No canes allowed on campus. We call it 'mobility training.' Canes become unwieldy inside homes or offices. It's too easy to knock something over, damage furniture, or whack someone in the shins."

"Mobility means no cane."

"You've heard the expression blind as a bat?" It was more a statement than a question. "Mobility emphasizes the reflected sound approach. In theory, when a blind or blindfolded person approaches an obstruction, like a large tree, car, or building for example, he or she will usually sense the object before crashing into it."

"Do we all have this er...sixth sense?"

"Not to the same degree, no. That's why I said 'in theory.' Very few have the confidence or makeup to fully develop it. Most people never get the hang of it."

"I see." The attendant caught his play on words and they both laughed.

That night Heron queued up in the mess hall, a faithful reproduction of an old English baronial hall. He was told that it was quite huge, large enough to accommodate all post personnel at one time. In the rear was a large floor where weekly dances were held. All the trainees were young and fit enough, they just couldn't see. Some had lost fingers or limbs. Many had experienced plastic surgery, though none had undergone anything as extensive as Heron.

The next morning after breakfast, the newcomers assembled in a small conference room to be addressed by the school's commanding officer, ophthalmologist Col. Fredrick H. Thorne. His manner was outgoing and ebullient. His audience could not see his gray-blue eyes peering at them through horn-rims filled with telescope-lens glass or his trim dark mustache and eyebrows that appeared to have been brushed on like a matched set. The receding hairline made him look fifty-ish though he could have been younger.

"Good morning, men," he began. "Old Farms occupies a unique position in the Army's program of caring for wounded servicemen. More of a school than a hospital, its sole function is to prepare you for readjustment to civilian life."

"We welcome you with the understanding of your needs and the problems you face as individuals. We offer many courses and those of you who work diligently will be amply repaid in the years ahead."

"Our goal is to have each of you leave here with the proper training and confidence in your own ability to live a useful life in your community."

That afternoon, Heron and a group of fellow students were treated to a tour of the facilities. He could smell the stables and hear horses whinnying well before he was told, "You are standing before a stable built in the style of an old Norman manor house made of stone and half-timber with a long sloping roof."

"Horseback riding is just one of the many recreations you will find here. You will learn to bowl, swim, roller skate, fish, go boating or golfing, whichever you desire."

"Just beyond the stables is a massive circular water tower made of red brick. It looks like a silo with a cone-shaped roof. It is a famous landmark rising majestically above the campus, and it blends with Old Farms high-style decor."

"Now we are standing in front of the motor pool," he said as they moved along. "It too looks like something you might find in the English countryside, though its purpose is to hold ambulances, buses, staff cars, and a fleet of trucks, which those of you who want to become mechanics will maintain." This latter comment elicited sounds of approval from a few of the more mechanically inclined.

At dinner that night, Heron learned that his fellow trainees ranged in age from 18 to 45, in education from fourth grade to PhD, and in rank from private to colonel. Except for being blind, most of the men had left the battlefield in fairly good physical condition. It was clear to Heron that he had been more severely injured and had spent more time in the hospital than the others.

Each day began with a half-hour session to air complaints about food, facilities, transportation, and the like. Frequently, CEOs from various companies like Champion Spark Plug, Royal Typewriter, and Fuller Brush came out to pitch their company and discuss job possibilities.

There were plenty of social activities. The men visited bars in town and attended weekly dances, where many would come into contact with their future wives.

Azelia visited Heron on the first weekend and marveled at how rapidly his confidence had returned. "How on earth do you get around without a cane?" She asked.

"I count paces and memorize directions – right, left, or straight ahead. Spin me around a few times and I'd be completely lost."

"You've always had a remarkable memory."

"I've walked these grounds every day until I have it mapped. But it's not without mishap. Notice the bruises on my face?"

"How did that happen?"

"Big Bertha. Come on, I'll show you."

He led her to a sturdy elm of considerable girth next to the main walkway by the school's entrance. "I was moving along at a good pace when *wham,* I smacked into this brick wall." He reached out and placed a hand on the bark. "Didn't know what hit me."

"I felt blood trickling from my nose. Just what I needed," he said sardonically. "Another scar."

"Then I heard a voice say, 'Sounds like you just met Bertha. She's got plenty of skin, hair, and blood on her. Sooner or later, every trainee makes her acquaintance,' he told me. He spoke almost affectionately of the damned thing."

Azelia grimaced. "I'd rather not look at it."

"It was my first day outside without a cane. I assure you it'll never happen again."

Azelia was overwhelmed by the beauty and majesty of the school. He led her past the ski hill, bowling alley, and golf course.

"Oh, look. Horses!" Azelia exclaimed.

"I wish I could look," Heron chuckled.

They stopped in their tracks while several horses were being led along a bridle path that had been plowed a few yards wide. Azelia was comfortable around horses, having ridden often at a friend's stable in Mendon. "The horses know their way around," Heron told her. "Most trainees prefer to wait until the weather improves before they'll ride them. Attendants go along to keep us out of trouble."

"I'm looking forward to the day when I can get back to such things as riding," Azelia said, patting her round protrusion.

"A month from now," he said encouragingly. "I can hardly wait."

"Neither can I," she laughed.

It was a beautiful morning and the air smelled like clean laundry pulled off a clothesline on a crisp winter's day. The sun's rays were warm and soothing. Azelia observed men on a bicycle-built-for-two peddling up the street, one guiding the other who was blind. She saw blind men working on engines in the motor pool, others practicing on instruments in the music room. Some trainees worked at carpentry while still others operated the school's switchboard.

It amazed her that these men could participate in so many activities. It raised her hopes that Larry would leave here with the knowledge that he had not been sentenced to a life of mental and physical torpor.

Heron took to training with ease. While many struggled with advanced Braille, he mastered it quickly, earning the highest grade ever awarded at the school in both Braille and typing. He spent a great deal of time working with leather and was soon crafting beautiful wallets and women's pocketbooks. He also worked on *The Quadrangle Review*, a newspaper published by trainees.

But mostly he strived to improve his singing. Encouraged by the trainees and faculty as well, he soloed at weekly post dances, at church services, and concerts. Col. Thorne met with him one day to discuss his future. "We think you should consider singing professionally. Many of the celebrities who come here to entertain us would be more than happy to help you get started."

Heron thanked him, but politely turned down the offer. "It would be an uncertain future at best and with success would come travel. I'm just looking forward to returning home with Azelia and raising a family."

Two months later Guido Noferi arrived home from the war. On March 15, his good friend, Ed Kalpagian, drove him and Azelia to Avon to pick up Heron and bring him home, so he would be there when the new baby arrived.

Fr. Carroll had no trouble spotting them the moment they entered the reception area, simply because Azelia stood out as the most attractive woman in the room and was, of course, noticeably pregnant as well. He quickly moved forward to greet them.

Fr. Carroll's eyes were the gray of wood smoke on a cold day in New Hampshire. Azelia saw the strength in them, a force that was uplifting. Following introductions he said, "Larry will be joining us shortly. We have someone going for him now and someone else bringing down his suitcase."

At that very moment, Heron was seated in the library. He lowered the book written in Braille and thought of how much he had learned since coming to the school. He now knew the true meaning of "mobility," and how to maximize the use of his remaining senses. Fr. Carroll had told him that his "sixth sense" was the most finely tuned he'd ever encountered. Heron had the uncanny ability to recognize people by their voices, even people from the distant past. And he could identify people by their walk and the shuffle of their feet.

None of the blind people gathered there that day had any trouble interpreting the meaning of the subdued bustle of changing shifts taking place as a sudden wave of orderlies, nurses, technicians, administrators, and doctors arrived while others departed. But only the most discerning ears could have known that the next set of footsteps were those of the orderly named Jim Hanson.

"Hi, Jim," Heron said, even before Jim had spotted him. The confused orderly answered, "Oh. There you are, Larry. Your wife's waiting in the reception area."

As they passed the time waiting for Heron to appear, Fr. Carroll asked, "Did you know that we offered to provide Larry with a Seeing Eye dog?"

"Yes," she answered. "He turned it down."

"To be honest, I don't believe he needs one. He gets around so well. I don't know how he does it, but he makes his way around town as though he had eyes."

The priest saw Heron approaching. "Ah. Here he comes now," he said proudly.

Azelia gave birth to Patricia Ann Heron on St. Patrick's Day, Sunday, March 17, 1946. Regrettably, Heron could only "see" little Patty with his fingertips. But when he finished counting her tiny fingers and toes, he said, "She's absolutely gorgeous."

Patty brought meaning back into his life and renewed his hope for the future. Before he had merely existed, now he had purpose, a reason to work harder and set new goals. Winter may follow summer in terms of his past, but having Patty proved that sunshine also follows rain. *Now I have a daughter. A raison d'être.* The sunshine was back in his life.

Azelia watched as he held the baby tenderly in his arms. But she agonized when she considered what he must be feeling in his heart. Though delighted to have a daughter, he was suffering inside because he could not see her. Azelia silently cursed the war and Hitler for his maniacal pursuits and prayed there would never be another war.

Heron returned to Old Farms filled with renewed hope for the future and immediately became involved in the forming of the Blinded Veterans Association, a historically significant organization that in 1958 would receive its charter from Congress to continue promoting the welfare of blinded veterans.

On Friday, Heron was invited to spend a weekend at the rectory with Fr. Carroll as part of his rehabilitation program. For dinner on Friday night, the chaplain prepared haddock that had been dipped in egg whites then coated with breadcrumbs, cornmeal, and lemon-pepper seasoning. He served it along with skillet-fried potatoes.

After dinner, they sat by a fire and listened to the crackling of logs cut from apple trees that now emitted a bewitching fragrance. Fr. Carroll poured two snifters of Janneau Grand Armagnac, Extra Old. The bouquet alone was enough to smooth the hackles of an angry bull. They lifted their glasses and Heron said, "Here's looking at you." Then they both laughed at his choice of words as he added, "I wish."

Fr. Carroll studied Heron for a moment before stating, "One thing I've noticed about you, Larry, is that you seem to have accepted your fate without bitterness or agitation."

Heron located a bare spot on the coffee table for his glass and leaned back in his soft wing chair. "I don't know. There are times, like when I listen to a football or baseball game, that I find it most difficult. I miss being able to run and catch a ball. I miss being able to drive a car, things like that."

"That's to be expected. You handle blindness better than most. Emerson wrote about greatness born of suffering. Being shoved around, bullied, even defeated, humbles us. It teaches the real facts of life. You seem more sure of yourself than people who can see."

"I don't dwell on the past and stew about things I can't control."

Fr. Carroll leaned his elbows on his knees and tented his hands. "You know, I've worked with blind people for most of my life and I find you quite unique. You have a quiet and singular confidence, perhaps a holdover from your earlier life. You seem well past the trauma associated with sudden blindness, much sooner than I would have expected."

"Believe me, I'm not always that sure of myself."

"You hide it well. I wonder if you'd mind answering a few questions. You see, I'm writing a book about my experiences working with the blind. Your answers could prove helpful."

"I'd be more than happy to try."

"I think you've already answered my first question which had to do with self-image. You're not like most people who suddenly lose their sight. The trend for most has been the significant loss of self-image."

"I haven't experienced much of that, perhaps because I am married to someone very special who has not allowed it to happen."

"What about the perception that people develop extra power in their other senses to compensate for the loss of sight?"

"Perhaps it's true. In my case, I don't know if it's because they grew stronger or that I simply rely on them more now. My hearing has always been exceptional and I have always been able distinguish people by their voices. Now that my life may depend on it, I lean more heavily on my other senses. But have they improved? Probably not."

Fr. Carroll shared that, "Understanding such feelings and addressing them is the key to learning how to live with blindness. I hope my book will prove helpful."

On Saturday afternoon, they sat around drinking beer and talking for hours on end about many subjects. Heron discovered that Carroll had studied Greek, Latin, and philosophy at Holy Cross. After graduating in 1932, he attended St. John's Seminary and was ordained in 1938. He had been working with blinded veterans since the start of the war and found it extremely rewarding.

He would later go on to win national recognition for helping the blind and training others using his tested methods. He would also one day found St. Paul's Rehabilitation Center for the Blind, St. Raphael's Geriatric Adjustment Center, and the American Center for Research in Blindness and Rehabilitation. He would become the National Chaplain of the Blinded Veterans Association and a member of the President's Council Committee on the Employment of the Physically Handicapped.

The priest was a kind and thoughtful man, and as Heron would learn firsthand, quite skillful at playing cards and board games. That evening, the priest introduced Heron to the new long white cane developed by Dr. Richard Hoover, the cane that would one day become the standard traveling tool for blind people nationwide.

When it came time on Sunday for Heron to return to his dormitory, Fr. Carroll presented him with the cane as a keepsake. "To remember me by," he said with a friendly chuckle.

Heron took it and they shook hands. "Thank you, Father." Carroll reminded him of Fr. Connors, in terms of dedication, strength, and spiritual fortitude. Both priests had a strong hand in helping him to hold on to his faith.

The following Friday was his last day at Avon Old Farms. The next morning Azelia would arrive to take him home. It would be difficult to leave, for the school had become a new home. Here he was surrounded by hundreds of men who shared the same afflictions, each capable of making his same missteps. It was OK if one of them screwed up; they could laugh openly at one another. These men were special and they understood what was going on inside him.

That night, he sat on a bench alone under a sky alive with stars he could not see and listened to the hollow barking of a dog in the distance. The world outside awaited him – an indifferent, unforgiving, even hostile world. The thought of leaving the shelter of Old Farms left him disconsolate and off balance, while at the same time he felt a certain need to get on with his life.

He was not alone. By the time the Army's occupation of the school would end in 1947, eight hundred-fifty trainees would pass through its portals. And every last man would experience the same feelings of sadness and fear when leaving the comfort and companionship of Avon Old Farms Convalescent Hospital.

They were waiting for him in the warmth of his kitchen on Wednesday, May 1, 1946, family, friends, and two-month-old Patty.

"Surprise!"

It was good to inhale the lusty smells of home cooking and to hear voices filled with laughter and good cheer. By now Heron had made some important adjustments. For one thing, he did not feel the need to apologize for what he thought was his ugly appearance. Neither did he solicit help from anyone - if he could in any way avoid it.

After the initial shock of seeing him for the first time, people quickly realized that he possessed as much guts and determination as he had before he left for war. Larry Heron was still fiercely independent, and as affable, sociable, and outgoing as ever.

One of the first things he asked of Azelia was to drive him to Milly Mitchell's on Nipmuc Pond for some heavenly New England-style fried clams. On their first visit, Milly stopped at his table to shake his hand. "Welcome home, Larry. This one's on me." To Azelia, she said, "I remember when you used to come here with your dad - such a nice man."

Heron asked, "Did you know that once you leave New England, it's like fried clams don't exist? The ones with the bellies, that is."

"Yeah, I know."

"All the time I was away, I had this craving. Nowhere, not even on the Cape, can you find fried clams that taste this good."

"Well thank you. Larry. That's real nice."

The next stop was Lowell's Dairy for a double scoop of homemade ice cream, chocolate over vanilla. The rich dark chocolate had a nutty cocoa flavor, and its creamy vanilla, second to none, was definitely addictive.

It was nice to revisit old haunts. Everywhere he went people rushed to welcome the returning hero. Rumor had it that Heron had thrown himself on a grenade to save his comrades. Not everyone knew the real story. He did not elaborate, mainly to avoid reliving the event. "The day started out awful and went downhill from there," is the most he cared to offer.

20
Life Without Light

On a Friday evening, Heron came down to the kitchen carrying the mysterious box Azelia had completely forgotten about. Now that she saw it again, her curiosity was piqued. "So what's in that box?"

"Open it," Heron said, handing it to her. Azelia slowly lifted the cover. It contained some objects wrapped in tissue paper. She smiled and tugged at the tissue. "Dear God!" she gasped. The box slipped from her grasp and crashed to the floor where two eyeballs rolled across it like huge marbles, each eye alternately searching the room.

"What's going on?" Heron asked.

"I dropped the box and these things rolled out that look like...eyes." Not having seen them, he could not imagine their eeriness. Their colors were flat and lifeless, lacking depth. They were monstrously huge outside their sockets.

"Larry, they're..." She couldn't find the words.

"They're samples. They will custom fit new ones to each socket using a gel..."

"Don't tell me any more, please."

"They gave me these samples so you could help me decide."

She gazed down at the eyes staring vacantly. "Honey, I prefer you just as you are."

"I thought if you liked them..."

"Your sunglasses are enough. These don't look real."

"If that's how you feel, it'll be a pleasure to skip the trouble and pain of having them fitted."

She lifted the eyeballs up one at a time, as though holding dead rats by the tail, and placed them back side-by-side in the box. On her next trip upstairs, she would load them into a shoebox and place it in the rear of his closet.

On Saturday, he pulled on a clean shirt and jeans that smelled of fresh air and they drove to Amelia's house on Dutcher Street for a visit and later a cookout. Less than a mile away was the Rustic Bridge. When Azelia told Amelia they had planned to check it out later, she suggested, "Why not now. It's a perfect day. Go. Go. You need a break. The kids are fine."

They left Patty playing with Amelia's daughter, Linda. They were the same age and got along better than sisters. Amelia would take the kids next door to visit with Mrs. Kalpagian then be back at the house in a few hours.

Amelia had been right. It was a lovely day. Temperature around 75 degrees. Sheer lace clouds drifted in a cerulean blue sky, breaking up lazily beneath a warm sun. When they reached the bridge, a slight breeze badgered tall clumps of marsh in the fen along the causeway.

It was good to breathe the clean air. Gentle breezes whispered through the pines and the warmth of sunlight fell on his face, easing the tensions and frustrations bunched inside him like storm clouds. "Tell me what you see," he said, as they settled on the warm stonewall along the edge of the bridge.

"It looks like something Thoreau would want to write about and Rockwell would love to paint. The sky is clear. The fish are jumping. There's someone fishing in a small boat on the other side of the pond."

The scent of pine was strong and they could hear the sounds of birds and a slight wind whispering through the pines.

"I did some ice fishing at Old Farms and found it quite relaxing."

"You are so amazing," she said. "You don't let anything slow you down."

"You are the amazing one."

"Me?"

"I used to lie in the hospital thinking what I would do if you'd left me," he said, wistfully. "Even now I'm amazed that you stuck with me. You are such perfection and I...I am damaged goods."

"Don't be silly. The only thing I ever wanted was to be with you. I will go on loving you, grow old with you, and die with you. Selfishly, I hope I am the first to go. I never could survive without you."

He hesitated a moment. "Everything's been taken from me except the most important gift of all. You are the one thing in my life that makes any sense. With you in my life, I can accept what's happened. Without you – well that would be another matter."

"That's something you'll never have to concern yourself with."

The following Tuesday, Ed drove Heron and Guido to Dave's Barbershop on Purchase Street in Milford. As with sound, the smells of life were acutely imbedded in his brain: cooking, smoking, exhaust fumes, flowers, ozone, and waste products. Heron could smell the barbershop from a half-block away, the accumulation of hair tonics, shaving lather, cigar smoke, and human musk were unmistakable.

Guido and Heron took seats facing a variety of tropical plants in two large windows on either side of the shop's entrance. Overhead, three ceiling fans rotated lazily, gently stirring the air and emitting a hum with a repetitious clacking as soothing as the motion of a moving train.

Ed, who was standing by the windows, spotted him turning off Main Street and heading up the hill toward the shop. "Hey, Larry. Here comes Charlie," he said mischievously. "He's wearing a Red Sox baseball cap, a blue sports jacket, and he's carrying a large brown paper bag." Ed quickly ducked into the storage room and Guido hid his face behind a newspaper.

A bell jangled as the door opened and in walked Charlie Barker. Heron said, "Hey, Charlie! You sure are a sight for sore eyes."

Charlie stared back in wonderment. Dave said, "Oh. Hi Charlie," and continued cutting hair. Charlie glanced around at the customers, who weren't paying attention.

"What? How?" Charlie sputtered. Dave stopped snipping and cocked a discerning eye.

Heron asked, "New jacket, Charlie? Blue looks good on you."

It appeared to Charlie that Heron was staring at him through the sunglasses. But it couldn't be. "What's going on?" he asked, a smirk crossing his face.

"Why don't you put that bag down and take a load off?"

"You must have heard the bag crinkle. That's it. Nice try, Larry"

"I like your Red Sox baseball cap. It looks...so official."

Charlie grinned, sheepishly. "You can't see. Can you? Nah. You're just putting me on aren't you? But how'd you know...?" He seemed all flustered.

Laughter came from the storage room, the door slightly ajar. Through the opening, Charlie confirmed that someone was back there. Guido's newspaper shuddered as he attempted unsuccessfully to suppress a laugh. Charlie pushed open the door and caught Ed with his hand covering his mouth to stifle his laughter. Then he pulled the paper out of Guido's hands. "You bastards," he snickered. "Having fun?"

The barbershop then erupted in spontaneous laughter.

Heron took pleasure from making light of his blindness. When someone would admire his necktie, he'd say, "Glad you like it. Picked it out myself." Then he'd wait for a reaction. Or when he'd drop by the soda fountain at the Hopedale Drug Store, he'd ask the friendly waitress, Joanie, "What did you do to your hair? I liked it better the other way."

On his daily walks about town, someone would invariably shout, "Hey Larry, how's it going?" Unless it was someone he'd never met before, he'd always shout back, "Just fine. How about you, Billy?" Then Billy, or Jimmy, or whoever would drop his jaw in wonderment and ask, "How did you know it was me?"

He accepted an invitation to march in the July 4th parade that was to start at the American Legion post and end at the town cemetery. Hopedale Street was dressed with flags mounted on ten-foot poles spaced every thirty feet. Red, white, and blue banners adorned the town hall. Caissons were towed behind black horses. Flags fluttered beside wreathes leaning on headstones in the town cemetery. Low-flying National Guard fighter jets made low passes and tilted their wings before heading for the South Shore.

Early that morning, Azelia left him with members of the American Legion and Disabled Veterans lining up at the head of the parade. He wore his best tan suit with a white shirt, maroon tie and a navy blue American Legion cap astride his head. She needn't worry, they told her.

She joined members of her family who had staked out a spot across from the pharmacy. Throngs lined both sides of the street as the band started up with *Stars and Stripes Forever*. Excitement surged through her in anticipation of watching Larry marching up the street. As the spirited music grew louder, she maneuvered herself into position for a better view.

"Well I'll be!" said Charlie Barker, standing on her right.

Azelia blushed with pride. He hadn't told her that he would actually be *leading* the parade - as Grand Marshal. He cut a neat figure with his head raised high and his cane held in his right hand like a baton. His left hand barely touched the sleeve of the officer marching beside him as he matched him step for step. A color guard followed fifteen feet behind them - an Air Force sergeant bearing the American flag and an Army sergeant carrying the American Legion flag. The standard-bearers were both flanked by navy men with rifles on their shoulders.

As word of his sweet tenor voice spread, he was invited to join the church choir. So strong and vibrant was his singing that he was asked to sing Ave Maria at Midnight Mass on that first Christmas Eve. The church that night was decorated with poinsettias, candles and greenery. People flocked from neighboring towns just to hear him sing.

The pleasant sound of his voice resonated throughout the church and was magnified as though he were standing in an echo chamber. When the song ended, there were enough tears to fill an Olympic-sized pool.

Soon he was invited to join the *Milford Area Singers,* and performed with them at hospitals, nursing facilities, weddings, and other events. He was frequently invited to functions as the honored guest, either as a singer or to deliver a patriotic speech – not just in Hopedale, but in neighboring towns as well. Meanwhile, he never missed a day of work at the Draper Corporation except to return to a veterans hospital for more operations.

When people would ask how he felt about blindness, he would comment, "One could get cynical about it or accept it. Long ago I chose the latter. Keeping things simple leads to a more rewarding life." At other times he'd answer, "It never pays to look back with regret, because you can't change the past. It's best to stay where we are, in the present."

Every few months he was readmitted to the West Roxbury Veterans Hospital where doctors continued to work on the reconstruction of his face. Perhaps to compensate, he paid very close attention to the clothes he wore. Everything had to be properly color coordinated and laid out each night before work. There may have been little that could be done to change his face, but he had total control over the clothes he wore.

Music was very special at the Heron family residence. Friends and relatives gathered often, especially on holidays. Sometimes Azelia's sister, Olga, and at other times Ed Kalpagian, would drop by to play the piano while the crowd that inevitably gathered would sing along. And as always, Heron would be coaxed into singing their favorite songs.

In late September, Fr. Connors called to ask if he could drop by for a visit. Connors confessed to hearing so much about Azelia that he felt he must meet her in person. When he first arrived, he lauded Heron for his great courage and demeanor in the face of all he had endured. "Your faith remains strong and I commend you for that. It is such a great lesson to those of us with less strength and perseverance."

"I died on that day you found me, Father. Then God gave me a second chance."

"That's a wonderful way to look at it."

"More than that. There's an aesthetic element to being blind. I used to judge people by their looks. Now, looks mean absolutely nothing. I go strictly by what's inside."

"Perhaps we should all experience blindness for a time," Fr. Connors surmised.

"Also, I am more sensitized to music and I'm a good listener – no visual distractions. On our drives to the beach, I smell the ocean sooner than anyone else."

"And another thing. He never has to drive the car," Azelia laughed innocuously.

The priest's gaze met hers over the rim of his coffee cup. "That's true," he said, lowering his voice to a confidential tone. "People don't just talk about one hero in this family. Your name comes up whenever they speak of your husband. Larry must have told you this – he might not have made it without you."

"*Would* not have made it," Heron corrected.

Connors continued. "Everyone had given up on him. But he held on. The thought of getting back to you was what kept him going."

Fr. Connors then told her how the men drew straws to choose who would put him out of his misery.

"Yes, I heard..." She teared up and reached for Heron's hand. "I would have died had he not come home."

"Your prayers seemed to have helped, Father," Heron said.

"I administered the last rites to so many young people in the war." He paused, staring into space. "I can count on one hand those who survived. I only hope I did some good for the souls of those who have moved on."

His voice suddenly became euphoric. "That brings me to another reason for my visit. On Sunday, November 12, I plan to hold memorial services for members of the 9th Division. The 9th lost 4,581 brave men who, like you, did not think twice about what was being asked of them. They lived their lives dedicated to their own faith, our faith, all praying together in a common purpose. The country, the world, owes them and you, Larry, more than it can ever repay. You risked your own life to save many."

"That's such a great idea, Father. No one should ever forget them," Azelia said.

"I plan to hold these services every year at this time. I expect soldiers of all faiths to attend. And I hope I will see you both there this and every year."

For a moment it seemed as though his mind had left the room. Just as quickly, it returned. "It's funny, on the battlefield, it never mattered which faith a man may have been. Soldiers would congregate around any chaplain to pray, no matter what his faith. Once, a Jewish chaplain called for me. He lay in a pool of his own blood on a battlefield in France. Knowing full well that he was dying, he asked for my blessings. Not absolution, mind you, just my blessings." Connors' eyes watered up. "He died a strong, dedicated Jew wanting nothing more from me than that. We should all have such faith. We must. And we must always stand up for it."

There was a moment of silence.

"I'd like it if we could pray together," Fr. Connors said. He reached out and they all joined hands. For a moment they sat in silence in a tight circle. All that could be heard in the background was the ticking of a grandfather clock in one corner of the room until Fr. Connors led them in a simple prayer.

"We must keep our faith in God strong," he said, with quiet finality. Then he spoke of love, love for one another. He prayed for the souls of all who gave their lives for love of family, mankind, and country. He ended by thanking God for His divine blessings. Heron could feel power and energy radiating through their hands as he prayed, as though a spiritual presence had entered the room and joined them.

Afterward, Azelia served cake and more coffee. It was then that Fr. Connors noted the pillow beside him with an intricate pattern woven into it. "What lovely colors," he said, holding the pillow with a floral design in front of him. "Did you do the crewelwork?" he asked Azelia.

"No. Larry did."

"You're kidding. Larry, this is beautiful."

"Well thank you, Father. But I'd appreciate it if you didn't spread it around."

They all laughed.

During the discussion that followed, Heron said, "The Gazette carried the story of how you won the Silver Star."

"Oh that. It was nothing."

"You rescued some soldiers. The article said that no one else dared go to their aid because you had to pass through a minefield to get to them. I'd say that was something."

"They said I was being brave, but I knew I was in God's hands the whole time." A pensive smile crossed his face. "You know, when they told me I was going to receive the Silver Star, I never gave it a second thought. In fact, they held a parade at which I was to receive it and guess what?" Before anyone could answer, he continued, "I was so involved in whatever it was that I was doing that I totally forgot and completely missed my own parade." He chuckled aloud. "More thrilling was the day I captured twenty-five Germans."

"You're kidding. Tell us about it," Heron said.

"It was rather bizarre. A soldier from the 9th Infantry was driving me through Aachen, Germany. The road was treacherous, full of holes and craters, doted with charred bodies, dust and rubble. Once tall buildings had been reduced to skeletons, mounds of brick, and blackened debris, some about to collapse. Fires burned, and black smoke billowed. Then came a clean stretch of road, only it was laced with fog. The driver shifted into gear and the engine took on a comforting rumble."

"That's when I began to doze. The driver became somewhat mesmerized as well. Suddenly, as we rounded a corner, we nearly plowed into a column of German soldiers who dodged to the side of the road to avoid being run down. The driver instinctively pulled the jeep to an abrupt halt to avoid hitting anyone. The Germans were just as surprised as we were and froze in place. No one raised a weapon."

"I asked the driver, 'What'll we do?'"

"He answered, nervously, 'Yell something at them, sir - as loud and brassy as you can!'"

"'Put down your weapons and surrender,' I commanded. That was the first thing that came to mind."

"To my amazement, the man in charge saluted and handed over his weapon. The others came forward and dropped theirs onto the back of the jeep. Then they all raised their hands. I couldn't believe it. They were surrendering to me, a chaplain."

"You're kidding," Heron laughed.

"Thank God they weren't SS. They would have killed us on the spot."

"What does SS stand for?" Azelia asks. "I've always wondered."

"Schutzstaffel, a wild, vicious cadre of animals whose role was to starve, brutalize, torment, torture and murder helpless civilians. They wore the same uniform as storm troopers: gray jackets with swastika armbands except for their black caps with a silver death's head badge and black ties. "

"When I led the prisoners into camp, the men couldn't believe their eyes. Word spread quickly that I had captured Germans and I took quite a ribbing. 'At least I take them alive,' I told them."

Connors drove home late that afternoon pondering what might have been. Heron had been born gifted beyond all dreams. But those gifts were consumed on that fateful day near Cherbourg. *Yet I never hear him complain.*

He overcomes major obstacles every single day and continues to endure painful operations. He marches in parades with battered head held high. With the loss of his athletic skills, he has unleashed a new talent – a beautiful voice that he uses for the enjoyment of others at hospitals, churches, and civic events. He speaks encouragement to young people and maintains his love of sports. He socializes with old friends and makes new ones.

And Azelia is a woman blessed with great beauty, courage, strength, and devotion. She too neither complains nor displays bitterness. She's been his crutch, his beacon.

And none of this has affected their belief in God or their sense of values. What a great country! What great people!

Fr. Connors suddenly realized that he was sobbing.

The following article appeared in the Milford Daily News on Tuesday, November 19: *At a well-attended meeting lasting two hours last night, the Milford VFW unanimously voted to present Lawrence J. Heron of Hopedale, a gift of $500 for Christmas. The drive to raise the money started last July with letters mailed to veterans in Milford and Hopedale.* The article noted that the American Legion had also started a drive for the purpose of doubling the amount.

On December 21, 1946, Heron was discharged from the Army. Ironically, his discharge papers listed his eyes as blue. And he was given a sever-
ance check in the amount of $154.77 along with the Purple Heart.

He quickly settled into life as a civilian, making his own way to and
from his job at the factory each day. When snowstorms hit, he'd be out shoveling snow. In the summer, he'd work around the house and perform mainte-
nance on the family car. On vacations to Marshfield, he'd swim in the ocean
and dig for clams. On weekends, he'd go fishing or to the golf course with
friends.

Norma Ripanti had married soon after the war, which changed her name to
Norma Thurston. She entered Azelia's kitchen to help clean up following a
Halloween dinner party in late October and asked, "Do you know what your
little daughter just said to me?"

"What?"

"She pointed to her own eyes and said, 'Daddy uh uh.'"

"Oh yes," Azelia laughed. "She's says that whenever she sees him take
off his glasses. She is very aware that her daddy is different and that he can't
see."

"Normally, she's a bundle of energy – into everything. I can't keep up
with her. But when she's around him, she calms right down. Takes his hand
the minute he stands up and leads him around like a Seeing-Eye dog."

Norma shook her head and smiled. "This family amazes me," she said.
"Especially you. You are so strong. I have always admired your courage."

"Me? How about you? Graduated from Temple in 1942. A master's in
physical therapy, and then off to join the Army."

"Yes, but I ended up safe at Walter Reed for two-and-a-half years until
my discharge in '46."

"You don't think that's something? You rehabilitated injured soldiers.
You became an officer for God's sake. You accomplished something with
your life."

Norma raised a brow. "Do I detect some...some discontentment here?"

Azelia blushed. "Not at all. I'm happy with my life. Oh, sure, now and then I wonder what goes on outside Hopedale, but I have a life, relatives, friends." She moved far away in her mind then swiftly returned. "When I really think about it, the only thing that's not being satisfied is my curiosity. It would be nice to be able to travel. I'd like to see Italy. But if I did, I know I'd just miss everything here and want to hurry back. It doesn't get any better than this, just...new and different perhaps. But I can live without change."

Norma turned her forthright eyes on Azelia and said, "How did you get so damn wise, Mrs. Heron? It takes most people years of travel and worldly experience to come to that very same conclusion."

On a lovely spring morning in 1947, they strolled arm-in-arm through town. The day was sunny and bright, the air clean. The sky was a vivid blue with temperatures in the low 70s. Ordinarily, it would take but a minute to pass through Hopedale, but nearly everyone they met eagerly engaged them in conversation, slowing them down. Azelia noted that Heron had little patience that day and was less talkative than usual.

What differentiated today's walk from others was that Heron had a surprise planned. They turned right at the corner of Hope Street and followed it a block to the Adin Ballou Park. In the rear right-hand corner of the small park, a bronzed Adin Ballou stood imposingly before the only remnants of the settler's original farmhouse, a doorstep and boot scraper.

"So tell me," Heron asked. "What do you think of this part of town?"

"One of my favorites. The homes are so lovely and it's right near the library, where I spend much of my time. Why do you ask?"

"Tell me what you think of this next house, the one abutting the park."

"The one on our right? It has a lovely yard. No one can ever build on the park side. It's almost like an extension of their yard."

"Our yard," he corrected.

"Our yard? Larry, what are you saying?"

"Yesterday, my boss told me the house was available and we are first in line if we want it. I told him yes."

"Oh, Larry!" Azelia squealed with delight.

"Our old place was fine before I joined the army, but that was before marriage and Patty. I swear the rooms have shrunk and the ceilings have dropped since then. Even the windows seem smaller."

A Draper representative was waiting at the front door to take them on a tour. The first floor had a huge kitchen and dining area, living room, family room, two bedrooms, and one-and-a-half baths. The second floor had two more bedrooms and a full bath. The move to Hopedale Street was completed in the summer of 1947, much to Azclia's delight.

Now that the war had ended, the country steered its resources and technology away from war, more toward developing products for a peaceful society. Now came television, frozen foods, stereos, 45-RPM records, chickens tidily wrapped in plastic. Doctors had stopped making house calls. Mail delivery dropped to once a day.

And on January 1, 1949, Carol Heron entered the world.

In the summer of '51, the Disabled American Veterans headquarters in Chicago, distributed an account of Heron's story to newspapers across the country: *the only living veteran in the history of the DAV to have a chapter named for him...overcame insurmountable handicaps to lead a normal life... outperformed his sighted peers as a quality control inspector at the Draper Corporation...survived injuries that would have killed an ordinary man...endured many complicated surgeries...serves as an inspiration to fellow members of the DAV and to handicapped people everywhere.*

Heron's notability was expanding. Celebrities and high-ranking officials were lining up to be photographed shaking his hand or to appear with him on television. A brief summary of his life was broadcast nationwide during a half-hour radio program.

Then on September 9, 1952, the Heron household boasted another new addition. This time it was a boy and they named him Lawrence J. Heron, Jr. Now there were two in the household who would answer to the name of Larry Heron.

21
Family Life

The following summer the Herons rented a cottage in Marshfield, Massachusetts. A few blocks away stood another cottage with a lovely view of the ocean that was for sale. It was in a state of disrepair, but nothing that a fresh coat of paint and some landscaping could not restore to life.

The problem was that the price was too high - nearly double what they felt they could afford. When Heron described the property to a close friend, the friend replied, "I was thinking of buying a place on the water. My wife and I should take a look. If we like it, perhaps we'll go in on it with you."

Azelia was not keen on such an arrangement. "A good way to lose a friend," she commented. But she eventually went along. Larry loved the ocean and swam like a marlin whenever he could get in it. He should not be denied, she decided. The next weekend, they journeyed back to Marshfield with the other couple. "We love it. A good deal," they agreed. "Let's do it."

So the following week the Herons put down a deposit. When they returned home, Heron phoned his friend. "You'll need to sign some forms and have them notarized," he told him. "Then we can set up a date for the closing."

"Gee," his friend said. "I wish you'd spoken to me before you put money down. We went over our finances last night and decided that we can't afford it right now."

"But I thought we had agreed."

"I'm sorry Larry. We changed our minds."

When Heron filled Azelia in on the conversation, she read the disappointment in his voice. "Let's go through the numbers again. It might be a stretch but we both expect raises this year."

They decided to complete the deal on their own. It turned out to be the best decision. Owning property with another party would have been a huge mistake, they now realized. They turned their attention to fixing up their second home.

Azelia had always liked to help her father in the garden and had learned from him the secrets as to why Italians grow the healthiest plants. Flowers and vegetables alike flourished under her skillful hands. She'd done so well with the house on Hopedale Street that it was difficult to tell where the park ended and their property began.

By the end of summer, she'd converted the rough shorn yard surrounding the cottage into the envy of the neighborhood. Guido applied his artistic talents to painting the outside of the cottage. Then he added a gorgeous stone fireplace to their spacious living room that lent coziness to it and helped extend the season well into the fall.

By now, area residents regarded Heron as a living symbol of everything the American soldier stood for. Admired for his heroic actions and courageous rehabilitation, he had become a role model for young people as well as for the handicapped.

People wanted to do things for him, like drive him to the Bright Oaks Club on Mendon hill where they could treat him to free drinks. Bright Oaks was a fun place where a blind man could socialize with sighted people on an equal footing. His beer glass was never empty, and he never had to reach for his wallet.

Bright Oaks was a social club where casual conversations and friendly arguments won the day. He loved the gregariousness of the place, the smell of the beer, the laughter, the loud voices, and the soft music. Here he could listen to discourses on everything from politics to how to best fertilize the garden. And he loved playing cards.

Braille-marked playing cards were kept on hand just for him. In time, people learned that he was unbeatable at various forms of poker. Whenever he played gin, he had his points counted sooner than his opponent. Pinochle was another favorite.

And all the while, he was developing a real taste for beer. More often than not, by the time someone dropped him off at home, he'd have difficulty climbing the front stairs then crawling into bed. On one such occasion, after Azelia had led him to his bed and had him safely under the covers, he heard her sobbing.

The next evening was a Saturday night. He walked past Azelia and went to the refrigerator and pulled out a bottle of Budweiser. "Care to join me, he asked."

"No thanks. I'm still working on a glass of lemonade."

He popped open the beer and set it down on the kitchen table, then took a seat and waited for Azelia to sit down opposite him.

"Do you remember that song I wrote for you after our...our one and only breakup?"

"Yes." She would never forget. It had happened when they were in high school. As part of the courting ritual he would drive her around town singing songs he'd created just for her, songs that sounded so good she didn't believe he'd made them up, but he had. This particular song was written on the heels of the break up.

It occurred right after his father had died. Heron invited Azelia to the funeral but she had failed to show. He became very angry because he felt she had not been there to support him when he needed her most.

They hadn't been dating long and she didn't know his family very well at the time. And her mom, Livia, thought that unless they had been going steady or were engaged, it would be improper for her to attend. That's how Livia had been raised in Italy. People shouldn't even date without a chaperon present.

Following that incident, they didn't speak for over a month. The problem for Heron was that Azelia was so attractive that plenty of men were queuing up to ask her out now that she was "free." One day a friend approached Heron and asked if he would mind if the friend asked her out, to which Heron replied, "Hell yes, I'd mind! Azelia is the girl I'm going to marry." He called her that night and invited her for a drive. And that's when he came up with his memorable song.

Now, as they sat quietly in the kitchen, separated by a bottle of beer, he asked her, "Did you ever write it down? Because I want to hear the words again."

"No. I never did," she answered.

"Oh."

She hesitated. "But I remember it. Every line."

"You do?"

"Sure." She thought for a moment. *"Sweetheart, I'm sorry that I made you cry, sorry for each little tear in your eye. I was mistaken, my whole heart is aching, please tell me you won't say goodbye. Now our dreams were broken, but soon they will mend. Kiss me again. Hug me again. Sweetheart, I'm sorry."*

The silence weighed heavy for what seemed a full minute before Heron spoke. "Take a good look at this bottle of beer," he said emphatically. "It's the last one you'll ever see me drink." It was his way of telling her that he hated himself for making her cry and that it would never happen again. Heron had always kept his word.

It was about this time that the Draper Corporation experienced its first layoff. Though the company's profits were eroding rapidly, it continued to live up to its image. Rather than downsize, it kept everyone working, though only three days a week.

On October 30, the Herons received an invitation to attend Fr. Connors' annual memorial Mass to be held for the men of the 9th Division lost in the war. Connors was now pastor of the Immaculate Conception in Worcester, Massachusetts.

Enclosed with the invitation was an article written by Fr. Henry Murphy under the synonym "Canon Pepergrass." The elderly priest, a close friend of Fr. Connors, described *Connors Coffee Shop* as a place on the battlefield where a pot was always brewing for any GI at any time, and where friendships were made and great bull sessions held. This bit of nostalgia from the Catholic priest set the stage for what would always prove to be an interesting and exciting event.

Over 450 people of all faiths attended the memorial Mass that year. Parents of the deceased came from as far away as Pittsburgh. On Saturday night there was a get-together, which allowed husbands to introduce wives and children to old army buddies. An hour later, Heron was asked to sing a few songs, and by the time the social gathering ended, he and Azelia had conversed with nearly everyone in attendance.

The services were emotionally charged and solemn, dedicated to the honor of veterans and their families, the nation as a whole, and the high moral purpose and idealism that had motivated the nation's call to arms. That evening an elaborate dinner was served followed by entertainment. As always, the Herons met new people and made new friends. They promised themselves that they would make a greater effort not to miss any of these events in the coming years. Each year, attendance would continue to increase, more than doubling over the next several years.

Azelia read from an article that appeared in the Boston Globe on December 24, 1954. "It says here that Dr. Murray performed the world's first successful kidney transplant at the Peter Bent Brigham. In fact, it goes on to say it was the first *organ* transplant ever performed."

"*Our* Dr. Joseph E. Murray?"

"The very same."

"Honey, that's wonderful. Everyone knew he'd do great things. What did he have to say?"

"He said he had been influenced by Dr. Brown's cross-skin graft of a pair of identical twins in 1937. His transplant was between identical twins as well."

"Just like him to spread the credit around."

On May 5, 1956, Debra Heron was born. Like any proud father, Heron doted on his new baby girl. His children's laughter always filled him with great happiness and joy. Vicariously, through his children, he was able to reclaim pieces of a life. As each child reached school age and began to encounter life's challenges, they would not hesitate to approach him for advice. His answers usually were aimed at helping them find their own answers. He was thrilled by their achievements and could be counted on to listen intently when they needed someone to lean on.

People claimed that young Larry was a chip off the old block and that Patty had his eyes and Azelia's smile. Others claimed it was the reverse. He was especially delighted to hear that Larry had his looks and shape and the girls Azelia's. "I would be very unhappy if it were the other way around," he said one day. What disturbed him most about blindness was that no matter how often people described his children, he could not put the pieces together to form a whole person. He could imagine but never know what they really looked like.

A letter arrived from Dr. Vance Bradford in April 1961 thanking Heron for allowing him to use photos of his face taken prior to his plastic surgery in England. Enclosed in the envelope was a copy of a paper the doctor had written. It had been published in the May 1961 Oklahoma State Medical Journal relating to medical problems likely to result from an atomic bomb blast. The article, entitled "Burns in Atomic Disaster," included photographs of Heron's head and face to illustrate what radiation burns might look like. It brought home to Heron just how serious his injuries were and how badly he had been disfigured.

In mid-September, eighty-year old Emma was placed in a nursing home over Azelia's objections. She required constant care and insisted on going. "You've got your hands full with the children," she insisted. "If I stay, everyone else will suffer. No. It's best this way." Emma passed away in her sleep at the nursing home on December 23, 1961.

"Why just before Christmas?" Heron wanted to know.

"Many people get depressed at this time of year. She loved the holidays so much, but the joy had gone out of living for her," Azelia said. "She was suffering. So much of her body had broken down."

"Yes. She lost the ability to enjoy her time with the kids, the singing and the laughter." Heron was hurting inside. He had been very close to his mother and loved her dearly. "Perhaps we shouldn't celebrate Christmas this year," he said.

"You know she would have wanted it. We need it more now than ever."

"Yes. I suppose you're right, though it could turn into an Irish wake."

More people than usual crowded into the Heron residence on Christmas Day that year. The Johnny Milans and the Jerry Dees arrived early. Olga and Fred Bresciani, Amelia and Jimmy DiSabito, Vera and Joe Pantini, all came with their children. By the time Ed Kalpagian and Pete Ferrelli arrived, Larry was anxious for their company. He greeted them with, "You guys sure are a sight for sore eyes." Everyone laughed.

Ed relieved Olga at the piano, playing Christmas carols while the guests sang along. The eggnog flowed and Emma was properly toasted. *Unbounded love and kindness...a great lady...hell of a cook...always there for you, especially for Larry...they were very close.*

In keeping with what had by now become a Christmas tradition, Johnny Milan delivered his rendition of *Rudolph the Red-nosed Reindeer*. When he had finished, everyone drank a solemn toast to Rudolph and his reindeer friends.

Jerry Dee was the first to leave, bidding all a "Merry Christmas and a Happy New Year, I hope to hell we'll all be here next year!"

Besides the holiday celebrations that usually took place at the Heron residence every year, there were summer vacations at the Cape, fishing, clamming, golfing, backyard barbeques with neighbors, and swimming in the Atlantic. Despite being blind, Heron could still swim like Johnny Weissmuller - farther out and for longer periods than anyone else. The only help he needed was for someone to direct him toward the shore when he was finally ready to quit.

22

Changes in Attitude

The years sailed by with alacrity. Before Heron knew it, Debbie was invited to her high school prom. Her date was a dream – she could not have hoped for better. But she seemed melancholy. The reason for her sadness was plain enough; her father could not see her in her gown, all grown up looking like a lady. He had never once been able to look upon her face. The fact that he's never laid eyes on any of his four children disturbed young Debbie as much as it did him. It was so unfair.

There were whole ranges of absurdities associated with blindness. At Christmas he could never fully appreciate the tree, the colorful gift-wrappings, nor the joyous looks that crossed each face when it was time to open the presents. He could never view a colorful sunset, nor look upon a snow-covered landscape. *But tonight, damn it, he will find out what I look like!*

When the time came for her to make an appearance, she looked in the mirror and tried desperately not to cry and spoil her makeup. She was dressed in a light blue taffeta gown, wearing nail polish, high heels, and make up. Her hair was swept back and gathered loosely in the latest fashion.

"You look beautiful," Azelia told her as she came down the stairs. "Yes," her father confirmed. "You're going to knock 'em dead." She walked straight up to him and took his hands, pulling as if to lift him from his chair. "Stand up, Daddy," she told him. With that, she took a deep breath and placed his hands on her bare shoulders. "You can't see my dress," she said.

193

"But you can feel it. It has a slight blue tint and fits perfectly," she said. She went on to describe every last detail, placing his hands strategically on the spaghetti straps, taffeta to her waist, low scoop in the back, and the flared skirt.

"Too well, perhaps," Heron replied, wearing a smile. She was still his baby girl. "That guy better have you home no later that one."

"Dad! This is a prom."

"I know. My little girl has grown up. You look lovely," he said, giving her a peck on the cheek.

"Thank you."

"No. Thank you." He hesitated. "And you smell of jasmine," he added. He could hear Azelia snickering in the background, or could it have been a sob?

Debbie was happy. Her father was pleased, she could tell, for that little episode helped him visualize his daughter all grown up in her prom gown. It's the best he could ever hope for in terms of imaging what any of his children looked like.

After she left, Azelia said, "Trust me, sweetheart, your daughter is blonde and beautiful. All your children are lovely. On a scale of one to ten, they're all elevens."

"No false modesty here," he replied, great joy registering in his voice.

The mood of the nation had shifted, and Heron noted that not all the changes were for the best. "North American Rockwell bought out Ben Draper and now owns the Corporation," he announced as he arrived home from work on a Monday in early 1967.

"What?" Azelia asked. "I can't imagine the place not being owned by a Draper."

"The market's gone dry. What little business there is, spare parts and such, has moved south to Spartanburg, South Carolina."

"Time has passed by the textile industry, I'm afraid. Draper looms have obsoleted themselves. The first ones sold over a hundred years ago don't look any different from today's models. They never breakdown. The world is saturated with Draper looms."

Heron's blindness had touched each of his children - more positively than negatively. Each learned at a very early age that their father was different, and each was very proud of him and his accomplishments. Their dad spent more time with them than most fathers, perhaps because he was a captive audience. He would take them digging for clams at the shore, just as his father often did with him. They marveled as he patiently fashioned fishing flies – more so when he took them fly-fishing and actually caught trout.

No Memorial Day, Veterans Day, Independence Day, Flag Day, or Armed Forces Day would pass without an article appearing in the newspapers about Heron - articles recounting his past accomplishments in sports, service to his country, sacrifices, courage and fortitude. There was enough written about his singing and celebrity to fill several scrapbooks.

Heron was gaining more celebrity now than when he was a sports star. So it was important that he maintain a certain flair for dressing well. For that purpose, he depended on family members to ensure that his clothes were always properly color coordinated. The socks had to be plain gray, black, or dark blue to match his gray, black, or dark blue suit respectively. His shirts must mostly be white or sometimes blue. "What color are these socks?" he asked Carol the night before the 1968 Memorial Day parade.

"Brown," she said, and then quickly added, "with blue flecks – to match the red stripes in your shirt."

"What?" he exclaimed.

"No. Red flecks in your socks to match the pink tie."

"Oh pipe down," he said, realizing he was being had. He secretly liked it when his children played pranks on him. It showed that they were not in the least intimidated by him or felt pity. The fact that he had been blinded never shocked them or caused them the least bit of embarrassment. And that was the way he wanted it.

Later that year, at a reunion held in New York for former members of the 87th Chemical Weapons Battalion, John Sears passed out copies of several articles he had written for newspapers serving towns south of Boston.

The first article explained how the 87th had landed on D-Day armed with mustard and phosgene gas. The men had been issued special fatigues dipped in wax and wore brown patches on their shoulders that would turn pink if exposed to poisonous gases.

As the war progressed, shells filled with poison gas of all types were discovered in German ammunition dumps along with thick rubber suits worn by gas handlers. According to Rommel, the Germans would have used gas if they could have developed a mask to protect their horses. Due to oil short-ages, the Germans relied heavily on horse-drawn wagons to transport ammu-nition, food, and medicine.

Once the Americans had taken Cherbourg, a captain approached Sears and said, "Get rid of all the poison gas we're carrying."

"How?" Sears asked.

The captain simply ordered, "Find a way."

Sgt. Sears pondered what to do. The ammo dumps would not accept it because it was too dangerous and no one wanted to handle it. So he took the only avenue left open to him. Over the next few days he had his crew collect all the mustard and phosgene-filled shells from each of the four companies. Then he located an open field with cattle grazing on it, which told him the field was not mined. He ordered his crew to dig a deep trench twenty-feet long and buried the shells. As far as anyone knows, that's where they remain today.

Sears' interest in the war led to several follow-on articles he had written. Azelia read some of them to Heron after they had returned home from the reunion. One particularly fascinating article, and also the most terrible, was about Nordhausen, a death camp. The story was one of deprivation and hor-ror that left them on the verge of tears.

As Sears came within a mile of one of the units, or sub-camps as they were called, he could smell the gagging, putrid stench of human death, unlike anything he'd ever encountered on the battlefield, a smell that would stay with him for life. When he reached the sub-camp, there were only about a hundred people still alive.

Their bodies were emaciated, their eyes hollow. None could have weighed more than 70 pounds. Their clothes were tattered and most went barefoot. The rest were dead bodies stacked six high on slabs set a few feet apart with nothing but purple, yellow, and green skin stretched over bones. He estimated about five thousand dead.

Records later revealed that of the thousands of inmates, only a few dozen were Jews, the rest were Poles, Czechs, Russian, French, Belgian, and Dutch. Inside, the stench was even more unbearable. Some inmates lay in their cots, right where they had died, others were approaching death. Nearly all the living suffered from typhus, and they were crawling with lice. Sores covered their bodies.

These men had been slaves forced to manufacture the V-2 missiles fired at London and other British cities. There were two long tunnels dug into the mountain for the transportation of rockets on railcars. The rockets were being assembled in smaller tunnels that interconnected these two. The inmates were being simultaneously starved and worked to death.

The Americans inadvertently killed a few of the survivors by feeding them food instead of starting them out with teaspoons of water. Many were already beyond help either way. German civilians from nearby towns were forced to bury the dead. Their denials of knowing anything about the camp fell on deaf ears, for the smell alone was enough to tell them exactly what had been going on here for years.

When Azelia finished reading the articles, any doubts that Heron may have had as to whether he and others suffered and died in vain were diminished. Freedom does not come without a steep price.

It all started with the Gulf of Tonkin, a body of water on the East Coast of North Vietnam, the staging area of the U.S. Seventh Fleet, the site that would lead to the escalation of U.S. involvement in Vietnam. In July 1965, there were 80,000 U.S. troops stationed in South Vietnam. By 1969, the number had risen to 543,000, with 400 tons of bombs and ordnance falling on Vietnam daily, the beginning days of the most vivid and memorable war in modern day history.

The longer the war continued to rage, the more the nation rebelled against US involvement. The country had lost faith in American leaders and American power. Attitudes toward the military had changed and veterans everywhere felt the scorn of advancing numbers of anti-war protestors.

By the time the war drew to a close, the US had committed 2.6 million troops, unleashed many times the tonnage of bombs dropped by both sides in World War II, and suffered 365,000 dead and wounded. And the Vietnamese, North and South, had suffered an estimated 5 million civilian and military casualties.

This was the beginning of a series of events that would turn Heron's life in a downward spiral.

22

Depression

On a Friday afternoon in November, the sun moved high overhead and a cool breeze swept down from the north. Heron stepped off the sidewalk onto the grass as one kid after another sailed past on a skateboard like dive-bombers peeling from the sky.

"Hey. Watch me," a voice called down from a rise on the hill. Heron heard skateboard wheels rumbling toward him on the rough pavement. That would be Glenn, whose board had a wobbly wheel. Billy's well-oiled board rolled smoothly, issuing a low hum. Walter's created more of a rumble, like rolling thunder. This was definitely Glenn.

"Hi Glenn," Heron said as the boy passed him.

"Yikes!" Heron heard the board skid out of control and heavy footsteps as Glenn's feet hit the pavement and pumped hard to keep him from falling. A final *whump thump* told Heron that the boy had crash-landed on the soft lawn.

"Geeze, Mr. Heron, how'd you know it was me?"

"Just a lucky guess," Heron said, trying to suppress a laugh. Heron was elated. Next Wednesday was Veterans Day, the day he would lead a parade through Milford.

It rained Monday and Tuesday, but on Wednesday morning the sky was a cool deep blue. Thousands lined the parade route through the heart of Milford's downtown. The veteran's groups were all there, as were the Police and Fire Departments, all led by their chiefs. The local selectmen, state representatives, and other local politicians had also turned out. In the mix were the Gold Star mothers of the Italian-American Vets, the DAV Colors and Contingent, the American-Armenian Vets, the VFW, and even a group of World War I veterans.

Each time a flag group passed, veterans lining the parade route removed their hats and held them over their hearts as a solemn tribute. Others tossed a salute, remembering whatever war they may have served in. Anyone could see that this was a very serious event.

"Here comes Larry Heron from Hopedale, for whom the DAV chapter was named," someone commented.

From the sidewalk in front of Billy Focus' Diner, a voice called out, "Hey Larry!" He recognized the voice. It was John Jakes. Without losing a step, the blind veteran yelled right back, "Hey John. How are you doing?" Jaws dropped in amazement, though many locals were already familiar with Heron's ability to recognize them by the sound of their voices.

As Heron reached the corner of Main and Central, he heard a commotion and the officer marching beside him told him to stop. A group of protestors were blocking the intersection. A fight broke out. People were chanting words like, "murderers, baby killers, stop the slaughter."

"What's going on?" Heron asked.

"Some jerks are burning the American flag in the middle of the street. Cops are trying to remove them."

A half-hour later, the parade resumed, but hearts and minds were now heavy. The country had never been this divided.

Heron was upset. A weekly column in the Milford Daily News quoted a woman who claimed Hopedale's "blind people" had registered complaints that they were being menaced by children on skateboards.

Azelia could not recall her husband ever being this angry. "Blind people? That would be me!" he exclaimed. "There are no other blind people in town. They're nice kids, doing what kids do. Now they'll think I've complained about them."

"Well why don't you do something about it?" Azelia suggested. "Let's phone the newspaper and set the record straight." She made several calls and finally had an editor on the line.

"And make sure you quote me," she heard Heron say to him when he was on the phone. "Those kids never once bothered me. Never ever came close."

The newspaper printed a formal retraction, quoting Heron as saying, "I had nothing to do with the article. No one spoke to me before printing it. If they had, they would have learned that I have no complaints regarding the children or their skateboards."

Young Larry turned seventeen on May 14, 1973. He was proud to be at an age when he could drive his father wherever he wanted to go. He especially enjoyed taking him fishing. It allowed for some quiet time together. Another enjoyable pastime was on the golf course where Heron amazed everyone with his long straight drives and putting skills. On their way home after a day of golf in Mendon, young Larry pulled into the parking lot of a grocery store to pick up a few items for dinner that night.

As they exited the car, a man approached shouting angrily, "What the hell do you think you're doing? That spot is clearly marked for the handicapped. Park it somewhere else." This despite license plates marked with a "V," which signified the ultimate in handicapped privileges.

Heron stepped from the car and curtly replied, "And what's wrong with you? Are you blind? Can't you see that I'm blind?" The man grunted something and walked off. The incident by itself would not have irritated him. But taken together with other events, like the skateboard experience and the anti-war movement, it signaled a major shift in attitude toward veterans, one that did not strike Heron as a change for the better.

This was further illustrated when Azelia replayed a conversation she'd heard recently between two people at the post office who didn't know she had doubled back for stamps. Earlier they had heard her asking if this month's disability payment had arrived.

"I can't believe he's still being paid disability," one was saying.

"You would think that after all these years, they'd quit wasting our tax dollars," the other replied.

"Enough is enough," her friend agreed.

Young Larry, built like his father and warmhearted like his mother, left the house early one Saturday morning to keep an appointment with the Milford dog officer. He was on his way to adopt a puppy from the pound after seeing it shown on television. It had the saddest look in its eyes that fairly begged for a home.

When they met face-to-face, the dog's tail thumped happily and she gave him a smile that melted his heart. He paid the thirty-dollar fee and headed home with his new charge seated proudly on a blanket beside him.

"Name's Maggie," he told his dad.

"What's she look like," he asked, bending down to pat the dog and scratch behind its ears.

"Part Golden Retriever and part German Shepherd. She's the tan of a Retriever and has the characteristic dark shading on her head, back, and tail of a German Shepherd. But she's not as big as either one, so maybe there's something else in the mix."

"Beautiful. Guess you're Maggie Heron from now on."

The tail thumped and Maggie licked Heron's hand. The dog's entire body oscillated in happy response to the kind hand stroking her head. She was home at last.

The story appeared in Monday's Gazette. Last night, three masked men, armed with a sawed-off shotgun, machete, and a knife, robbed the Immaculate Conception church in Worcester, Massachusetts. The Reverend Edward T. Connors and two young volunteer workers had been tied up with rope and wire that the men had brought with them and forced to lie face down on the floor.

Money from the day's collection, approximately three thousand dollars, had been taken from the rectory safe. The two women, who had been loosely tied, were able to free themselves and then the priest shortly after the robbers had left the scene.

After Azelia read the article to Heron, he phoned his friend immediately. "I'm so glad no one was hurt," he said to the priest.

"If anything happened to either of the nurses, I could never live with myself," Connors told him.

"Think they'll recover the money?" Heron asked.

"I doubt it. So far the investigation has turned up nothing. There was not much distinguishing about them. The police think that at least one might be in our congregation. They seemed to know the how, when, and where of the collection money. God forgive them."

Nothing like this ever happened in these parts before. It was a sign that did not bode well.

Heron waved goodbye as his brother-in-law drove away from the house. He started up the front steps and tripped over a newspaper that was deposited there, falling forward and smashing a knuckle against the wooden step as he reached out to break his fall. "Damn," he cursed, holding the knuckle to his mouth, tasting blood.

He was tired of having to depend on others for rides, never able to drive himself anywhere - to a friend's house or grocery store, or to take Azelia for as spin. So many things he'd love to be able to do, things others took for granted. A complaint finally escaped his lips, though there was no one to hear it.

"Why me?" he asked aloud.

Dusk was falling, chilly and grainy, as he continued to mount the steps. He crossed the porch landing and reached for the doorknob, smashing the sore knuckle on the knob. When he had the door open, he called, "Hey Maggie! Where's my girl?"

He heard a thump as she leapt off the sofa in the living room, and he could hear her claws on the wooden floor as she ran to greet him. Heron could not see the smile on her face nor the sparkle in her eyes but he could hear her tail whacking the front of the commode in the hall and that helped lift his spirits.

Maggie was so friendly that both ends of her body wagged at once, her head, ears, and tongue at one end and her tail and butt at the other. Normally she had more of a calming effect on him, but not so much today. The deep depression started in the pit of his stomach and clawed upward until it squeezed his heart. The pressure building inside was like a volcano preparing to erupt. "Why me, Maggie?" He bent to stroke her neck and pat her head. "Tell me why?"

He plunked down on the sofa and leaned back resignedly as Maggie flattened obediently at his feet then dragged her body closer.

"Most of my buddies went on to college on the GI bill. They drive BMWs and Mercedes. Ironic isn't it - cars made in Germany, I mean." He sighed. "Think what might have been..." His voice trailed off. Knowing it was fruitless to continue down this path, he did so anyway. "They can afford fancy cars, maids and nannies to care for their kids. I just want to send mine to college."

Maggie came to a sitting position and sent a lick in the direction of Heron's knee that missed entirely.

"Wouldn't it be wonderful if I could afford nice things for my sweetheart, eh? She deserves a break, wouldn't you say?"

Maggie could stand it no longer. She answered with a yelp.

"You agree then? The best I can do is to not be a burden." He paused, then leaned down and rubbed behind her ears. "That's why I go walking around town alone and make my own toast in the morning and ask for no help unless it is absolutely necessary. How can I ask any more of her? Know what I mean, Maggie?"

Maggie let out a low whine. It was as though she understood that her master was crying. No person could have detected it. Her master's tears ware falling inside where they couldn't be seen, only tasted. But nature gave Maggie special senses. She knew when he was unhappy and she would do anything in her power to lift his spirits. She drew closer and placed her head on his knee, looking up with soulful eyes, sensing misery in her master's heart.

Why shouldn't he feel down? There were no promises in his future. He felt like flotsam being tossed in a rough sea, with no bearings, no destination, no dreams or ambitions. His skin felt clammy, sallow. A cold sweat pervaded his body, void of substance.

Finally, he stood and made his way to the rear door and dropped to a sitting position on the back stoop; Maggie slipped past him to visit the outdoors and do her business. A breeze bathed his moist flesh, cool and invigorating. He drew in a deep breath and tasted the fall air.

Get hold of yourself, damn it! You can't run but you can walk. You can't see but you can feel and hear, and your senses are acute. You don't look beautiful but what the hell - you have Azelia. And she'll always look to you like she did at age twenty-three. Who else do you know that is that lucky? So stop feeling sorry for yourself. She deserves better than that. Get on with your life.

Heron welcomed the jangle of the phone and rushed to answer it, nearly knocking over a plastic garbage can in the process. He tried to calm down as he moved with the speed of a sighted person to pick it up. The caller was Mrs. Harry Rubenstein. Strange. In all these years he'd never heard from her. "I just called to see how you're doing, Larry."

"Fine. Just fine. And you?"

"Oh, I'm having one of my mood swings," she said. "I got to thinking about David and it made me think of you."

A long pause. "Can you tell me something, Larry?"

"If I know the answer – sure."

"Tell me how it happened? I need to know how David died. The Army told me nothing really. I would like to hear the truth."

He understood. It was not the first time someone had called to ask how a loved one had died. He had heard the experts on TV talk about closure. *There is no such thing,* he thought. But knowing the truth might help lessen the pain.

"Would you like to come over to talk about it in person?"

"Oh. That's nice of you. But I think I'd rather hear it now. I may not be good company – you know."

"Yes." He had heard the whole story at one of the 87th Battalion's reunions. "I was not there but I understand it happened so quickly that none of those killed ever knew. They were relaxed and eating breakfast when a shell came in unexpectedly and hit a tree above them. The fragments killed them all instantly. There was no suffering."

"Are you sure?"

"Positive. They were killed where they sat, some with spoons still held in their hands. They never knew."

There was a moment of silence, then, "Thank you Larry. I am so sorry for what happened to you. You are very brave. If there is ever anything I can do..."

"I appreciate it, Mrs. Rubenstein. My wife told me how nice you were to her at the train station when we were leaving together - David and I. She'll always remember you for that."

They said their goodbyes and Larry made a move to attend to Maggie woofing at the back door.

It was a perfect fall morning. The limitless blue sky held only an occasional puff of cotton on a Saturday in 1974. Last night, Debbie worked until two a.m., sprucing up the apartment she shared with another student off the Framingham State College campus. Her mom and dad would be arriving at any minute and she wanted to impress them. A floral afghan covered the coffee stains on the living room sofa. Although it wasn't her turn, she had scrubbed the bathroom (ugh) and replaced soiled linens. There were no dirty dishes in the sink. A fresh fragrant bouquet of flowers graced the table by the entrance. She had thought of everything.

Everything, that is except the bare floors that reverberated with the loudness and intensity of a Jamaica kettledrum whenever anyone crossed it, the first thing her father noticed as he crossed the room. After giving her a hug and asking how she had been, he moved about the room stomping his feet. "You need some carpeting in here," he stated, flatly. "That will keep the noise down"

"I know dad."

"It's so loud when someone walks, you can't hear yourself think," he said later. "I couldn't study with all this racket going on." He stomped a bit more to make his point.

Their stay was brief, just a short visit to drop off a care package consisting of food, blankets, and other essentials."

After they left, Debbie went to the library and then out to dinner with some friends. When she returned at eight that evening, her roommate, Linda, was waiting impatiently for her. "Debbie, you aren't going to believe this."

"What?"

Linda stepped aside and pointed to the living room. "Look. Your parents bought us a new rug."

"They what?"

"Your dad and mom stopped at a rug store in Nobscot and purchased the rug. It was delivered three hours after they'd gone."

"It fits perfectly. How did they know the size?"

"You got me."

"My mom probably paced it off when we weren't looking. She's good at things like that."

"Your father is something else."

"Oh no, what did he do?"

He called a little while ago. "When I told him I really liked the color, that the color matches everything in here, he said, 'Of course. I picked it out myself.'"

They both laughed.

He felt so strongly about his children that he always wanted them to have the best money could afford. The most important thing in his life was his family. So when, Patty, his first daughter married, it was a big deal for Heron. He sang *Daddy's Little Girl* as the bride and groom danced together. People were more than moved by it. "Isn't it just beautiful?" Norma asked. When he finished, people rushed to take his hand and pat him on the back.

The next year, young Larry entered the University of Massachusetts and like his father excelled in sports, namely baseball and basketball.

24

The Slide Continues

The shrill sound of a siren cut through the morning air like an ax through butter. Eastbound traffic on I-90 southwest of Boston swerved to open a path as the ambulance sliced across three lanes to access the Prudential Center exit ramp. Moments later it pulled to a stop at the emergency entrance to the Jamaica Plain Veterans Hospital and a scene of controlled chaos erupted. The doors to the emergency vehicle were flung open and a gurney pulled from the rear with dispatch.

The doors to the emergency room opened almost simultaneously and a doctor rushed forward, took one look at the patient and felt his own pulse quicken. A member of the EMT filled him in on what little he knew as they rushed the patient inside. His neck and face were grossly swollen. His skin was feverish. His responses to questions were slurred and barely intelligible. The team had no idea what was wrong with him.

When they rolled him into the ICU, the doctor listened to his chest then ordered the nurse to hook up an IV for re-hydration and to take his temperature. "It's 100 and climbing."

"Tell me when it hits 103. I want some stat blood work and film of the swollen area," he ordered. It seemed clear that the patient was suffering from a massive infection that had sent him into shock.

Fortunately, this hospital boasted the man who that same year had made major contributions to the new field of craniofacial surgery. He would later establish the craniofacial program at Children's Hospital to correct deformities and cleft palates. The emergency room doctor wasted no time in summoning that doctor for a consult. Fortunately, the surgeon was on duty and available.

"It doesn't look good," he told the craniofacial expert who arrived within minutes of receiving the call. "I think we should operate, but frankly I wouldn't dare. I have no idea what's wrong. It could possibly be a pituitary adenoma, requiring transsphenoidal surgery."

The moment the consulting doctor, Dr. Joseph Murray, saw the name on the patient's chart, he had a sense of deja vu, suspecting right away what might be happening. "It's very likely something else. Do we have X-rays?"

As if on cue, a nurse arrived and said, "Here are the X-rays."

"Just as I thought. See this?" Murray pointed to a dark spot close to where the pituitary gland was located. "It looks like a piece of metal. No doubt shrapnel. It's been in his body for years. This man is Larry Heron, an old friend. Our paths seem to cross whenever he's in trouble. Let's get him into surgery immediately and see if we can find a way to extract that thing."

"Temperature's 103!"

Murray knew he must act fast. Heron was losing consciousness. He feared his patient might soon lapse into a coma, with potential for brain damage or death. First, the doctor took steps to drain fluids. Then he formulated a plan. He could open the skull and go in, but the procedure was too intrusive and inherently the most dangerous. He could try to reach in though the sphenoid sinus, one of the facial air spaces behind the nose, but that would not get him close enough and the shrapnel appeared too large to be extracted through that small a space. He decided to use a direct transnasal approach. He'd make an incision in the back wall of the nose. Judging from the location on the X-ray, he should be able to get in and make the extraction.

After a lengthy and delicate operation, he was able to remove the piece of metal causing the problem. He made sure that he had removed all possible sources of infection. If this had gone on for one more day without attention, Heron would surely have died. Or would he? This was, after all, Larry Heron, the man who defied death.

As the anesthesia wore off, Heron was greeted by an old acquaintance –

pain, intensely visceral pain. But he was used to it by now. Since being admitted to VFGH, he had endured thirty-six major surgeries counting this one. With the help of an old friend, morphine, he slept well that first night. By morning he was ready for some breakfast – except that the doctor had denied him anything but liquids. Over the next few days he managed a speedy recovery.

On the day of his release, Dr. Murray came by to wish him well.

"We've got to stop meeting like this, doctor," Heron joked.

"What are the odds?" the doctor asked.

Heron extended his hand. "Thanks, doc. You saved my life."

"Someone else helped, another someone from your past. He's right here."

"Hi, Larry," a voice said.

"Dave? Dave Tredeau?"

The doctor and Tredeau exchange astonished glances. "How did you know it was me?" Tredeau asked.

"Never forget a voice." He said, drawing a breath. "Well I'll be. This is like an episode from *This is Your Life*." Dave had played shortstop on St. Mary's baseball team with Heron. They had both competed against Dr. Murray when he played for Milford High.

"You were the guy who threw me out at home plate the day of the slugfest," Dr. Murray laughed.

To commemorate a new wing being added to the West Roxbury Veterans Hospital, Heron had been asked to sing to the accompaniment of the famed Army Band at an outdoor ceremony. The tape was set. Patty was put in charge of hitting the record button right after her father was introduced.

She sat ready at a table beside the grandstand trying to stay awake during the endless speeches when suddenly an awful drone swept past her ear. She held perfectly still, hoping it would fly away, but more wasps appeared. As she backed her chair from the table, she spotted the attraction – a garbage can parked a few feet away.

The opening speeches by dignitaries ended and Heron stepped to a microphone to begin singing The National Anthem. His voice was deep and resonant - never better. This was the best performance of his life, in fact. Thank heavens he had decided to make a tape of it.

The music wasn't making the wasps very happy; in fact, it stirred them to action. They were circling now like planes locked in a flight pattern around a busy airport. One buzzed so close that she thought it would go in her ear. She swung at it with her program guide, which only seemed to anger it more. It began altering its flight pattern to circle closer to her head. They were getting organized. It was only a matter of time before she'd be stung. She waved the guide with one hand and dragged her chair back further with the other. Finding a shady spot far enough from the garbage can, she unfolded the chair and sat down.

"Did you get it?" Heron asked before she was finally settled.

"Get what," she asked. Then, she stood. "Oh no. I forgot to turn it on. Oh. No. Was it good?"

"Just my best performance ever," he said, confidently. "But you're kidding me, right?"

Patty cried, "No Dad. I didn't turn it on. I'm so sorry."

"What?" he asked, incredulously.

"I was so distracted by a bunch of wasps that I forgot to turn on the recorder. I'm really sorry, Dad."

"Did any bite you?"

"No."

"Well I'm glad of that. No big deal, sweetheart." He encircled her shoulders with his arm. "I'll just have to do better the next time." He hid his disappointment so well that it almost had her convinced. Almost.

"I'm so sorry, Dad."

Heron was already smiling and talking to some dignitary as though nothing had happened. But Patty Heron would never forget that day. Everyone she ran into commented on how wonderful her father sounded. Someone said, "I wish I'd recorded it. To which Patty replied, "Yeah, me too."

The downward spiral of the Draper Corporation that began in 1967, when the company was sold to Rockwell, had gained momentum. Besides market saturation, Draper looms had become too expensive. Three-and-a-half foreign looms could be bought for the price of one Draper loom. By 1978, the plant closed and the era of the great company town came to an end - the likes of which would never be repeated.

"The one good piece of news I learned today," Heron told his wife, "was that they are going to let us, and all the people renting houses, buy them at below market prices, just to get them off their hands." After he relayed the price, she replied, "We can't afford not to buy our house for that amount."

The closing forced Heron into retirement. Young Larry would complete college that same year and begin teaching biology at Hopedale High School. The Herons were now living off their savings, disability, and social security payments. Azelia accepted a job as a librarian at the Bancroft Memorial to supplement their income.

Though patriotism had been on the decline, traditions remained strong in Hopedale. On May 28, 1979, Heron played a central role in Memorial Day commemorative services, after which members of the press asked him how he felt about the war. "I don't believe in war but when my country calls... well I love my country. I gave a lot for my country." When asked about the incident that left him so badly damaged, he responded, "We had to return fire, so someone had to unload the truck. The decision was mine." That was all he would say about the ephemeral events that had changed his life forever.

Father Edward T. Connors retired from the priesthood in 1979 at age 73. In November of 1980, his predecessor, Fr. Joseph W, McKiernan, invited him to return to Immaculate Conception to continue his 9th Division "annual pilgrimage" to celebrate Veterans Day. Retired Chief of Staff General William C. Westmoreland, a long-time admirer of Connors and the man who had headed up the 9th Division at the end of World War II, presided over a ceremony in which the names of the division's 250 Vietnam War dead were sealed inside a tan brick monument in front of the church.

At a similar ceremony in 1966, Westmoreland had presided over the sealing of microfilm containing the 4,581 names of 9th Division soldiers killed in World War II. Also participating this year was Major General Louis A. Craig, the commanding general of the division during most of the war. This year, Members of the Worcester County Chapter, Vietnam Combat Veterans, and Combined Allied Forces all took part in the parade that kicked-off at the Worcester Fire Department on Grove Street and ended at the church overlooking Gold Star Boulevard. Everyone present was invited to attend the annual division banquet to be held later that day in the Sheraton-Lincoln Inn.

During Mass, Fr. Connors hailed all veterans "who laid down their lives in the cause of peace." To the Vietnam Veterans, he added, "Your lives have been far more difficult than ours because we were allowed to win our war."

General Westmoreland, affectionately referred to as "Westy" by the men who had served under him and the priests he has befriended, gave the final address. The Supreme Commander of Allied Forces in Vietnam for more than four years, praised veterans of the conflict saying that U.S. troops were in Vietnam "to stop the ruthless Communist regime of Hanoi from overrunning South Vietnam." He added, "Now all Americans understand that was a noble cause, especially when they see what is happening in Indochina today. Nobody wants to go to that part of the world today – they all want to get out."

He termed American withdrawal from Vietnam a fault not of the soldiers who were there. "They did the job they were sent to do. It was not our soldiers who failed. As in World War II, the men who fought in Vietnam supported a principle that has always characterized Americans: peace."

At the close, Heron sang the National Anthem. Then from a church balcony, bandleader, Harry L. Bullens played *Taps,* the bugle call for the military dead, while a second bugle player, hidden in a distant location, played a second, haunting *Taps* echo, sending chills tracing down spines.

At the completion of ceremonies, Fr. McKiernan was introduced to the Herons. "Last June," he told them, "in a surprise celebration, the Catechetical Center at Immaculate Conception was renamed the *Reverend Edward T. Connors Center*."

"That is so nice," Azelia said. "He certainly deserves it."

"Besides, no one could pronounce 'Catechetical,'" the priest joked. "At the celebration, Father Connors said he was 'embarrassed but grateful' for the tribute. The parishioners love him. They refer to him as 'mister-one-in-a-million,' and his soldiers still call him the Godfather of the 9th Division."

"He's a hard act to follow," McKiernan concluded.

In the summer of '84, the National Veterans Wheelchair Games were held in the town of Brockton, Massachusetts. And what better tribute than to have Lawrence J. Heron open with the National Anthem accompanied by the 18th U.S. Army Band from Ft. Devens?

Cardinal Bernard F. Law gave the Invocation.

Then World Middleweight Boxing Champion, Marvelous Marvin Haggler, appeared with George Lang, Congressional Medal of Honor winner, for the lighting of the torch. Following the ceremonies, the owner of Ben's Tavern offered Heron and his friends, Guido, Ed, and Pete Ferrelli, free coupons for food and drinks at his tavern.

Ben's was located off Bellevue, near Main. The crowd on Saturday night was noisier than usual, perhaps because it was "Buck-A-Burger" night. Azelia was attending a Bingo tournament in Milford with her sister, Olga.

Above the cacophony of laughter, music, conversation, and Red Sox play-by-play, came the gravelly voice of a heavy-set man at the bar. His acquaintances were calling him Bubba. Bubba was in a foul mood because the Red Sox had just lost to the Yankees.

Heron was seated at a table near the piano at the back of the room. The piano player was playing *Heart of My Heart* and the Heron crowd was singing along. After *Four Leaf Clover* ended, there was a call for Heron to sing *Forty Shades of Green.*

As he began singing in a soft mellow voice, the noise in the room abated. Everyone quietly listened – except Bubba. "Hey, bartender, another bourbon!" he bellowed. He swallowed the bourbon, savoring its sharp descent then followed it down with a swig of beer from a frosted mug. Wiping his mouth on the sleeve of his green and brown-checkered polyester, he let out an exaggerated burp and plunked his empty beer mug down noisily. "Gas 'er up," he said. "And how about some quiet so's we can hear the TV?"

The bartender frowned and said, "Hold it down, please. You're disturbing the customers."

"You mean the blind guy? He's disturbing me!" Bubba said it loud enough for everyone to hear.

"I am asking you politely, Buddy." The bartender said again.

Bubba slid his glass forward. "Just pour me another."

The bartender complied.

Upon request, Heron began singing *Danny Boy*.

"When's the blind guy going to give it a rest?" Bubba shouted. His friends laughed encouragingly.

Heron raised his voice and the patrons threw disgusted glances Bubba's way. When the singing ended to applause, a woman at a table near the bar leaned toward Bubba and said, "Show some respect. That man's a war hero."

"War he-ro? Hey, Audie Murphy," Bubba shouted. "How many babies you kill?" His cronies slapped their thighs. Thus encouraged he continued, "So what's with the blind guy anyway? How'd he get his face messed up?"

The woman at the table rose in protest. "That's an awful thing to say."

"Pipe down," Bubba blurted.

Pete Ferrelli, built like a linebacker, pushed his chair back from Heron's table. "That's it!" he said. "I'll shut him up."

"No!" Heron extended a hand in protest. "Let the blind guy do it." As he tapped his way toward the bar with his cane, the room became pin-drop still.

"The blind guy leaving us?" Bubba asked his friends.

His voice was a beacon.

Heron homed in.

Suddenly, Bubba grew still. He could smell his own fear as the blind guy drew closer to him with the bearing of a soldier, head held high. The nearer he drew, the more he could swear the blind guy could see him through his glasses. The scarred face was ashen and the mouth was curled into a crooked smile. For just a brief moment, he wondered if perhaps he had gone too far.

"You should apologize to the lady," Heron said flatly, his nose inches from Bubba's. Though somewhat unnerved, Bubba nonetheless felt safe. After all, this man was totally blind and he had friends to back him. Instead of apologizing, he said, "I don't see no lady."

"You have three seconds," Heron said.

"You'd better go back to your buddies." The blind guy appeared to be confused. His hands were groping for the bar. Bubba suddenly felt more in control. "Think 'cause you're blind I've got to take your crap?" He jabbed Heron sharply in the chest with an index finger to punctuate his claim.

Heron counted, "Three, two, one."

Pete, Ed, and Guido were all on their feet as they saw Bubba rise above the crowd like Tinkerbell. The big man's eyes were bulging. A split second later he was airborne, flying over the bar, clearing the glasses and bottles, and crashing down on the floorboards behind. When he opened his eyes the bartender was smiling down at him

The blind guy was leaning over the bar and appeared to be looking down at him, "How's that for a blind guy?" he asked.

A cheer erupted as Ed took Heron by the arm and led him triumphantly back to the table where the singing commenced immediately. Now everyone joined in as Bubba and his friends quickly settled up and departed through the front door.

A patron leaned forward and asked the woman who spoke up earlier, "What the hell just happened? Who is the blind er...gentleman?"

"A living example of why this country is so great," she answered.

25

Fr. Connors Last Farewell

Tuesday, January 28, 1986, opened bold and blusterous and continued to worsen as the day unfolded. When Father Thomas O'Malley stepped from his car in the visitor's lot of St. Francis Home, the wind was groaning like an organ off-key. As he trudged over crusty snow, he ignored the freezing temperatures and inhaled the freshness of the cold night air. The call had come in the middle of the night, as often was the case. This time the summons was to the bedside of his dearest friend, the ailing Father Edward T. Connors.

Connors had been preparing for death for a long time and did not fear it. His faith was strong. If he could no longer be up and about to help others, then perhaps it was time to go. Nevertheless, when he thought back to the life he had lived, sadness overtook him. For there was so much more he wanted to accomplish before leaving this world forever.

Fr. O'Malley leaned forward to look down upon this once vibrant priest and dear friend lying flat on his back for the first time since he'd known him. His face was drawn and his eyes were hollow. His arms appeared too frail and his face had taken on a deathly pallor.

But the kindly smile was still there.

Never before had he spoken about his past, but tonight was different. Time was running out. So he talked of old times and revealed a few secrets.

Connors' love of sports, and the kids he helped shape into responsible men, meant more to him than simply winning games. He believed a great deal could be learned on the playing fields, and that every young person could benefit from being involved in sports. Every kid deserved the opportu-

217

nity to achieve a "personal best."

But it wasn't simply healthy bodies and minds that concerned him. He was convinced that playing sports builds character, that it teaches respect, trustworthiness, honesty, responsibility, fairness, caring, and good citizenship. He looked up at Fr. O'Malley, and asked through eyes that were blurring, "Remember the Sullivan brothers?"

Fr. O'Malley answered, "There were three of them. It surprised me when they all went to college and turned out so well. As kids, they were a handful."

"They certainly were." Connors eyes looked up at the ceiling. "Well, this one time the boys turned pretty rowdy after a basketball game. In those days, there were no shower rooms or lockers, just old Flanagan's barn rigged with a shower."

"I remember it well."

"I heard a commotion that day, and when I went to investigate, I found the boys teasing poor old Randy Cowan, the janitor who used to clean up after them. Cowan was mentally impaired but it never stopped him from working hard and it didn't mean he wasn't sensitive. The boys didn't know that or didn't seem to care. They were jeering and snapping their towels at him – teasing the heck out of him. Cowan was really upset. It looked to me like he was crying. That really got to me."

"So I lined them up in that barn and went right down the line from left to right, slapping each and every one of them across the face, including Bobby Sullivan. By the time I finished, my hand hurt. Then I sent them home thinking about what they had done."

"The next day I received a call from Mrs. Sullivan. She said, "Robert tells me you slapped his face yesterday.""

"'Yes I did,' I replied."

"Good. I just called to tell you that if he ever does anything like that again, I want you go right ahead and whack some more sense into him. Keep him straight."

Fr. O'Malley flashed an amused smile.

Connors grinned up at him. "Can you imagine what that would cost me today?"

O'Malley was having trouble holding back a flood of tears. "Times have changed a great deal in our lifetime," he said. "And I'm not sure it's all for the better." Then he added, "Someone should write a book about you, Father Connors. You've helped so many confused kids straighten out their lives and go on to become responsible adults. And the way you volunteered to serve alongside them in battle..."

"I have often prayed that when my work here is done, which it appears could be at any minute now, He will say to me, 'Well done, Edward, well done.'"

Fr. O'Malley stayed by his side, talking to him while Connors' eyes involuntarily closed. O'Malley would not leave him until the end, which he knew was not long in coming. And when it was finally over, when Fr. Connors was finally gone from the earth and the people he loved so dearly, O'Malley just sat for a long time remembering the man who had been his dearest friend.

The next day, he and Fr. George Rueger discussed some of what had passed in Connors' time. Fr. O'Malley said, "When the boys would not come to confessional, he would bring the confessional to them – in the rear of his beach wagon," the vehicle that gained overwhelming popularity throughout New England. "The kids would sit on the tail of the wagon while Father Connors listened through a drop-down canvas sheet. He even took confessions behind trees and in open fields."

"Sports played a major role throughout his life," Rueger said. "But I think the place he felt he did the most good was in the war as a chaplain."

"Yes. You know he took great pleasure poking fun at himself. He used to say that he was the man who never got the bird of a colonel or the red of a monsignor. And then Westy conferred upon him the honorary promotion to *Green Colonel*."

"I remember," Rueger laughed. "He was very proud and quite moved by that. The general thought quite highly of him, didn't he?"

"Yes. In August of '66, Westy sent him a wire from Saigon. He asked his old and valued friend if he would be willing to accept an award on the general's behalf at ceremonies that were to be held in Miami Beach. The general was fighting a war and could not attend. Fr. Connors wired back that he'd be honored."

"Without a doubt," Rueger said, "he was the most popular and widely known priest in the diocese. He'll be sorely missed."

On Wednesday, April 16, 1986, Massachusetts Governor Michael Dukakis waited on the steps of the oldest building on Beacon Hill for the arrival of a state hero, Larry Heron. The State House, completed in 1798, sat atop a parcel of land once owned by John Hancock, the state's first elected governor and signer of the Declaration of Independence. Overlooking Boston Common and the Back Bay, the State House had been designed by native-born architect, Charles Bulfinch and featured a copper dome coated with 23-karat gold.

The governor, local representatives, and DAV officers had gathered here to give special recognition to Larry Heron, the now legendary hero. At the conclusion of ceremonies, the governor accepted a POW-MIA cap and key chain presented to him by Heron in memory of those from Massachusetts still missing in action.

The governor was amiable and seemed quite honored to meet Heron. He asked about his experiences and they were soon swapping views on subjects ranging from the raising of children to what was taking place in sports. When Heron mentioned that his wife's name was Azelia, Massachusetts State Representative Marie J. Parente said, "She was named after the flower, but her parents had just come over from the old country and misspelled it."

Governor Dukakis smiled and said, "After seeing her picture, I believe the flower was named after her."

After posing for photographs, Dukakis took his guests on a guided tour. Heron was especially impressed with the central chamber of the House of Representatives, its massiveness echoing in his sensitive ears.

On June 6, 1990, a week after Memorial Day, Representative Parente referred to Heron in her monthly State House Report, which was published in the Milford Daily News. *Children could learn a lot about the importance of saluting the flag from Lawrence J. Heron, for whom the Milford Disabled Post is named.*

Each time the American Flag and its bearer approaches his "parade spot" (guided by a whisper from a friend) Larry's quick salute gives viewers a glimpse of what he "sees" in its beauty and significance. It is because of sacrifices like those of Larry and his counterparts, that Old Glory still waves and stirs the hearts of his Blackstone Valley countrymen. Larry, on behalf of children (and all of us), thanks for your lasting and selfless devotion to our well-being.

That about summed up the feelings of the people in southeastern Massachusetts for Larry Heron. He was still an icon, a living symbol of the proud veteran who loved his country enough to surrender everything he had to preserve it.

"Oh my!" Azelia exclaimed.

"What?" Heron asked.

"Dr. Murray made the headlines again. Listen to this." Her voice trembled with pride as she read from the October 9, 1990, issue of the Boston Globe. *"Joseph E. Murray, 71, of Wellesley, professor emeritus of plastic surgery at Brigham and Women's Hospital is the Recipient of the Nobel Prize in Medicine for his discoveries concerning organ and cell transplantation in the treatment of human disease."*

"It's for performing the world's first successful organ transplant in 1954, and for proving it possible to transplant organs between non-identical relatives and from the deceased to the living. The estimate is that 20,000 people a year are being given a new lease on life because of him."

"Here's another article in today's Worcester Telegram and Gazette where he mentions you, how he came upon you at Valley Forge and didn't know it was you until he read your name on the chart. It says, *Working with burn victims at Valley Forge General Hospital during World War II inspired the doctor to steer his medical career towards tissue and organ transplanta-*

tion."

"The Nobel Prize. More than the money, it's the prestige. He's climbed the Mount Everest of prestige," Heron said, with admiration.

"Funny you should say that. It says here that he once scaled the Matta-horn."

"Quite a man."

26
Died on the 4TH of July

After finishing their grocery shopping in Milford on Thursday, the Heron's found young Larry waiting at the door. "Some guy from Boston called about an hour ago, Dad. Didn't leave his name. He said he'd call back later."

"Wonder what he wanted?" Azelia said, as she plunked two bags of groceries down on the kitchen counter. Heron was right behind her with two more bags that she took from him. "If it was important, he'll call again," she said.

The phone rang again at 7:10. The man on the other end identified himself as the artistic administrator for the Boston Pops; he was calling on behalf of Keith Lockhart, conductor of "America's Orchestra."

"Some of us sense a resurgence of patriotism, something the country sorely needs. I've seen Mr. Heron's picture in the paper and had the opportunity to listen to him sing the National Anthem at Memorial Day services last May. No one stirs patriotism more than Mr. Heron. We would be honored if we could persuade him to sing the National Anthem to open this year's 4th of July ceremonies."

Words suddenly formed a traffic jam in Azelia's throat. "Why, er, ah, just a moment. He's right here."

Azelia watched his face light up. "At the Esplanade?" he responded. "That would be..." He hesitated. "Quite an honor," he said at last.

When he was off the phone, Azelia threw her arms around him. "I'm so proud of you," she said giving him a firm hug. She knew how dearly he

223

loved his country and how honored he must have felt. No greater patriot had ever walked the face of the planet. "I can't wait to tell our friends."

She left him sitting in the kitchen for a few moments while she went upstairs to change. Heron headed straight to the back door, opened it, and stood breathing in the raw freshness of the rain. Suddenly he felt exhilarated. It was the first time he had felt so alive since the birth of his children. When Azelia came back down, she heard him humming softly.

He was very happy these days. All three daughters were married and the Herons now had several grandchildren. All were delightfully well-adjusted, and brought great joy to their grandparents. Not surprisingly, Carol's son, Matt, was a sport's all-star in high school. Several colleges were already pursuing him. Heron attended as many of his games as possible and delighted in chatting with Matt about his play.

Life seemed to be going well until a week later, when Heron suddenly collapsed on the kitchen floor and was admitted to the Milford Hospital after being diagnosed as having suffered a major stroke.

Two days later, Azelia answered the phone. It was Heron. "Come get me out of here," he begged.

"What's wrong?"

"Just come and take me home. Please. I don't want to stay here another minute."

During the drive home, Azelia asked, "What happened?"

"Nothing's like it used to be," he said flatly.

"Did somebody do something? What's wrong?"

Slowly, she drew it out of him. One of the new nurses had yelled at him and was treating him shabbily. She had called him both a "pain in the neck" and a "spoiled brat."

"Did you do anything?"

"Nothing on purpose." Too embarrassed to use the bedpan, Heron had climbed out of bed to find his own way to the restroom. But the nurse had moved things around while he had been napping and he tripped over a stool.

After that, the young nurse chided him repeatedly. She accused him of wanting special privileges and gave him strict orders as to how he was to behave.

Azelia vowed to keep him at home after that incident and to look after him herself from then on. Times had changed and so had attitudes. In the old days her husband had been treated differently, with great respect, not with humiliation.

Heron sensed that the end was near. He was back where it had all started fifty years ago, on his back, waiting to die. Where had the time gone? If only he could have gotten some of it back. He was not ready to die. There was so much more he wanted to experience, like singing at the Esplanade, attending more of Matt's football games, being there when the next grandchild came along.

When the next series of strokes hit, he refused to be hospitalized and Azelia did not push him. The doctor concurred that in his present condition, it was better for him to remain at home. He was in need of constant attention now. Azelia could not leave his side unless someone came to take her place. This continued for several weeks. He ate very little and couldn't seem to hold anything in his stomach. When Azelia wasn't caring for him, she was cleaning up after him.

One day, after giving him a sponge bath, Azelia said, "I've got to go downstairs and prepare supper."

"Go. I'll look after him," Debbie told her mother.

When Azelia was out of earshot, Heron asked, "Who was that woman?"

"That was Mom." When he failed to show signs of recognition, she added, "Azelia – your wife."

"Oh."

Moments later, he drifted off to sleep. Debbie stayed by his side, looking down at him. He had never looked this vulnerable. For all these years he'd been her rock, someone who could not be kept down for long. If only there was something she could do.

Suddenly he was eighteen again, wearing saddle shoes and khaki's. His hair was cut short. Three white stripes graced his blue and gray letterman jacket. He was the captain of St. Mary's football team, a cocky one at that, with always a gleam in his eyes. "Today I'm going to score two touchdowns," he said to her. Her eyes were smiling as he added, "Just for you."

The game was played again in his mind. He scored the winning touchdown and the crowd was cheering. And that night, he strutted up Mendon Hill like many other nights, cold air cutting through his jacket like a knife. He stuffed his hands into his jacket pockets then withdrew them. He found he could move faster with his hands swinging by his sides. And there she was, practicing field hockey on the front lawn, as lovely as a summer's breeze.

She stopped when she saw him coming and rushed towards him with her arms outstretched. Then she vanished into thin air like a ghostly apparition. And he was cold, very cold. There was a bright light ahead. Maybe if he moved closer, he could get warm. He headed for the light.

Everyone in the household heard Debbie's screams and came running. The cause of death was listed as subarachnoid (brain) hemorrhage.

Azelia was stunned. The absence of his company, the silencing of his voice, the void that no other person could ever hope to fill was like a giant sinkhole that abruptly opened and sucked away her life. He will never sing with the Pops but he made it past July 4th. Ironically, perhaps mercifully, the end came on July 7, 1995.

Letters of condolence poured in from friends, relatives and people who had served with Heron. Many came from people Azelia didn't even know, and from far away. A typical letter arrived from Hopkinton, Massachusetts. An old news clipping was enclosed.

The writer referred to Heron as an unforgettable and formidable competitor. *Though we only met on the playing field, I always kept up on Larry and admired the courage and determination you both demonstrated in forging a solid family life. As a fellow veteran, I appreciated how he faced ordeals and daily challenges.*

Larry was an outstanding athlete in every way. He had speed, durability, and was tough to bring down. Our games with St. Mary's were intense and fiercely competitive. Larry was the difference. He was a clean player, aggressive, and I suspect had an innate determination to succeed at whatever he attempted. I also recall that he was very handsome – and I suspect very popular. It seems he faced life as he faced every contest in which he participated. May he now rest in peace. My sincere regards to you and your family.

The highlight of the funeral was a eulogy delivered by young Larry who expressed in glowing terms the tremendous pride, love, and admiration his family felt for him. His children had learned so many lessons from a father who had overcome every obstacle thrown in his path, and a mother who stood gallantly beside him every perilous step of the way. They could only hope that perhaps now their father could see what his children looked like.

The funeral ended with the melancholy strains of taps. Its restful vibrations lingered in the hearts and minds of the hundreds of people gathered there, long after the last note had gently stirred the air.

A single tear made its way down Azelia's cheek. Last night and this morning, she had cried her eyes out. Her beauty was still striking despite the gray threads in her hair. The years of worry and stress had aged her gracefully, like a fine wine. She was now grand dame, incongruous amongst her peers, as gracious still as she was wise, the matriarch of the Heron family.

She was magnificent, regal on the outside, but within, she was dying, a little piece at a time. *Goodbye my love. Someday soon I will return to be with you - forever.*

The following November marked the first time in nearly half a century that Heron did not appear as the central figure in a patriotic event. But he was not forgotten. In newspaper articles and at public observances such as Veterans Day and the 4th of July, Larry Heron would continue to be remembered as "one of the most courageous of America's World War II heroes."

People remembered his athletic achievements, the long suffering, the painful operations, the blindness, the singing, and his deep religious faith. They talked about the characteristics that had inspired the nation's Disabled American Veterans to honor him as the only living veteran to have a chapter named after him.

At the same time, Azelia was lauded for her courage and strength. On November 5, 1995, Daniel P. Reilly, the Bishop of Worcester, conducted a Pontifical Mass in her honor and presented her with a special award at the Sacred Heart Church of Hopedale. Pastor Raymond Goodwin said, "It is indeed a precious moment because she is a person who over these many years has given her heart to the Lord, to her family and friends, and especially to her husband, Larry. Azelia remains a living example of God's gift to His church, and in a special way, to our Sacred Heart family." The event was reported by the news media. It meant a great deal to Azelia because it helped keep the memory of Heron's sacrifices alive.

Two weeks after receiving her award, Azelia's sister, Olga, passed away. The stress of losing yet another loved one left Azelia weak and drained, but did not prevent her from driving to the Marshfield cottage for a pre-arranged meeting with her children. As she stepped from the car, she collapsed onto the driveway unable to walk. When her son suggested he take her to a hospital, she insisted on climbing into bed instead, believing that she was merely suffering from exhaustion.

Her throat felt raw and she had flu-like symptoms, so she asked him for some nasal spray. He rushed to a drug store and when she applied the spray, she immediately began to scream and cough up blood in large amounts.

Blood was pouring from her mouth and nose. Family members crowded into two cars to take her to the Jordan Hospital in Plymouth, where doctors took one look at the blood-soaked towels Patty held to her nose and the bloodstained front of her dress, and estimated she had lost roughly three pints.

Jordan was a small hospital with limited facilities. Since the bleeding continued and she was having difficulty breathing, she was rushed by ambulance to the Framingham Union Hospital where doctors were at a loss as to what was wrong. A doctor stuffed her nostrils with gauze and she was then transported to the Milford Hospital.

"Perhaps it's lupus," one doctor surmised. "Perhaps her carotid artery is blocked," ventured another. Two years would pass before her condition would be diagnosed as pulmonary fibrosis. During her many checkups, it was discovered that she had sustained a fracture of the spine from osteoporosis and she was placed on heavy doses of steroids.

Pulmonary fibrosis is a debilitating lung disease that hits heavy smokers. Since Azelia never smoked, she attributed the disease to the reddish-brown particles of dust that had been billowing from Draper smokestacks over the years, to settle on rooftops, cars, and outdoor furniture like fine snowflakes. Several people who lived close to the factory had developed respiratory problems, many in the same families.

On Saturday, May 13, 2000, young Larry came home carrying a large bouquet for his mom. Tomorrow was Mother's Day. He found her in the living room tethered to an oxygen tank via twenty-five feet of plastic tubing that snaked ubiquitously behind her wherever she went. Today she looked so frail and unhealthy that Larry grew more concerned than usual. A constant diet of pure oxygen had rendered her cheeks aflame and face pale, yet her bright eyes were as cogent as ever and she was dressed as if she expected to go calling.

"Ohh! What beautiful flowers," she told Larry. "You're so thoughtful. Just like your father."

She pondered a bit, then added, "They've forgotten him, haven't they?"

"Of course not," he said, unconvincingly. "They'll never forget him." The Herons celebrated Thanksgiving and Christmas at Azelia's that year, since she couldn't travel anywhere without a supply of oxygen. Larry was still living at home so that he could continue to look after her.

Just as the moon reaches the far right side of her hospital window, an alarm sounds and a nurse moves swiftly down the hall to Room 201. She notes that Azelia's vital signs are erratic and that her gasps have intensified. A doctor is summoned who administers medications knowing that it is not life the stimulants are prolonging, but a slow death. He orders a new array of tests then leaves to check on other patients.

Azelia sees Heron's face now, so handsome. His bright blue eyes are smiling at her, beckoning. His arms are open wide. There are no scars. He looks just as he did at age twenty-three. She runs to him and their lips meet.

He holds her close and she is smiling through her tears.

On that morning, July 4th 2000, the family was notified that Azelia Heron had passed away peacefully in her sleep – which was not true. She hadn't slept. She had lain awake throughout the night, following the moon until the end, hoping that from somewhere up there, he was looking at it too.

She died on America's most patriotic day, almost five years to the day after her beloved husband had passed on. It seemed their lives had meshed like clock gears from the start, always in unison, always keeping good time. And now, at last, they were united once again.

The crowd that gathered at the Heron residence on Christmas Day 2000 had thinned out considerably but was no less joyful to be with than in prior years. The only guests from the old crowd were Norma, Amelia, and a few other close relatives.

There were many grandchildren now, ranging in age from nine to twenty-one. Carol's son Matt would be playing football for Maryland next season and would eventually wear a Miami Dolphin's uniform. After Christmas dinner, they gathered in the kitchen where the conversation drifted back in time.

"And do you know, one night he promised she'd never see him drink beer again?" Carol asked. "Well, she never did and he never came home with liquor on his breath after that."

"There are so many amazing stories about them," Debbie said. "Like the poem Dad wrote for her."

"What poem?" Patty asked.

Carol told about their one major breakup after Azelia had failed to show up at John Heron's funeral. She read the words of the song she had scribbled on a tattered piece of paper after her mother had recited them for her. When she finished reading, she folded it and returned it to her purse. The room was quiet and eyes were moist.

Patty asked, "Remember the time he sang *Rudolph the Red-nosed Reindeer* at Johnny Milan's funeral?"

"Tell us. Not everyone's heard it," Carol said.

"Every Christmas, Johnny Milan would come by with his wife, Ester and before they'd leave, he'd sing *Rudolph*. So when he died, Ester asked Dad if he would sing *Rudolph* at the funeral. Dad thought it might be in bad taste but she insisted. After all, she told him, it was his favorite song.

"Well you had to be there. When he started singing, people thought he had lost his mind. Some laughed out loud – you know, nervous laughter. Others were outraged. It took months for Dad to live it down."

Debbie asked, "Did Mom ever tell you the story about Grandma Livia and how she came to this country?"

Heads shook negatively. "Tell us," Larry said, leaning forward encouragingly.

It was a Cinderella story. She told how the mayor of a small town outside Pisa had presented the widowed Livia with a business/marriage proposal. He said to her, "You're a good mother in need of an income and I want a child. Marry me and I'll care for you and your children. And we'll have a child together." The mayor lavished everything he had on the child born to them, while Livia was condemned to a life of picking grapes in the fields. Along came Grandpa Noferi, a Draper Corporation salesman who could speak fluent Italian. He took one look at Livia toiling in the vineyards and was smitten. Debbie closed with, "They moved to Hopedale and the rest is history."

"I had never heard that one before," Larry said. Now it was his turn. The women began filing out of the room as soon as they knew it was about his father's football games, but the men and his three sisters remained spellbound. When he finished, Patty, who had been staring pensively ahead, said, "Dad was quite a sports star, wasn't he?"

"God, if he had only gone to Notre Dame," Carol said, wistfully, "who knows what might have been?"

"He was the best," Larry said, his eyes glistening. "Mom was too. They both were."

EPILOGUE

On February 23, 2001, John Sears parked his car outside the Plymouth post office. The front license plate on his vehicle read "Camel Green." In his hand was a package he intended to mail to Keith and Mary Ostrum in Erie, Pennsylvania, regarding the 87th Battalion's upcoming reunion. He made it as far as the curb in front of the post office where he collapsed on the sidewalk and died.

The 87th held its last reunion in Gettysburg on September 16-17, 2002. Like many of the ninety surviving members of the 87th, Roger Burt and Angelo Bastoni chose not to attend because Gettysburg was difficult to reach and would have required several modes of transportation.

A small group of surgeons came together at a symposium in Baltimore in June 2003 to place into permanent record their experiences while working with World War II veterans at VFGH. In attendance were doctors Bradford Cannon, in his nineties and Joseph Murray, in his eighties. Both are retired but in amazingly good health. To this day, they continue to write articles, publish books, and make significant contributions to the field of medicine. In addition, Dr Murray was named Honorary Chairman of the U.S. Transplant Games to be held July 28-August 1, 2004, in Minneapolis-St. Paul, and invited to appear as a special guest.

BIBLIOGRAPHY

Alexander, Bevin (2000) *How Hitler Could Have Won World War II.* New York: Crown Publishers.

Ambrose, Stephen E. (1995) *D-Day.* New York: Touchstone.

Ambrose, Stephen E. (1999) *The Supreme Commander.* (2nd ed.) Jackson: University of Mississippi.

Ambrose, Stephen E. (1999) *The Victors.* New York: Touchstone.

American Printing House for the Blind (2002) *Father Thomas Carroll.* Key word: Avon Old Farms + World War II. [Online] http://www.aph.org/hall_fame/carroll_bio.html

Astor, Gerald (1999) *The Greatest War.* Novato: Presidio.

Benison, Saul, and Barger, A. Clifford, and Wolfe, Elin L. (1987) *Walter B. Cannon: The Life and Times of a Young Scientist.* Cambridge: Belknap Harvard.

Bradford, Dr. Vance A. (1961) *Burns in Atomic Disaster.* Oklahoma: State Medical Journal.

Bradford, Dr. Vance A. (1944) "Heron's Medical Records." Doctor's Report while Heron was a patient at #158 General Hospital, Salisbury.

Breuer, William B. (1981) *Bloody Clash at Sadzot.* St. Louis: Zeus.

Brookesmith, Peter (2000) *Sniper.* New York: St. Martin's.

Cannon, Dr. Bradford (2000) "Heron's Surgeries." Valley Forge General Hospital Archives 1944-46. Phoenixville

Carroll, Andrew (2001) *War Letters.* New York: Scribner.

Carroll, Rev. Thomas J. (1961) *Blindness: What it is, What it does, and How to Live with it.* Canada: Little, Brown & Company Limited.

Chase, William H. (1950) *Five Generations of Loom Builders: A History of Draper Corporation.* Hopedale: Draper Press.

Connors, Father Edward T. (1942-45) "Letters to Bishop during World War II." Personal accounts of activity from the battlefield during World War II.

Curtis, Dr. Robert H, (1993) *Medicine: Great Lives.* New York: Atheneum.

Dale County Stories (2003) *A History of Fort Rucker, Alabama.* Key word: Camp Rucker. [Online] http://www.graceba.net/~library/Dale.County.Stories /a.fort.rucker.html

Dunnigan, James F., and Nofi, Albert A. (1994) *Dirty Little Secrets of World War II.* New York: Quill William Morrow.

Gawne, Johnathan (1999) *Spearheading D-Day.* Paris: Histoire & Collections.

Gilbert, Martin (1991) *The Second World War* (First Owl Book Revised ed.) New York: Henry Holt and Company.

Global Security (1976) *Vietnam War.* Keyword: Vietnam War. [Online] http://www.globalsecurity.org/military/ops/vietnam.htm

Greenleaf, Robert L. (1945) *87th Chemical Mortar Battalion, U.S. Army.* Key word: 87th Chemical. [Online] http://www.4point2.org/hist-87A.htm.

Heaton, Lt. Gen. Leonard D. (1964) *Medical Department, U.S. Army Surgery in World War II: Activities of Surgical Consultants, Vol. II.* Washington: U.S. Government Printing Office.

Heron, Azelia. (1999) "Life Stories." Taped interviews. Hopedale.

Heron, Carol, and Heron, Debbie, and Heron, Larry, Jr., and Heron, Patty (1999) "Anecdote's." Interviews. Hopedale.

Heron, Lawrence J. (1935-39) "Personal Scrapbook." Sports and World War II clippings. Hopedale.

History 87th Chemical Mortar Battalion, Motorized. (1943-45) Battalion Daily Journal.

History of Chemical Disarmament. (2003) History. Key word: History of Chemical Disarmament. [Online] http://www.opcw.org/basic_facts/html/bf_int_main_frame_history.html

History of Hq. & Hq. Company, 87th Chemical Bn. (1943-44) Company Daily Journal.

Holts, Major, and Holts, Mrs. (1999) *Battlefield Guide to the Normandy Landings.* South Yorkshire: Leo Cooper.

Kortegaard Engineering (1969) *History of the 4.2" Chemical Mortar.* Key word: 4.2-inch mortar. [Online] http://www.rt66.com/~korteng/SmallArms/4pt2.htm

Miller, Russell (1993) *Nothing Less Than Victory.* New York: Quill.

Pravos, Edward F. (1998) *Neptunus Rex: Naval Invasion, June 6, 1944.* Novato: Presidio.

Ramsey, Gordon Clark (1984) *Aspiration and Perseverance: The History of Avon Old Farms School.* Avon: The Avon Old Farms School, Inc.

Roosevelt, Jr., Gen. Teddy (1943) *Love Letters to his wife, Bunny.* Keyword: Famous Love Letters. [Online] http://www.theromantic.com/LoveLetters/rooseveltjr.htm

Ryan, Cornelius (1994) *The Longest Day.* New York: Touchstone.

Schmitt, Hans A. (1989) *Treaty of Versailles: Mirror of Europe's Postwar Agony.* Key word: Treaty of Versailles. [Online]

http://www.nv.cc.va.us/home/cevans/ Ver-
sailles/papers/Schmitt_paper.html

Scripps-Howard (1944) *Reporting World War II.* New York: The Library of
America.

Spann, Edward K. (1992) *Hopedale: From Commune to Company Town
1840 – 1920.* Ann Arbor: Braun-Brumfield, Inc.

University of Notre Dame (1940) *Knute Rockne's "Win One for the Gipper"
Speech.* Key word: The Gipper. [Online]
http://www.google.com/search?hl=en&ie=UTF-8&oe=UTF-
8&q=the+gipper&btnG=Google+Search

US Seventh Army Report of Operations (1988) *Approach to the Siegfried Line.*
Key word: Forbach. [Online]
http://www.trailblazersww2.org/approach_to_the_siegfried_line.htm

Printed in the United States
20580LVS00001B/61-330